MURDER
IN THE
SCOTTISH
HIGHLANDS

BOOKS BY DEE MACDONALD

DEE MACDONALD

MURDER IN THE SCOTTISH HIGHLANDS

bookouture

Published by Bookouture in 2024

An imprint of Storyfire Ltd.
Carmelite House
50 Victoria Embankment
London EC4Y 0DZ

www.bookouture.com

ISBN: 978-1-83525-506-3
eBook ISBN: 978-1-83525-505-6

ONE

The sun had risen over the top of the distant blue mountains, some still capped with snow, and glistened on the tumbling waters of the Altbeag River as it made its way west, crashing over boulders, towards the sea. It was a perfect April morning in the Western Highlands of Scotland.

It was against this background that Ally McKinley, on holiday from Edinburgh, had fallen in love with an old malt-house, a two-storey stone building just outside the tiny riverside village of Locharran, and had decided to retire there. Leaving city life behind was not something that she'd ever considered before that moment, but seven years after the death of her dear husband Ken, standing in the heather with the sun on her face and the lovely old building rising up in front of her, she had realised that she was ready for a new adventure.

Ken, a greatly respected headmaster, had been the kindest and best of men, a wonderful husband and father. However, in their forty years together, Ally had had to come to terms with the fact that her husband lacked an adventurous spirit. Her ideas of going round Europe in a motorhome, or packing up and going to live in an old farmhouse in the South of France, had fallen on deaf ears. What would they live on? he'd wonder. We'd be self-sufficient, she'd counteract; grow fruit and vegetables, olives and grapes! 'You could teach English while I'm treading the grapes into a fine wine!' He'd guffaw gently, as usual, and continue correcting exercise books or doing his crossword. She hadn't minded; they had created a wonderful life together in their old Victorian semi in Edinburgh, raising two children and building fulfilling careers, Ken as a teacher and Ally as a researcher for a TV studio in the city.

But there were only so many times you could research other people's adventures and exploits without wanting to embark on one of your own. And so two years after she stood in the heather, after months of living amidst building rubble, here she was, the proud owner of The Auld Malthouse Bed and Breakfast. Converting the malthouse had been an adventure in itself but it had not been cheap. Ally had needed to supplement her meagre pension and pay back the overspend on the conversion and, as she liked people, decided she'd rather enjoy looking after guests. Three en-suite bedrooms would surely be perfectly manageable.

It was 10 a.m. on this particular morning in The Auld Malthouse, as Ally caught sight of herself in the hall mirror rushing from the kitchen towards the dining room, a breakfast plate in each hand. As was her habit, she straightened herself up to her full five feet ten inches. She had to constantly remind herself to walk tall – even with a plate in each hand – because, at sixty-eight years of age, she most definitely did not want to develop a 'dowager's hump', or whatever the name for that unfortunate condition was.

She deposited a loaded breakfast plate in front of each of her two guests.

'Beautiful day!' she said cheerfully.

'It certainly is!' agreed the diminutive, elderly man in horn-rimmed glasses.

'I believe it's going to cloud over later,' said his wife, the aptly named Mrs Frost.

These two did not believe in getting up early, in contrast to the nice American guest in Room 1, who liked to be out and about by eight or nine each day.

But not this morning. Ally wondered why.

On the way back to the kitchen, she studied herself more critically in the mirror, which was placed on a north-facing wall and not nearly so flattering as the south-facing one in her bedroom. Now that she'd left the expertise of Edinburgh's hair-stylists behind, she knew she needed to find someone to sort out her rapidly greying locks. Still, her make-up looked OK. Ally rarely went out of the door without her make-up on, and she was quite sure that her guests would enjoy their breakfasts more if they weren't confronted with aged, sun-damaged skin and unadorned eyes. And it was important that every detail was correct in this new venture of hers! How many people had the opportunity to come to live in such a beautiful place, in such an impressive old building, and start a new career?

Back in the kitchen, Ally wondered again about her American guest in Room 1. Where *was* he? Was he having a lie-in after a heavy night at the bar of the nearby Craigmonie Hotel perhaps? At this rate, Ally could see breakfast dragging on all morning, meaning that Morag, her cleaner, would have to do the bedrooms single-handed. Then a thought struck her: perhaps poor Mr Carrington was ill? Should she investigate?

Ally stood hesitantly in the kitchen, sipping the rapidly cooling coffee she'd made five minutes earlier, and wondered what to do. Morag was late; not that she'd be able to do Mr Carrington's room anyway because, presumably, he was still in it. She should really take a look. What if he'd had a heart attack or something?

Ally made her way up the curved wooden staircase. The bedroom door was closed, and there were no sounds from within. Mr Carrington had a key to his own room, of course, as did all her guests, but she knew that he never used it because he always left the door unlocked and the key lying on the desk in front of the window.

Ally tapped gently. Then, getting no reply, knocked more loudly. 'You OK, Mr Carrington?'

No response. She opened the door.

The room was empty. The bed had not been slept in, the curtains had not been closed and the complimentary tea tray had not been touched.

Bewildered, Ally was making her way back towards the door when she heard a loud scream from somewhere below, outside at the back of the building, where the old malthouse outbuildings – now her laundry room and shed – surrounded a cobblestoned courtyard. Leaning out of the window, which overlooked the courtyard, Ally spotted Morag in her familiar purple anorak, her hand over her mouth, staring in horror at the prone figure spreadeagled at her feet. Straight away Ally recognised his distinctive greying-red hair, and the newly acquired Barbour and tartan scarf. What drew her eye most especially, however, was the horn-handled dagger protruding from the centre of his back.

Mr Carrington's back.

Wilbur S. Carrington, as he liked to sign his name.

Morag looked up at her in shock. 'Oh my God, Ally. He's dead!'

TWO

Ally raced downstairs, moving faster than she had in years, and joined Morag in the courtyard. Morag was shaking and could barely speak. 'It's the American,' she said after a minute, her blue eyes wide with horror.

Ally nodded wordlessly. It certainly *was* the American.

Ally had knowledge of some basic first aid and so checked his wrist for a pulse. Nothing. And he was very cold. She wondered how long he'd been there. She had no inclination to touch him again and, besides, she knew she shouldn't. Let the police do all that.

They were both in shock as they arrived in the kitchen. Morag sat down, her normally pink face white as a ghost and her sturdy little body visibly shaking. She was sixty years old and had been working as a cleaner in the local hotel until Ally had appeared on the scene and offered her fewer hours for more money.

Ally picked up her phone and called the police.

'Ally McKinley at The Auld Malthouse in Locharran here. One of my guests has been murdered.' She paused for a moment. 'Yes, I'm quite sure he's been murdered,' she said in exasperation. 'There's a bloody great knife sticking out of his back!'

As she ended the call, there was a knock on the door which led into the dining room.

'We've not had our *toast!*' Mrs Frost, from Room 2, said petulantly, trying to peer in. 'And what was that noise all about?'

Ally took a deep breath. 'Oh, just a death on our doorstep, Mrs Frost. Quite took my mind off your toast for a minute, but I'll see what I can do. By the way, neither of you must leave the building. The police are on the way.'

Mrs Frost's mouth fell open as she retreated into the dining room.

Ally closed the door and headed towards the toaster.

'I could do with a wee drop of whisky,' said Morag, her voice wobbling.

'That makes two of us,' Ally agreed, withdrawing a bottle of Glenmorangie and two glasses from the cupboard.

'I'm that shocked!' Morag accepted her glass and took an enormous gulp. 'Who on earth would do that to a tourist? A nice man he was too.'

Ally shook her head. 'I've no idea, Morag. The police said not to touch him or anything around the body. But I suppose we'd better check that it doesn't rain, or we'll need to lay some plastic or something over him.'

Morag shuddered. 'I don't want to look at him again. I'll see that knife and all that blood until my dyin' day!' She took another enormous gulp. 'I've forgotten ma phone, so I canna even ring Murdo! He'll still be on his rounds, but I canna remember the number offhand.'

Ally had a feeling that not a great deal of cleaning was likely to be done today. Not that Room 1 was going to need much cleaning. She removed the Frosts' toast from the toaster and carried it into the dining room.

. . .

'Run through that again, would you, Mrs McKinley?'

Detective Inspector Bob Rigby blew his nose lustily and regarded Ally with heavy eyes. He obviously had a bad cold and was not looking particularly joyous at this call-out. He was a chubby man, about fifty, and several inches shorter than Ally – as were most people – so she could see how his black hair was thinning on top. He had a very pronounced Birmingham accent and Ally wondered what had brought him to the Highlands. Presumably he'd come up to Inverness for a few quiet years before he retired and he probably hadn't reckoned on much in the way of crime in this part of the world.

'Like I said, Mr Carrington was normally an early riser, and I was a bit worried that I hadn't seen him yet so went upstairs to investigate, and then I heard Morag screaming. I saw him from the window with what appeared to be a dagger sticking out of his back, which, on closer inspection, looks like a skean dhu.'

Rigby looked a little confused. 'Isn't that the dagger they put in their socks?'

Ally nodded. 'Yes, it's part of the full Highland dress.'

'And, in your opinion, he was definitely dead at that time?'

'I'm no medic, Inspector, but he was stone cold, no pulse and I reckon he must have been dead for some while.'

Rigby turned to Morag. 'So, Mrs McConnachie, you were heading towards the back door, and...?'

Morag nodded, her eyes still wide. 'Aye, I was in a rush because I was a bit late, ye see. Murdo – that's ma husband – hadnae reset the alarm and I never woke up till gone *nine*. Murdo's Locharran's postman, ye see, and he's up and about at five, and then he resets the alarm and—'

'Yes, yes,' the inspector interrupted impatiently. 'So, what time did you finally arrive?'

'Well, gone ten. Maybe about quarter past.'

He turned back to Ally. 'How come you didn't see the body earlier?'

'Because the courtyard's round the corner from the back door, and I had no reason to go out there.'

'Hmm. Any idea where he might have gone yesterday evening?'

Ally thought for a moment. 'He did say he'd be having some supper at the Craigmonie Hotel, and I daresay he might've had a few drinks at the bar as well. He was very keen on the malt.'

'And you heard nothing during the night?'

Ally shook her head. 'My room's on the other side of the house though. Perhaps the Frosts heard something; they're the English couple staying in the room opposite his.'

Rigby made a note on his pad. 'I'll have a word with them in a minute. Can we see Mr Carrington's room now?'

Ally led him, and the young police constable who was with him, upstairs. The young constable was noticeably nervous, and he had the most prominent Adam's apple that Ally had ever seen. She watched with fascination as it bobbed up and down when he replied to Rigby's commands.

'As you can see,' she said, 'he's hardly used this room at all in the past twenty-four hours.' Ally crossed to the window and looked down at the white-clad team who were examining the body.

Rigby looked around for a second and then nodded to Ally. 'Thank you, Mrs McKinley; you can leave us now.'

With relief, Ally left them to it and made her way down the stairs. She wondered if she'd been a bit sharp with the Frosts, so she bypassed the kitchen and went straight into the sitting room, where they'd been asked to remain.

'I'm sorry if I was a bit abrupt earlier,' she said, 'but it's not every day that I find one of my guests dead in the courtyard.'

'Who died?' asked Mrs Frost.

'Our American guest, Mr Carrington.'

'Oh no!' Mrs Frost's eyes widened and she clutched the carefully tied pussy-cat bow on her blouse. 'Did he have a heart attack or something?'

'I rather fear it was the "or something", Mrs Frost, seeing as there was a dagger sticking out of his back.'

'A dagger?' Mr Frost asked tremulously.

'A skean dhu, to be exact,' Ally explained. Then, remembering that they were English, added, 'That's the knife that's tucked into the man's stocking when they wear full Highland dress.'

'Oh, my goodness!' Mrs Frost was tugging at her bow again. She frowned. 'We need to get away from here as soon as we can, Walter! I'd *thought* this place was more genteel!'

'Well, I don't think there have been any murders round here before,' Ally said, a little annoyed.

'He seemed such a nice man,' said Mr Frost. 'I didn't think this sort of thing happened up here in the Highlands!'

'Neither did I,' admitted Ally. She was beginning to wonder what she'd let herself in for with this venture. Her first guest had just been killed!

THREE

Reluctantly, Morag heaved herself off the kitchen chair and went to tackle the bedroom upstairs, just before Murdo pulled up in his little red van.

He arrived at the front door and, as he handed a couple of letters to Ally, asked, 'What the hell's goin' on? There's police everywhere and they wouldnae let me anywhere near the back door.'

Ally took the letters and left them on the hall table for now. 'Come in for a minute. Morag forgot her phone, so she couldn't call you.' As she led him into the kitchen, she proceeded to inform him of the morning's events.

'Oh my! She must be awful upset!' Murdo wiped his brow, visibly shocked. Like his wife, he was short and sturdily built. Unlike his wife, he had a prolific moustache and was almost bald.

Just then, Morag came rushing back down the stairs. 'Oh, Murdo, you wouldnae *believe* it!' She then burst into tears as her husband put a consoling arm round her. 'It was horrible, horrible! Like you see on the telly, but that sort of thing just disnae happen round here!'

'But it just did,' Murdo said, turning to Ally. 'Did you hear any wailing last night?'

Ally rolled her eyes. 'Oh, Murdo, you don't believe all that old nonsense, do you?'

Ally had, in fact, heard some strange noises as she'd drifted off to sleep, but it had been a windy night and she hadn't yet become accustomed to all the sounds of the house. She shook her head, determined not to add to the local gossip about Wailing Willie.

Wailing Willie was her ghost. Back in the early 1800s, a certain Willie Morrison, who was extremely fond of the drink, had broken into a room above the main malt store, where it was known that there was a stockpile of the end product. Willie was the local piper and, for reasons best known to himself, had taken his bagpipes with him and, in between working his way through several bottles of the finest Scotch, he'd blasted out a few tunes. As Willie became more and more inebriated, so his repertoire evolved into a series of long, mournful wails. He died with a smile on his face and the blowpipe still in his mouth. Now rumour had it that Willie's ghost still haunted the malthouse, complete with his bagpipes, which emitted a spine-chilling wail at the approach of a local death.

'Well now,' said Murdo, scratching his head, 'I'm not sure if I didnae hear a funny noise myself in the middle of the night. Then again it might've been the cow.' He hesitated. 'Would I hear him half a mile away?'

Murdo and Morag had a cottage, with a little piece of land, down by the river, where they had nine chickens, a goat and a cow. Not to mention four cats.

'I wouldnae be too sure,' Morag said dubiously.

'So, who was it that was killed?' asked Murdo.

'An American,' Morag replied. 'A Mr Carrington. A nice man.'

'He was an author,' Ally explained, 'writing a book about

the local area and researching his family tree. Apparently he had Scottish ancestry, and seemed to think that he was in some way related to the owner of Locharran Castle.'

'Och, I've heard about him!' Murdo said dismissively. He thought for a moment. 'Was that American's room the one where Wailing Willie met his end?'

'No,' Ally replied. 'That's now an en-suite bathroom to another bedroom – the one the Frosts are in.'

'Where are the Frosts now?' Morag asked.

'They're in the sitting room, waiting to be interviewed by Detective Rigby. *She* is not well pleased.'

'I'd better go and finish their room then,' Morag said, 'before they get back up there and that awful woman finds somethin' to complain about.'

Morag and Mrs Frost had not got off to a particularly good start. Mrs Frost had acquired a very grand accent – compared to her husband anyway – and spoke with the proverbial mouthful of marbles. While Morag rolled her Rs at great length, Mrs Frost rarely pronounced hers at all. So, when she'd asked Morag for more 'wotaah', Morag had been at a loss to know what she wanted. Furthermore, Morag was not one to say 'pardon' – which Ally constantly encouraged her to do – and had wrinkled her nose up and asked, 'Eh?' After Morag had eventually produced a jug of water, Mrs Frost had then asked her for some extra packets of 'sugaah', because her husband, 'Waltaah', had a very sweet tooth. Morag had duly obliged. 'Your sugarrrr, Mrs Frost!'

Later, Mrs Frost had asked Ally how long Morag had been her 'cleanaah'.

'Morag's been a cleaner ever since she left school,' Ally had informed her, 'and she's brilliant. She worked at the Craigmonie Hotel for years until I arrived here.'

'Hmm,' Mrs Frost had said.

Though she was grateful for their custom, Ally would be

relieved when the Frosts left, which was hopefully at the end of the week. However, this could, she reminded herself, be delayed due to Mr Carrington's unfortunate demise and the resulting police procedures.

Murdo, after gawping out of every likely window, none of which overlooked the crime scene other than the one in the victim's room (which Rigby had locked), got bored. Unable to see what was going on, he set off round the village to spread the news. No need for town criers up here. This never-been-heard-of-before event would be round the village in minutes, doubtless embellished by Murdo's insistence that he'd been forewarned of this incident by Wailing Willie, although how he might be able to hear it from half a mile away would doubtless not be explained. He'd be unlikely to mention the cow.

This soon became obvious when groups of locals began arriving at the gate with phones and cameras. They couldn't see anything, of course, because the rear of the house was now cordoned off, so they entertained themselves by taking photos of police cars and the tape. When the ambulance arrived, there was a flurry of excitement until it drove round to the back and out of sight, but no one moved just in case it might come back again, with a *murdered corpse* inside! Eventually the ambulance did reappear, moving at speed with the windows covered, and headed off, presumably to Inverness or Fort William.

DI Rigby came back into the kitchen just as Ally was busy heating up some beef broth for her own and Morag's lunch.

'That smells good, Mrs McKinley!' He sniffed in appreciation.

'Would you like a bowl, Inspector?' Ally asked.

'That would be lovely, but I have to be on my way.' He sighed. 'Now, I've already spoken to Mr and Mrs Frost, and I'm about to question everyone at the Craigmonie Hotel, but

Constable Chisholm will stay here for the moment. He'll make sure none of the public come snooping around. The body's gone, of course, but we'll keep the yard cordoned off for the moment. I've locked Mr Carrington's bedroom and taken the key, because I don't want anyone in there, or anything touched. We've done a preliminary, but we will need to come back. Did you have any further bookings for that room?'

Ally shook her head. 'No, he booked it for a month but said he might want to stay longer. But whenever he decided to leave, I wouldn't have any problems letting the room because it's the beginning of the tourist season.' She thought for a moment. 'What about notifying his relatives?'

'Leave that to us. We have his mobile phone, which was in his pocket and has all his telephone numbers. Did he ever speak to you about anyone? Like a wife? Or a brother or sister?' He withdrew a neatly folded white handkerchief from his trouser pocket.

'No,' Ally replied. 'I only know he came from somewhere near Boston, but he never mentioned any family. He did refer to the Locharran estate, though, and seemed to think he might be related to the family who own the castle.'

'Did he now?' Rigby raised his eyebrows.

'Yes, and he asked me to list all the ancient churches in this area because he wanted to check some records or other. I told him to ask the local minister – that's the Reverend Donald Scott – because I'm a relative newcomer here.'

'Have you any idea why he might have wanted to check on records in old churches?' Rigby asked.

Ally shook her head. 'I can only guess that there might have been records somewhere containing the details about his family tree, which he seemed to be after. It was only yesterday, when I asked him if he'd found anything, he said he had got *some* of what he wanted. That was the last time I spoke to him.'

'I wonder if he told anyone what he'd found?' Rigby said

thoughtfully, rubbing his chin before sneezing twice. 'Right-oh, let's just hope we can get this sorted out quickly. I need to have a chat with the earl next. Thanks for your help – just hope you don't catch this cold.' And, with that, he was off.

Ally took a mug of soup out to Constable Chisholm, who looked like he'd rather be anywhere else on earth than here. He thanked her profusely, his Adam's apple working overtime.

Back in the kitchen, Ally stood gazing out of the window. The sun had come out so perhaps she needed some fresh air to clear her head and, hopefully, dim the memory of that poor man's body. Murdo would doubtless have spread the news, so she decided against heading down to the village yet and being pestered for all the gory details. She'd have a short stroll across the moor and then walk down to the village while Morag got on with the cleaning.

As always, the fresh air calmed her. There was moorland on both sides and above the malthouse, from where there was a panoramic view of her little lane which, after joining the road to and from the castle, meandered down to the village, where houses, shops, the church and the hotel were dotted along the riverside. She laced up her boots, zipped up her jacket, and headed out, determined to clear her head and gather her thoughts.

FOUR

As she made her way through the heather, Ally questioned for the first time her own sanity at opening a guest house and living under the same roof as a bunch of strangers.

In fact, her family all thought she'd gone completely bonkers when Ally announced that she'd fallen in love with a remote village on the rugged west coast of the Scottish Highlands, where there was an old malthouse just *asking* to be renovated: set against a picture-postcard backdrop of blue mountains and heather-clad foothills. It wasn't a 'pretty' building, as it had been built to be functional, but it was impressive, and Ally had known it could be made to look really beautiful. It became The Auld Malthouse B&B, because everyone referred to it as 'that auld malthouse'.

There was even a hilltop castle, visible for miles around, which had been owned for generations by the Sinclair family. Hamish Sinclair was the current owner and also happened to have the title of Earl of Locharran. The eighth earl. He was, according to local gossip, a somewhat raffish, debonair sort of fellow, fond of country pursuits and women. To date, Ally was told, he'd married only once and had no offspring, but had had countless lady friends since. Later, Morag had informed her, 'Ye'll need to keep yer distance, Ally, because he's a right old groper!'

The earl aside, as far as the malthouse and the village of Locharran were concerned, it had been love at first sight for Ally.

Her son, Jamie, had stared at her, uncomprehending. 'You're planning to leave *Edinburgh*?'

Ally nodded, and Liz, Jamie's wife, asked, 'So what's brought this on?'

'You remember when my friend Maggie and I had that holiday last year, when we drove up through the Highlands and stayed in all those little bed and breakfasts?'

Liz nodded, and Fiona, her then sixteen-year-old grand-daughter said, 'I saw the pictures you took. It looked lovely.'

'It *was* lovely,' Ally confirmed, 'and, for some time now, I've been wondering what it might be like to leave the city and live somewhere like that.'

'You'd soon get bored, Mum,' Jamie pronounced. 'No cinemas, theatres, restaurants – you'd go barmy. And all that *rain*! It's always raining on the west coast.' As far as Jamie was concerned, Edinburgh was the centre of the universe.

'But it's milder,' Ally said defensively, 'and it would be nice to get away from the cold east wind.'

'And what exactly would you *do*?' asked Jamie.

'Well, the old malthouse I liked so much is for sale.'

'And…?'

'I thought it could be converted into a nice B&B. It's got planning permission and nobody seems to have shown much interest in it – so far anyway.'

Jamie stared at her in disbelief. 'You're *sixty-six* years old!'

'Well, I've always been a late starter. You know *that*! Heavens, I was considered to be ancient at thirty-three when I had you, even more so at thirty-five when I had your sister because everyone was having babies in their twenties then! Luckily, I'm still fit and well and it's seven years since your father died. I'd like to do something interesting with the rest of my life.'

There was a hushed silence as everyone's eyes swivelled in Ally's direction.

'So you're seriously planning this?' Liz asked.

Ally nodded firmly. 'Yes, I'm seriously planning this. The agent's coming round tomorrow morning to put my flat on the market. I want to buy the malthouse before anyone else does. It's going for an absolute *song*!'

'So, when you've finished all this *singing*, what will you do with the place? Don't tell me you'll have your hard hat on knocking down walls and the like!' Jamie asked, looking down from his six-feet-two-inches viewpoint.

Ally shrugged. 'No, I'll let the local tradespeople do that, after I've found a good architect. Anyway, I've made an offer on the malthouse, which has been accepted, and I've enough cash in the bank for that, thanks to your dad, but I'll need to sell the flat for all the renovation work.'

Jamie laughed. 'Dad would have thought you'd gone completely crazy.'

'I daresay he would,' admitted Ally, 'but since he's no longer with us, that's hardly relevant.'

'Well, I think it's a lovely idea,' said Fiona. 'Can I come up in the holidays please?'

Ally laughed. 'Of course you can! I'd love that! You *all* can! I'm hoping to get five bedrooms out of it, most with en suites; three for paying guests, one for myself, and one for friends and family.'

'And where will you live while all this building work is going on?' Liz asked.

'I shall probably rent a nearby cottage while the building work is going on, which will give me time to get to know the local area and the people, and to supervise the conversion, of course.'

Jamie raised his eyes to heaven. 'My mother, the project manager!'

'You've got it in one!' agreed Ally.

There were, of course, setbacks. The solicitor in Inverness, who was handling the sale, had spent a fair bit of time trying to locate the particulars. 'No one else has shown much interest in it so far,' he explained apologetically. Ally wondered why. The solicitor shook his head. 'Don't know. Nice-looking building, though. Perhaps it's the ghost that's put people off.'

'Ghost?' Ally had asked.

'So they say but a lot of nonsense, I expect.'

Ally decided not to mention this to her family.

Then the first offer on Ally's flat fell through and, for a few anxious weeks, Ally was terrified someone would step in, with more money in the bank, and steal the malthouse, ghost and all, from under her very nose. The missives weren't yet concluded, meaning that if someone came in with a higher bid in the meantime, she could lose the property. It wasn't hers yet. But miraculously, out of the blue, a cash buyer for the flat appeared and was in a hurry to move in.

And so her conversion from Lowlander to Highlander had begun.

Ally, now walking down to the village, observed the stone cottages, the sheep on the hillside on their endless quest for grass amongst the heather, the imposing castle with its turrets above and the cheery greetings from everyone she met, and decided she loved living here. How could a murder have taken place in such an idyllic spot? She was not going to let this incident put her off, and she was going to make a success of it by hook or by crook.

FIVE

Locharran Post Office and Stores was run by two spinster sisters, Queenie and Bessie McDougall. Ally reckoned they must be well into their seventies. Probably not a great deal older than herself, but they'd certainly let nature take its course, with no adornment.

Queenie was the elder – and the boss. She'd acquired a permanent stoop, due to years of stretching across the counter in order to catch every word that any customer might utter, in any part of the shop, no matter how quietly. She was therefore well informed on everyone and everything and, if she ran out of gossip, she was a dab hand at making some up. If you wanted to know what was going on in Locharran, Queenie was your woman. Bessie, on the other hand, said little and did most of the work. She spent much of her time wiping her nose, an affliction that seemed to be permanent.

Ally braced herself as she ventured into the shop mid-afternoon, hopeful that Queenie might be taking a nap which, according to rumour, she'd lately begun to do. But Queenie was behind the counter as usual, looking wide-eyed and excited, and certainly not about to nod off.

'Och, Mrs McKinley!' Queenie clapped her hands in glee. 'Och, it's grand to see you after *all* you've been through!' She beamed expectantly.

'I'm fine,' Ally said, 'but it's Morag who's had the worst of it, because she found the body.'

'Aye, Murdo was telling us she was in a bit of a state. Poor Morag. She usually pops in about this time.' Queenie looked hopefully towards the door. 'Is she still working up with you?' She nodded in the general direction of the malthouse.

'She's gone home. She only does an hour or two for me in the morning. Two pints of milk please, Queenie.'

Queenie didn't move. 'Now, tell us, what did the body look like? Was there lots of blood?'

'Yes, there was some, of course. Otherwise he just looked like he'd fallen flat on his face.' She didn't mention the skean dhu.

'He was that American, wasn't he? Was he the one that thought he was a relation of the earl?'

'I believe he was writing a book,' Ally said, 'and researching his family tree.'

'Writing a book,' Queenie repeated slowly, looking towards her sister, who was halfway up a ladder arranging tins on the top shelf, her pink bloomers on display under her droopy grey skirt. 'Did you hear that, Bessie? He was writing a *book*.' She turned back to Ally. 'He came in here once, you know, wanting to post stuff to America. To Mass... Massa... Masser...'

'Massachusetts,' Ally provided. 'That's where he came from.'

'Fancy that,' said Queenie. 'Now, who would want to be killing him?'

'That, as they say, is the million-dollar question. How about my milk? Two pints, please.'

'Aye, I'll get that for you in a minute.' Queenie stretched even further across the counter. 'Ye'll be getting all thae newspaper folk now. Well, *I* could tell them a thing or two about what goes on round here!' She cackled with laughter and looked across at Bessie, now at ground level. 'And I could that, couldn't I, Bessie?'

'Oh aye,' said Bessie, tugging down her skirt and giving her nose a quick wipe.

Queenie got the milk out of the fridge. 'Now, was he writin' murder stuff, Mrs McKinley?'

Ally shook her head. 'I don't think he was a novelist. He was writing about the local area, because he had some ancestry round here.' She picked up the milk.

'Och,' guffawed Queenie, 'they *all* say that! If he was thinking he had a claim to be a relative of the earl, then he must have had kinfolk up here. I'm beginnin' to think he should have kept his mouth shut about that.' She narrowed her eyes and nodded sagely.

Ally got home to find no fewer than six reporters at her gate.

'Hey, Mrs McKinley, is it true you found the American's body?'

'What was he like? Why was he here?'

'Is it true he liked a wee dram or three?'

'Can you show us where you found him?'

Ally didn't want to be rude because, after all, these guys – including one young woman – had a job to do which, at times like this, did little to increase their popularity. She'd been warned by Rigby that the press would arrive and not to give them any details, only basic facts. She confirmed that her cleaner had found the body, that he was an American, he was very nice and that he was writing a book. She avoided mentioning Morag's name, in case she got pestered too. But they already knew.

'It was a Mrs McConnachie that found him, wasn't it?'

Ally finally made it into the kitchen and deposited her milk in the fridge. There was no sign of the Frosts, but their car was still there, so they'd obviously not done a runner. She sat down wearily in a chair beside the log burner.

Ally loved this big, warm kitchen with its large, oil-fired Aga, as well as the log burner, its original oak beams and the long, old pine kitchen table from a shop in Fort William which had cost a fortune to have transported to Locharran. The units were all made of wood, and the kitchen had a cosy, welcoming feel. It was Ally's favourite room, and it was all hers for the remainder of the day because she didn't serve lunches or evening meals for her guests. There were plenty of options in Locharran: the Craigmonie Hotel, with its restaurant and bar food, The Bistro (owned by her new friend, Linda), and there was Concetti's restaurant and takeaway, owned by a second-generation Italian family and known locally as 'the chippy'. Ally knew she couldn't compete on variety or price, and so decided to leave it to the professionals and save herself a great deal of work.

The kitchen, along with the entire ground floor, had once been part of one enormous store, which the architect had cleverly created into rooms while retaining the old ceiling beams and stone walls where possible.

She peered out of the back door but could see no sign of Constable Chisholm or the police car, so he'd probably decided to call it a day. Gingerly she ventured out, round the corner into the yard. It was still cordoned off with only a partly faded chalk outline of where the body had lain. Ally shivered and returned to the warmth of the kitchen, then peeped out of the front window to see if any of the reporters had gone.

Coming in the gate, with a reporter close on his tail, was Callum Dalrymple, the manager of the Craigmonie Hotel, which was situated a short walk down the winding lane to the village, and on the riverside, close to the shop, the school, the church and the eating places. Callum was a short, well-built man with cropped, prematurely greying hair and hypnotic blue eyes. Ally opened the door.

'Sorry to bother you, Mrs McKinley,' he said, 'but the police have only just left us, and I wondered how you'd got on with them?'

'Oh, I'm fine, Mr Dalrymple, just a bit shell-shocked, as you can imagine. Would you like a cup of tea?'

'That would be lovely, and please call me Callum.'

'And I'm Ally.'

Having ascertained that Callum liked milk and two sugars in his tea, Ally sat down opposite him at the kitchen table. He really had the most beautiful blue eyes, which reminded her of Paul Newman's.

'Well, well,' said Callum, clearing his throat. 'I don't know what to make of all this. The police have questioned all the staff, most of last night's customers and guests, and myself.'

'I only have one elderly couple staying here now,' Ally told him.

'How long have you been here now, Mrs... er, Ally?'

'Just over a month,' Ally replied, 'but I hardly think I'll give you much competition.'

'Oh, competition's always good,' Callum said cheerfully, 'and you should get plenty of visitors as we come into summer.' He thought for a moment. 'Although, of course, all this furore might not be doing your business any good.'

Ally hadn't thought of that. 'You really think this will put people off coming here?'

Callum sipped his tea. 'I certainly hope not, but folks can be funny at times.' As an afterthought, he added, 'It might well have the opposite effect because they might find the site of a murder a gruesome attraction! Particularly if you include the ghost!'

Ally looked at him in astonishment. 'You don't really believe that baloney about a ghost, do you?'

He pulled a face. 'Who knows? But it could well be good for business.'

Ally was speechless for a moment. 'I think the ghost folklore is nonsense, but I must admit I hadn't considered the murder affecting bookings.'

They talked briefly about Mr Carrington for a few minutes before Callum said, 'Well, he had a good dinner, on his own, in the restaurant last night. Venison pie, he had.' He grinned. 'I suppose you could call it the last supper? I have to say that he had far too much to drink, and he was prattling on about being a relative of the earl, and how important he thought he was. He was upsetting quite a few of the other customers, and I had to ask him to leave, but he became a bit belligerent.'

Ally nodded. 'So, whoever stuck a knife in his back must have followed him up here, I suppose?'

'I expect they'll establish a time of death,' Callum replied, 'which would seem to be somewhere around midnight, because he must have left the bar around eleven. Unless, of course, he was waylaid on the way back or chose to go elsewhere. His body could have been dumped here, I suppose.' He studied her for a moment. 'You might be feeling a little nervous, up here on your own?'

'Nervous?' Ally hadn't even thought about being nervous. 'No, I'm not nervous, and I do still have a couple of guests here, so I'm not exactly on my own.' Nevertheless, she doubted that either of the Frosts would be very likely to defend her from a dagger-waving madman.

'Oh, that's all right then.' Callum set down his mug on the table. 'I'd best be getting back. I hope you didn't mind me popping in?'

'No, not at all,' said Ally truthfully. 'It was kind of you to think of me.' She wondered if he was married. Imagine waking up to those Paul Newman-type blue eyes every morning! He might be six inches shorter than her, but she'd have given his wife or girlfriend a good run for her money if she'd been thirty years younger.

'Keep safe now!' he called as he left through the front door.

Back in the kitchen, Ally sat down and considered what he'd said, suddenly becoming aware of being pretty much alone in a large five-bedroomed house with a killer on the loose. Her thoughts suddenly turned to her late husband. What would Ken have said to all this? Probably something like, 'Well, whatever possessed you to leave your nice, comfortable life in Edinburgh in the first place?'

It was with some relief that she heard the Frosts coming back, Mrs Frost loudly ordering her husband to wipe his feet on the mat.

Then the phone rang.

'Mum! Are you all right?' Jamie, of course.

'Yes, I'm all right! Why wouldn't I be?' Ally tried to inject some cheer into her voice.

'It's all on the *news!*' he exclaimed. 'One of *your guests!*'

'Yes.' Ally was amazed at the speed with which the media had gleaned the details. 'But it wasn't in the house here, you know. The body was found in the yard at the back.'

'But that means there's a killer on the loose in your area, Mum, and you're an elderly woman in a bloody big house! They've even shown it on the telly – The Auld Malthouse!'

'It's not that big!' Ally protested. 'And I do have other guests.'

'I feel I should come up there, you know. It's just that—'

Knowing he was about to begin a long discourse on how chaotic everything was in the building industry, Ally cut in, 'Jamie, I'm fine! Really, there's absolutely no need for you to worry.'

'You're quite sure?' She could detect the relief in his voice.

'I mean, Liz might be able to take a day or two off and drive up.' He didn't sound too sure about that, either, which was no surprise, since Liz had a small boutique selling vastly overpriced women's outfits and, as far as Ally could remember, she only had one part-time assistant.

'*Of course* I'm sure. All the doors have good locks on them, and, as I told you, there are other guests.'

'Well, if you're all right...' He hesitated. 'Perhaps you should consider getting a dog, Mum.'

'I'm all right, so stop worrying!'

'I expect you'll have Carol on the phone in a minute if she's watching the news.'

Ally sighed. 'I expect I will.' She wondered if the news had filtered down as far as Wiltshire, where her daughter lived with her pilot husband and three children. Again she thought of Ken: would he ever have agreed to come up here in the first place? After this incident, would he now be trying to persuade her to pack her bags and return to civilisation?

Sure enough, she'd hardly replaced the receiver when Carol phoned. 'Mum, are you OK? It's all on the news, you know. Would you like me to come up for a bit? I'd have to bring the children, of course, because Simon's on a long trip, but you wouldn't mind that, would you?'

Much as she'd like to see her daughter, Ally had a vision of three lively kids running around the malthouse while a murder inquiry was taking place. Definitely not! She'd hardly finished assuring Carol that she was perfectly all right when her brother and three of her friends phoned in succession. She was truly grateful to have so many people caring about her, but by nine o'clock, when she wanted to watch a much-acclaimed drama on television, she'd had enough. She switched off her mobile and took her landline off the hook.

SIX

In the morning, Morag phoned to say she was going to be late – again. This time she was having her hair done because she was going to be 'on the telly'.

When Ally walked into the dining room, Mrs Frost said she was quite off her food with all this 'nasty business' going on. She could probably manage a croissant, she said, but she couldn't face an egg. Mr Frost was having no trouble facing two eggs, along with sausages, bacon, black pudding, tomatoes and mushrooms.

'We won't be extending our stay,' Mrs Frost informed Ally as she poured coffee. 'We originally thought we might stay another week, but *not now*.' She regarded her husband and his breakfast plate with distaste. 'I'd really have liked to do some photography as the scenery round here is so spectacular.'

'I didn't know you were a photographer,' Ally said.

'Oh, I wouldn't say I was any kind of expert,' said Mrs Frost, fluttering her eyelashes modestly. 'I just dabble a bit.'

'Well, if you change your mind, the room is available next week. Have the police said that it's OK for you to move on?' Ally asked.

Mrs Frost stared at her in horror. 'Are you suggesting that we may be *suspects* for this appalling crime?'

Ally shook her head. 'Of course not! I'm not suggesting any such thing, Mrs Frost, although doubtless we may *all* be regarded as suspects until they find the killer.'

'How tiresome! Yes, they have asked that we stay on for a couple of days, and we've had to give them all our details and answer so many questions. Where are we going next? Where do we live? When will we be back there? All very tiresome. Incidentally I heard some strange sounds emanating from our bathroom a couple of nights ago, probably the pipes. You should have them checked.' She looked again at Mr Frost, who was still wolfing down his breakfast. 'You heard it, didn't you, Walter?'

Walter swallowed a forkful of sausage and shook his head. 'Can't say I did.'

This was definitely not an appropriate time to mention Wailing Willie. 'I'll look into it,' Ally said vaguely as she made her way back to the kitchen. Wailing Willie indeed! She was becoming as daft as the locals and must have been out of her mind to even *think* of it!

It was nearly eleven before an unrecognisable vision appeared in the kitchen. Morag sported blonde, bouffant curls, in place of her normal mousy, greying mop, plus bright-blue eyeshadow, and a floral summer dress. The dress might have fitted her once, but it now clung to her ample curves and showed up her knicker line. Ally reckoned she must be freezing because it was still very chilly outside.

'Where's the party, Morag?'

Morag gave a wry smile. 'I *told* you I was going to be interviewed for the telly. They should be here any minute now.'

Ally realised, for the second day running, that not a lot of cleaning would be taking place today. 'Look,' she said, digging an apron out of the drawer and handing it to Morag, 'you don't want to get any marks on that dress, so if you could finish off the

Frosts' breakfast stuff, I'll get going upstairs. You can obviously take off the pinny for your television appearance!'

As Morag donned the pinny, the phone in the hall rang. It was Rigby.

'Just wanted to let you know, Mrs McKinley, that we've managed to contact Mr Wilbur Carrington's brother. As we speak, he's probably somewhere over the Atlantic, heading to Prestwick, I should think. Anyway, he wants a room with a shower in the en suite.'

'Here?' Ally asked.

'Yes, why not?' Rigby asked.

'Isn't that a little insensitive, seeing as his brother was murdered here?'

'Well, Mrs McKinley, so far as I know at the moment, that man could have been killed anywhere between the Craigmonie Hotel and your place, and the brother's got to stay *somewhere*. I thought that, as you're just starting up at The Auld Malthouse, you might like to have the honour? But I must remind you that Room One will remain locked for the time being, so you'd need to accommodate him in one of the other rooms.'

'Thank you,' Ally said. 'Any idea when he might be arriving?'

'None at all,' replied Rigby cheerfully.

Ally hung up and went to start cleaning the Frosts' bedroom. Within minutes, Morag came upstairs, pulled off her apron and said, 'They're wantin' to interview me *now*!' She was shivering with excitement.

'Well, off you go!' said Ally. 'Don't worry – you'll be fine.'

'Ah told them all about Murdo no settin' the alarm and that,' said Morag the next day, 'but they didnae show that bit on the telly.' She was back in her checked trousers and floral wrap-around apron, her blonde curls rapidly reverting to frizz.

'Well, well,' said Ally, feigning surprise, 'I guess that's another jewel ending up on the cutting-room floor, as they say.'

'Eh?' said Morag, still basking in the glory of her brief television appearance.

'It's just an expression in the film business, Morag. I used to work in television, remember, as a researcher.'

There was still no sign of either Rigby or Wilbur Carrington's brother. Ally felt as if she was in limbo, as the Frosts were still occupying Room 2, she had to keep Room 3 vacant for the brother and she couldn't use Room 1 at all.

'Wouldn't you think you'd hear *something* from *somebody*?' Ally grumbled to herself as she polished the hall mirror.

Ally needed visitors. She'd overspent on the malthouse conversion, and she badly needed income to repay the loan that the bank had grudgingly given her. So long as the Frosts left on Saturday, she could at least take bookings for Room 2. But would the police allow the Frosts to leave and would anyone want to book a room at The Auld Malthouse knowing that one of the guests had just been murdered? There was always the bedroom adjacent to her own, which was supposedly reserved for family and friends. It was a large, sunny room, but whoever occupied it would be obliged to share a bathroom with herself. She sighed. How long were the police going to take to solve this?

Perhaps it was time to take matters into her own hands...

After Morag left, Ally located the extra key for Room 1, which she kept hidden in the kitchen drawer, and ventured upstairs. Rigby had never actually *asked* her if she had any other keys, but, in fact, she'd got several extra ones for each room.

To be on the safe side, in case Rigby would be able to detect any new fingerprints, Ally donned her yellow Marigold rubber gloves. There must *surely* be a clue in that room.

The room was, of course, more or less exactly as she'd last

seen it. Ally had always liked this bedroom best out of the three, because it was dual aspect, one window facing south and the other facing west, and so got the sunshine all day. She'd opted for a lot of cream, with dark blue as an accent colour, and had some golden oak furniture along with some painted pieces.

Ally locked the door behind her and ventured warily across the wooden floor with its large white sheepskin rugs, and wondered where to start. She sat down in front of the oak chest of drawers and gingerly pulled out the top one, which contained a man's wristwatch and some folded white handkerchiefs.

The next drawer down was full of neatly folded socks and boxer shorts in plain colours. The third one contained some sweaters, mostly cashmere. And the bottom drawer contained some newspaper cuttings about the area and the earl in particular, and some old photographs. Nothing very exciting. Had the police checked this? She'd have to replace each item very carefully as they might well have taken photographs. She seemed to remember the police liked to take photos of everything.

Most of the photos in the drawer were very old and faded. Could that severe-looking, tight-lipped woman possibly have been his mother? And the two little boys, with their all-American haircuts and toothy smiles: could they be the Carrington brothers? It was difficult to identify either boy as the elderly man she'd known so briefly. She looked hopefully for a passport, but there was no sign, so Rigby had most likely taken that.

Then Ally remembered the antique desk in front of the window. They'd inherited it from Ken's grandmother, so it had to be at least one hundred years old. It was oak, with carving on the legs and the back, and was probably worth a lot of money, but Ally could never bring herself to sell it. She'd always been intrigued by the fact that it had a secret drawer and had almost forgotten that she'd mentioned it to Wilbur. 'If you have any private documents, Mr Carrington,' she'd said with a smile, 'there's a hidden drawer in here. Let me show you.' She'd released the little catch so the drawer slid open.

'Well, if that ain't the *cutest* thing!' Wilbur Carrington had exclaimed.

There was a slight chance that he just *might* have put something in there, Ally supposed. She felt for the catch, and out came the drawer, in which was a slim green cardboard folder with 'Earls of Locharran' scribbled in black ink on the cover. She withdrew the file and opened it to find more photographs, many of which were of documents, and lists of churches throughout the West Highland region.

Ally sat down and briefly studied the contents, looking guiltily around just in case Rigby had decided to suddenly return. But, she thought, these could be important and were plainly not meant to be found, and Rigby was certainly unaware of the drawer or the folder's existence. She pondered for a moment. Should she tell Rigby? She had some private doubts as to his efficiency, although perhaps she should make allowances for his cold. Then her old research training kicked in. This was no TV programme but could be more important than any whodunnit!

She picked up the folder, popped it under her arm, pushed the drawer shut and left the room, locking the door carefully behind her. She'd replace the folder and inform Rigby about the drawer later.

As she made her way downstairs, she experienced a little shiver of excitement at the prospect of what she might find. In the meantime, she'd lock it away in the drawer where she kept her personal papers, in the little office off the back of the kitchen. When she got a moment, she'd study the folder and its contents in detail.

. . .

Ally had met Hamish Sinclair only once since she'd arrived, in Locharran Stores, when Queenie had taken great pleasure in introducing them to each other. 'This is the Earl of Locharran,' she'd gushed importantly, and then with less enthusiasm, 'And this is Mrs McKinley, who's just bought the old malthouse.'

'Oh,' he'd said, his eyes lighting up as he'd extended an age-spotted hand. 'I'd heard that a lovely lady had bought the malt-house.' He'd given her hand a little squeeze. 'You must come up to the castle for tea now that you've settled in,' he'd added, still firmly holding her hand.

He was about her own height with a shock of white hair, a little white beard and mischievous brown eyes, and had been clad in a kilt of mainly green tartan, presumably the Sinclair hunting tartan. With this he'd worn a jaunty little sporran, a green tweed jacket and matching green knee-high socks. Knowing his reputation with the ladies, the last thing Ally had wanted to do was let him think that she was in any way eager to further their acquaintance. Now, however, she was curious to know if Carrington had visited him, and what the earl had thought of the American.

Maybe, she thought, *it's my research training taking over*. When she'd worked in television, Ally had never been quite sure what she might have to research next. Sometimes it had been historical research, for a costume drama when it was essential to get all the dates right. Sometimes it had been for a murder mystery when she'd had to find out about police proce-dures, and sometimes it had been about a famous figure, when she'd had to get all the facts spot on.

When she'd got home from Locharran Stores, she'd googled Hamish Sinclair and discovered that he was the eighth Earl of Locharran, educated at Eton and Cambridge (which explained his upper-crust accent), widowed and the owner of thirty thou-sand acres in the Scottish Highlands. It hadn't mentioned his reported fondness for the ladies.

. . .

The next day, Thursday, after she'd finished the necessary chores, Ally decided she needed some fresh air, and she wondered how to 'accidentally' bump into the earl. She had a feeling that he might well know something about what Carrington was researching. It would certainly come into the conversation, she felt sure, because that was all everyone was talking about.

It was a beautiful day – the sun was shining, and the birds were singing. Above the village were miles of heather-clad moorland, affording wonderful views of the mountains and the sea loch in the distance. She wished she had a dog; Jamie's suggestion wasn't a bad one. Perhaps she'd get one eventually. She'd feel more secure with a dog, and she'd enjoy the walks.

Looking at the views and breathing in the pure Highland air, Ally found it hard to believe that any murder could take place in such an idyllic spot.

She climbed up, stumbling occasionally on the dense heather, until she came across a little hut built into the hillside. It was a roughly built wood cabin, measuring probably about nine feet square, doorless, but with a couple of benches inside. Presumably it was used as some sort of shelter in inclement weather.

Ally had just sat down on one of the benches to admire the view when a large black Labrador appeared, full of excitement and enthusiasm, tail wagging frantically. Within seconds, he was joined by another large golden one, barking wildly and also greeting her with enthusiasm, followed by an equally friendly springer spaniel. Ally, laughing, stood up to try to ward off their muddy paws and found herself face to face with Hamish Sinclair.

'Oh, hello!' he said, smiling broadly. He was wearing some form of breeches today, tucked into his stockings, and carrying a walking stick. 'How nice to see you again!' He shouted at the dogs to *get down*. 'I hope they haven't covered you in mud?'

'No, no,' said Ally hastily. 'It's fine. I'm wearing old clothes. I hope I'm not trespassing or anything?'

'Of course not,' said the earl. 'These moors are for everyone, unless we're out shooting! We always put notices out on such occasions. We met in the shop, didn't we?'

'Yes, we did.'

'Mrs McKinley, isn't it?'

'That's right. That was before all this dreadful business took place,' Ally said, hoping to open up the subject.

'Oh, indeed. And I understand the poor man was found at the malthouse?'

'Yes, he was. Did he come to visit you?'

'Aye, he did indeed. Tracing his ancestors, he said.'

'Was he a Sinclair then?' Ally asked.

Hamish shrugged. 'Who knows? Who cares? Anyway, you must come up for tea at the castle one of these days, so we can get to know each other better.'

'That would be lovely,' said Ally, knowing he was changing the subject.

He turned away, shouting for the dogs. 'I'll be seeing you soon,' he said, giving her a wink.

SEVEN

On Friday, four days after the killing, a letter was pushed through Ally's letterbox, her name just decipherable in the scrawled handwriting. It had been delivered by hand.

With some difficulty, Ally made out the contents of the letter, which was written on expensive top-quality writing paper, headed 'Locharran Castle' and further adorned with the Sinclair crest which featured a cockerel and read 'Commit Thy Work to God'.

Dear Mrs McKinley,

I was charmed to make your acquaintance briefly in our local shop and on the moor yesterday, and would be delighted to further that contact. Perhaps you would be kind enough to join me for afternoon tea here at the castle on Sunday, say about 4 p.m.?

Do let my housekeeper, Mrs Fraser, know if this is convenient. I hope to see you then.

Kind regards,

Hamish Sinclair

Underneath was scrawled what was presumably Mrs Fraser's mobile number.

Well, thought Ally, *I wanted an opportunity to ask him a few questions, so I have to go.* She phoned Mrs Fraser to say she'd be delighted to attend.

The Frosts departed the following day, having given all their contact details to DI Rigby.

'It is quite disgraceful that we could even be *considered* as suspects,' Mrs Frost told Ally haughtily as she settled the bill. 'We are law-abiding citizens and have been all our lives, let me tell you! I've never had as much as a *parking ticket!*' She tut-tutted whilst shaking her head in despair.

'At least the police are letting you move on, Mrs Frost. Surely that's better than having to remain here indefinitely until the killer is found?'

Mrs Frost sniffed. 'And when will that be, pray? I haven't seen many police around here or a great deal of action going on.'

Ally refrained from agreeing with her, although she'd been thinking much the same thing. She wished the couple well, and breathed a long sigh of relief as she saw their little Nissan disappear down the drive and out of sight.

Morag had arrived and was preparing to work on the Frosts' bedroom. There was as yet no sign of any further visitors, and Morag asked if it would be OK if she didn't come back until there was, because she'd been approached by Mrs Fraser, up at the castle, to see if she could do 'a wee bit of cleaning up there'.

'That's absolutely fine, Morag,' Ally said. 'There's nothing for you to do here until we get some guests.' She grinned. 'I might see you if you're working there tomorrow because I've been invited for afternoon tea, would you believe?'

'Oh, I *would* believe,' said Morag, nodding and narrowing her eyes. 'We've all been wonderin' how long it would take before the old groper tried to get his hands on you. Ye'll need yer chastity belt before ye go!'

Ally laughed. 'Surely he's not that bad – I'm only going for a cup of tea!'

'That's what you think. You mark my words!'

Ally wondered what one should wear for such an auspicious occasion. It wasn't every day she got invited to tea with an earl. The weather in April being unpredictable and, although bright, not particularly warm, she finally settled for some smart trousers, one of her two cashmere sweaters and a matching patterned scarf draped, as artfully as she could, round her neck, plus some plain pearl earrings. Best to look as classy and under-stated as possible, she supposed, slinging on her trench coat.

Locharran Castle was an enormous, imposing structure, built very much in the manner of the French chateau, complete with turrets at every corner. Ally had viewed it from afar but had never ventured up the driveway and had certainly never been anywhere near the huge, oak front door, accessed by a flight of stone steps on either side. There was a large iron bell, with a pull-chain, on the right of the doorway, and Ally could see no other method of announcing her arrival. Nervously she gave it an experimental tug and was almost deafened by the peal which, she felt sure, must be audible for miles around. It must also have been heard in the castle, as a matronly grey-haired lady in a pink dress and white apron arrived at the door.

'Mrs McKinley? Do come in. I'm Mrs Fraser, the earl's housekeeper.' She stood aside, and Ally was conscious of being surveyed from head to toe. 'The earl is expecting you in his study. May I take your coat?'

Ally nodded, and Mrs Fraser hung it up carefully on a hanger in the outer lobby.

Ally was ushered into an enormous stone-floored hall, with a gigantic stone fireplace taking up most of one wall. Above the oak-panelled lower walls was an impressive array of stags' heads, mounted equidistant from each other, or so it looked. She didn't have time to count them, but there must have been at least fifty.

She followed Mrs Fraser along a chilly stone corridor for what seemed like miles, before she was finally ushered through another oak door into a book-lined room, which was presumably the earl's study and where Hamish Sinclair was standing in front of a glowing peat fire. For a brief moment, Ally was transported back to childhood holidays at her grandmother's house near Fort Augustus, where a peat fire burned in every room. It was a wonderful smell, like no other.

Her host stepped forward with a smile and an outstretched hand. Again, Ally was aware of him holding her hand just a tad longer than was necessary.

'Do sit down, Mrs McKinley. I'm so glad you could come.' He turned to Mrs Fraser. 'Perhaps you could bring in the tea things in a minute or two, Jean?'

Mrs Fraser disappeared, and Ally sat down on a tartan-covered armchair and took stock of her surroundings. The room was too large to be considered cosy, but at least it was warm. The bookshelves, which stretched from floor to ceiling, were packed with tomes of all shapes and sizes, many of them old and leather-bound. There was a huge mahogany desk in front of the leaded window, on which was a jumble of paperwork, and several crystal decanters containing golden liquids which Ally took to be Scotch.

As for the Earl of Locharran, he was again resplendent in a kilt – a different one from before, predominantly red – which he'd topped with a red V-necked pullover. His thatch of white hair had been neatly brushed, and Ally could decipher a considerable amount of expensive aftershave in the air.

'I hope you're all settled in now, Mrs McKinley,' he said, still standing in front of the fire, his legs spreadeagled in a proprietary manner.

'Yes, thank you, sir.' Ally wondered what she was supposed to call him.

'Oh, do call me Hamish,' he said, as if reading her mind. 'I think we should be on first-name terms, don't you? After all, we are neighbours!'

'Um, yes, if you think so. I'm Ally, short for Alison.'

'Well, Alison,' he said, moving a little closer, 'I'm sorry the village has been so preoccupied by this wretched crime, and so soon after your arrival in this beautiful part of the world. Such a nasty business. I gather it was you who found Carrington's body?'

'No, no, that was Morag McConnachie. She cleans for me sometimes.'

'Ah, Morag.' He smiled. 'Nice wee lady. Cleans for us now and again too. Must have been an awful shock. I understand that the Carrington fellow was actually staying with you at your bed and breakfast?'

'Yes, sir, er... Hamish.'

'I believe you've converted the malthouse very sympathetically.'

Ally smiled. 'I tried, because I didn't want to lose any of the character.'

Hamish sat himself down in the tartan-covered chair opposite her own. There was a wild explosion of colour between the mainly red of the tartan in the kilt along with the greens and blues of the chair.

'Oh,' he said, 'there was certainly plenty of character within those walls of yours. The malt was formed there for centuries, you know, in the steeping pits, and produced a very fine whisky.

Finest whisky on earth. We still make it locally, but it now has to be stored in modern containers, approved by health and safety and all that, and it does not taste the same, believe me. And, of course, you've got the ghost, which adds even more character.'

'Oh, I don't believe all this nonsense about a ghost!' Ally said, smiling.

'Well, my dear, maybe you should. Ah, here comes our tea!'

After a brief tap on the door, Mrs Fraser trundled in a big, old oak tea trolley, loaded with tea things, from the dainty china crockery to the mountain of smoked salmon sandwiches, cut in tiny triangles, along with scones, jam, butter, cream and a selection of cakes and pastries. She placed the trolley between them.

'Would you like me to pour?' Mrs Fraser asked, wielding a tea strainer. Proper tea then.

'Yes please,' Hamish replied, 'and I would ask that you please put the milk in the cup *first*.' He glanced at Ally, as if for approval.

'I don't actually take milk,' Ally admitted. 'Just one spoon of sugar please.'

Mrs Fraser obeyed, carefully pouring the tea through the strainer before passing it to Ally. She then poured the earl's milk into the cup in a slightly exaggerated manner before filling it up from the teapot.

'Shall I leave you to it then?' she asked, looking towards the door.

'Yes, that'll be all for now, Jean,' said Hamish.

As the door closed behind Mrs Fraser, her host said, 'Do have some of these sandwiches, Alison. Did you know we smoke the salmon here ourselves?'

'No, I didn't,' Ally admitted, taking a couple of tiny sandwiches and placing them on her plate on the table alongside her chair.

They both chewed silently for a moment before Ally, after

dabbing her mouth daintily with the white linen napkin (and hoping not to leave traces of lipstick), said, 'These are delicious.' She paused. 'I'm very sad about poor Mr Carrington. He seemed a very nice, harmless sort of person. I believe he visited you at some point?'

'Oh, indeed he did! He was a bit of a nuisance, here every five minutes. Very taken with the castle and the clan.' He pushed the plate of sandwiches towards her. 'Do have some more.'

Ally wondered if she should admit to looking through Carrington's effects. She decided she would. 'I had a look through some of his things,' she said casually, 'and he had a file full of photographs and cuttings all about you and the castle.'

Hamish had now moved on to the scones where he busied himself shovelling on jam and cream. He took a hearty bite and nodded.

'He told me he was writing a book about the Highlands and this area in particular,' Ally continued, 'and he seemed to think his ancestors came from here.'

'Apparently he thought the *Sinclairs* were his ancestors,' said Hamish, giving a perfunctory wipe of his mouth and a stroke of his beard, presumably to remove crumbs. 'Of course, all Americans like to find out where their ancestors came from and some, like him, have these fanciful ideas. Aren't you having a scone?'

'No thank you,' Ally replied.

Her host leaned forward. 'You don't need to worry about your weight, Alison. You're in very fine shape! Can't stand all those skinny women you see on the television.'

Ally smiled nervously. She could see some distance up his kilt but not enough to be able to see if he was wearing anything underneath. She sincerely hoped he was.

'Perhaps you'd be kind enough to permit me to pop into

your malthouse sometime, as I'd very much like to see what you've done with it,' he said.

'Yes,' Ally said hastily, 'but getting back to Wilbur Carrington—'

'Must we?' he put in. 'After all, the poor man must have upset somebody, I suppose.'

Understatement of the year, Ally thought. 'Yes,' she agreed, 'but do you have any idea who might have wanted to kill him?'

'Not a clue. Do try one of the pastries, Alison. They're delicious. Maggie Jamieson, our cook, is an excellent baker, did you know?'

Ally thought it might appear rude if she refused a cake as well, so she carefully selected the smallest, taking a little bite and nodding in agreement that it was indeed delicious. 'What sort of questions was he asking you, Hamish?'

'Oh, all about the Sinclairs, you know. He had no idea that we originated from France as the Saint Clairs, and that we own land all over Scotland. Stuff like that. He wanted to check on some old churches in the area, so I told him that Ian – that's my chauffeur – would be happy to ferry him around. I don't suppose poor Ian was particularly happy, but at least it got Carrington away from here because he was becoming a bit of a nuisance. More tea?'

What Ally wanted was more information, so she'd have the tea as well. 'Yes, please.'

He stood up, poured the tea through the strainer and remarked, 'Many Scottish people drink their tea without milk. I wonder why that is?'

Ally shook her head. 'I've really no idea.' He passed her the refilled cup and saucer but remained standing, and she had the distinct impression that he seemed to be peering down the V-neck of her sweater. She hastily rearranged her scarf and took a sip of her tea.

'You're not nervous down there, on your own, with a killer on the loose?'

'No, I have good locks on the doors, and I usually have guests.'

'You'll need to get a dog,' he said. 'It would keep you safer.'

'I've been thinking about that,' Ally said. 'It would be good company in my old age!'

'May I ask how old you are?' enquired Hamish, sitting down again and patting his sporran. At least that was what Ally hoped he was patting. 'I do realise,' he went on, 'that that's not a question one should ask a lady, but I'm guessing you might be nearing a very youthful sixty?'

Ally almost dropped her cup. The temerity of the man! Was he being deliberately flattering in the hope of some sort of seduction?

'You're right, Hamish,' she said, 'ladies don't discuss their age.'

'Oh well, never mind.' He didn't look particularly disheartened by her reply.

'I wondered what sort of things Carrington was asking you?' she persisted.

'*Asking* me?' Hamish had come alive now. 'No, he wasn't *asking* me; he was damned well *telling* me! Trying to convince me that the elder brother of my great-grandfather had secretly wed one of the housemaids and sired a son with her, before dying shortly afterwards. Then she and the baby were banished off to New England, would you believe? And the story goes that it was the new earl, his younger brother, who was *my* great-grandfather, who banished her. Carrington claimed he was on the verge of getting the truth. He was telling me that he was the rightful heir to the earldom and to the estate, if you can believe it!'

EIGHT

For the second time in as many minutes Ally had to steady her cup. She quickly drained her tea and replaced her cup and saucer carefully on the trolley. 'More to the point,' she said, 'do *you* believe this?'

Hamish waved his hand dismissively. 'Stuff and nonsense! Housemaids were forever becoming pregnant by their masters, for God's sake! Par for the course.' He didn't appear to be in the least bit perturbed.

'But they didn't all marry them, did they? Do you really think Carrington might have been able to prove it?' Ally asked, shivering with excitement as she thought of the contents of the folder, which she'd not yet examined. 'I got the impression that Wilbur Carrington had most of the proof he needed to prove his ancestry, but that he wanted to find the local church so he could dig into their records.'

'Just a lot of rubbish!' Hamish stood up again. 'If we must talk about the wretched man, can we at least do so with a drink?' He consulted his watch. 'It's definitely cocktail time, Alison, and I make a pretty good cocktail, if I say so myself!'

Ally was keen to find out more but felt she might be wise

not to outstay her welcome. 'I should be going—' she began, to be interrupted with, 'Nonsense! Have you a houseful of guests awaiting you, Alison?'

'Well, no,' she admitted ruefully, 'but—'

'In that case, we shall have a drink. I'll get Jean to collect the tea things.' He pressed a bell on the wall.

'Well, thank you.'

'That's a girl! What's your poison?'

'A small Scotch would be lovely, with water please.'

'A woman of taste,' said Hamish approvingly, heading in the direction of the desk and the decanters just as Mrs Fraser reappeared through the door.

'Shall I remove the trolley, sir?' asked Mrs Fraser, looking towards the desk and then at Ally.

'Yes, please. Mrs McKinley and I are going to sample some of Locharran's finest malt.'

The woman cast a further glance at Ally before pushing the trolley out through the door.

Ally supposed that this visit would be all over Locharran before long: the earl entertaining the new lady with lust in his eyes. She'd have to brace herself.

The earl handed Ally a crystal glass, filled to the brim with the golden liquid. 'I did add water,' he reassured her, sitting down opposite again with a large glass for himself. This he raised in the air before uttering the Gaelic toast. '*Slàinte mhòr!*'

'Cheers!' Ally replied, taking a sip. He was right; it was indeed a beautiful malt, and the main ingredient might even have been stored under her very own roof! Feeling emboldened, she asked, 'So, it doesn't worry you that a passing American might lay claim to your name and estate?'

'Well, he's hardly likely to *now*, is he?' Hamish said with a broad smile.

'True,' Ally agreed, wondering whether this could be the motive for his murder. She was keen to hear more about this claim of Carrington's but felt it might be wise not to stay too long. She was also aware that, since the trolley had been removed, the earl was slowly inching his chair towards hers. Did he honestly think that a glass of whisky, no matter how sublime, could pave the way towards seduction?

Ally was not easily affected by alcohol. She'd always enjoyed it, imbibed a glass or two of wine most evenings, and when she'd occasionally overindulged had always managed to keep her wits about her. She was unlikely to be influenced by the attentions of this rather silly man. She decided to enjoy what remained of her drink and then make her escape before he made it all the way across to where she was sitting.

'Has DI Rigby been questioning you?' Ally asked.

'Yes, that damned detective keeps asking me questions. And not only me, but he's been interrogating poor Mrs Fraser, and Angus, my gamekeeper, and Ian, my chauffeur, and goodness knows how many others who work for me. He's making himself a perfect nuisance.'

'Surely Rigby didn't think any of you had anything to do with the murder?'

'The thing is, Carrington began telling anyone who'd listen that he was the rightful earl and, furthermore, he was going to prove it. Then he was going to turn my entire estate, including the castle, into some sort of giant theme park!'

'That's unbelievable!' Ally exclaimed, wondering if the malthouse was part of his estate and whether she should be worried.

'*He* certainly seemed to believe it, Alison! Now, tell me about *yourself*,' he said, edging his chair another inch closer.

Ally kept it brief. Widowed, two children, four grandchildren – one in Edinburgh and three down in Salisbury, Wiltshire. She'd been a TV researcher until she retired.

'So what brought you to Locharran?'

Ally was aware he'd managed to move forward another

couple of inches. How potent did he think his damned whisky was?

Trying to finish her drink as quickly as she could, Ally told him about how she'd fallen in love with the malthouse and the area, wondering at the same time if she'd have loved it quite as much if she'd been pre-warned that it would come with an over-attentive earl.

Gulping the remainder of her whisky, Ally stood up. 'This has been most enjoyable,' she said before he could open his mouth to protest, 'but I must go now just in case I have a queue of prospective guests.' *And chance would be a fine thing*, she thought.

Hamish got to his feet, clutching his glass. 'Oh, surely you could stay a little longer?'

'I'm afraid not, Hamish, but thank you for a lovely tea and wonderful whisky.'

'Oh well.' He sounded resigned. 'It's been a great pleasure, and I look forward to visiting your malthouse in due course. Let me escort you to the door.'

She followed him along the corridor and through the enormous hall, to the entrance area, where she'd left her coat. As he helped her into it, he said, 'I'd be delighted to drive you back to the malthouse.'

'Thank you, but it's only a ten-minute walk and it's all downhill. I shall enjoy the fresh air.'

Afraid that he might make some move towards kissing her, Ally held out her hand.

'If you're sure?' He gripped her hand tightly again.

'Quite sure, thank you.'

Ally set off down the drive, sorely tempted to look back to see if he was still watching from the doorway, but she resisted the urge.

. . .

Ally got home to the large, empty malthouse with no prospective guests in sight and hoped that none had come while she was out. There were no messages on the answer machine or on her mobile. She sat down in the kitchen with a black coffee, to counteract the whisky she'd gulped so rapidly, and thought about the visit. Perhaps Hamish could become a bit of a pest, but she was old enough and wise enough to deal with men like him. She'd dealt with a fair few in her life, usually with a hefty kick in the shins, or a knee to where it hurt most, if necessary, long before women's liberation.

What was really perplexing her was how relaxed the earl appeared to be, in view of the fact that Wilbur Carrington had laid claim to his estate. Was this just an act? Had Carrington produced some sort of evidence? What if Hamish Sinclair had really felt threatened?

With such a possible motive, was it likely that Hamish Sinclair, the Earl of Locharran, could actually be the killer? Given that Rigby had interviewed the earl and questioned people on the estate, he obviously had considered it likely.

Ally couldn't get her head round the fact that the earl was so relaxed about it all because, in his shoes, she'd be seriously worried about being the chief suspect because the American's claim might be valid.

NINE

Later that evening, Ally poured herself a glass of wine and sat down in the kitchen. She had an armchair on each side of the log burner, which she'd let die off, although the Aga was still on. It was still cool in the evenings and the Aga was the source of the central heating and, even when on low, provided a comfortable warmth.

She thought about Rigby. He seemed like a nice man, but she had some doubts about the accuracy of his suspect list. Apart from anything else, he hadn't seemed to even consider *her* as a possible suspect, and yet Carrington's body had been found near her back door! *Was* she on his list?

Having spent most of her adult life in research, Ally was becoming more and more curious about who, out of the likely suspects she was aware of, could possibly have carried out this heinous deed. When she'd been doing her TV research, she'd used little Post-it notes for all her ideas, which she'd attached to a board and then eliminated as necessary. She'd like to do that again now, to list her own ideas about who the suspects might be, but she could hardly have that on display in the kitchen; it needed to be hidden somewhere. Ally looked around and remembered her large, much-loved still life painting of oranges, lemons and grapes. It had once belonged to her grandmother, who, she'd been told, had brought it back from Italy, although what her grandmother had been doing in Italy had never been made clear. It had been one of the first things she'd unpacked on moving into the malthouse and looked just right hanging on the wall behind the old oak table.

Turning the painting over on the kitchen table, she saw to her delight that it had a smooth wooden back, the perfect place to stick her ideas when she was on her own. Morag was extremely unlikely to take the picture down at any time, as she normally just flicked a duster at it.

Ally got out her little book of Post-it notes and decided to write the name of a possible suspect on each sheet. Where to begin? When she'd done her TV research, she'd always put the problem in the middle, and the possible solutions around the centre, like the numbers on a clock face; the most likely candidate at the top of the dial at 12 o'clock, and the least likely at 6 o'clock. It had worked well in the past, so why shouldn't it work well now? It was her version of a compass – something to guide her – because she could never keep 360 degrees in her head.

She put her first Post-it note in the centre, with 'Wilbur Carrington – Victim'.

She knew that the earl, Hamish Sinclair, just *had* to be the chief suspect. He was, without doubt, the person with the most to lose: his castle, his land, his estate, his title. She knew, too, that she must not let her own feelings get in the way. She liked the man, as a friend, and her gut feeling was that he was innocent. But gut feelings could not come into this, and so, without doubt, Hamish had to be the chief suspect. And, doubtless, he had no shortage of skean dhus. She placed him directly above Wilbur, at 12 o'clock on her imaginary clock face.

Then there were the two women up at the castle: Mrs Fraser and the cook, Mrs Jamieson. She didn't know the cook but decided she should find out about her as soon as possible. Both ladies would be out of a job, and out of the castle, if Carrington had had his way, and no doubt both of them had access to the earl's skean dhus. Most likely Mrs Fraser had overheard a great deal of the conversation between the earl and Wilbur Carrington, and it was entirely possible that she'd shared this with the cook. Perhaps it was a conspiracy between the two of them? The cook certainly wouldn't baulk at the sight of blood, since she was probably used to cutting out various joints of meat from the animals slaughtered by the earl and his hunting guests. Ally wrote 'Mrs Fraser' on one note and 'Mrs Jamieson' on the other, and stuck them on the board, side by side, at 1 o'clock.

Then there was Angus Morrison. He, too, had an estate house, although Ally had no idea of his circumstances. He was soon to retire, she'd been told, and perhaps he expected to keep his house. Did people in tied houses, on estates such as this, save up for their retirement, or was it a foregone conclusion that the house would be theirs for the remainder of their lives? There was so much she didn't know, but nonetheless Angus had to be a suspect. He was perhaps not such a strong suspect as the others, so she'd stick him on the board at 6 o'clock.

Ally hated herself for even having to *think* of Murdo and Morag, but their house was estate-owned, and they had some land as well for their menagerie of animals, and it was Morag who had found the body. They had just as much reason as everyone else to want to preserve their lifestyles. She couldn't quite see Morag wielding a skean dhu, but Murdo could. Ally had visions of Murdo waiting for Wilbur to come out of the Craigmonie, following him, stabbing him and then instructing Morag to make a big fuss when she found the body outside of the malthouse the following morning! Ally wrote 'Morag' on one and 'Murdo' on another, and stuck them, side by side on the board, at 4 o'clock.

Who else? Well, there was Queenie and Bessie, of course, although it was difficult to imagine either of them moving at any kind of speed, far less brandishing a dagger. Queenie rarely moved anyway, so it would have to be Bessie, as usual, who'd do the dirty work. Again, it was only a possibility if they were in league with someone else. She wrote 'Queenie' and 'Bessie' on a Post-it, and on another wrote a large question mark and placed them side by side at 8 o'clock.

The back of Ally's still life was now nearly full of Post-it notes, but it was still almost impossible for her to believe that any of them could have done the deed. She'd feel a great deal better when she could begin to eliminate them, one by one, and tear them off. Until then, she'd try to do some more research on her suspects. There were four spaces on her clock available for anyone else, but nothing came to mind at the moment.

Ally studied the board for a while, then turned it round again to face the wall.

TEN

On Monday morning, DI Rigby appeared just after nine o'clock.

'Just a few further questions, Mrs McKinley.'

Ally led him into the kitchen and placed the kettle on the Aga. 'Tea? Coffee?'

'Thank you. Tea please, two sugars.' Rigby stood in front of the log burner, rubbing his hands. 'It's chilly again today.' His cold appeared to be on the wane.

'Yes,' Ally agreed. 'Not very springlike at the moment. How's the inquiry going?'

Rigby rolled his eyes. 'Tricky. I have to ask: did Carrington say anything to you about having proof of some claim or other on the Sinclair estate?'

'Only that he was looking around old churches, apparently searching for some old records, presumably regarding his family.'

'Hmm,' said Rigby. 'And on the Sunday evening, did he *tell* you he was going to visit the Craigmonie Hotel?'

Ally nodded. 'Yes, he said he fancied some of the local

whisky, and he'd have a meal in the restaurant while he was there.' She'd already told him all this.

'At what time would you say he went out?'

'I reckon it would have been about half past seven. I saw him walking down the path to the main road, and that was the last I saw of him until...' Ally was still trying to delete from her mind the sight of Carrington's lifeless body and the bloodied skean dhu.

'Right.' Rigby accepted the mug of tea and cupped his hands around it.

Ally offered him some shortbread, which he wolfed down in seconds. She wondered what time he'd started work and if she should offer him some breakfast.

'I imagine incidents like this are very rare in these parts,' Ally remarked. 'Have you had many to deal with?'

There was silence for a moment while he finished off the shortbread, then he cleared his throat and replied, 'Actually, this is my first up here.'

'What an initiation!' Ally exclaimed, suddenly feeling sorry for the guy. 'I was talking to the earl yesterday,' she added, 'and he too mentioned about Carrington claiming that the estate was rightfully his.'

Rigby shrugged. 'Moot point. We haven't found much proof of that yet. I found the earl to be a very straightforward man. Quite impressive. He'd surely be an expert on his own family's ancestry.'

'And I understand Carrington planned to make the whole estate into some sort of theme park,' Ally continued, 'which I imagine must have gone down like a lead balloon with most of the locals.'

He groaned. 'Indeed it did,' he said, gulping his tea. 'Most of the villagers' homes here are owned by the estate and, on his visits to the Craigmonie Bar, I understand he informed everyone what his plans were. I believe the malthouse here is *not* on the Sinclair estate?'

'No, it's not,' Ally confirmed. 'I must admit I double-checked the malthouse deeds when I got home yesterday. Apparently, the freehold was bought years ago by the local distiller, and now belongs to me.'

'Nevertheless,' Rigby said with a grin, 'I don't suppose you'd like some sort of Disneyland all around you?'

'No, I can't say I would. But I don't think I'd have felt strongly enough to have stuck a knife in his back, even if I'd *known* about it while he was alive. But at least I'd be likely to get some customers!'

He sniffed. 'Talking of which, Tyler Carrington, brother of the deceased, should arrive here in the next few days. He's in Inverness at the moment, having identified the body, and has expressed a wish to see where his brother spent his final days.'

'Isn't that a wee bit ghoulish?'

Rigby shrugged. 'Each to his own.'

'And is he aware that all my rooms are doubles? His brother didn't seem to mind.'

'He doesn't seem to be short of money. Just one point: on *no* account must he be allowed into Room One. He may want to see his brother's stuff, but he is *not* to go in there. I've locked it up, of course, and I'm assuming you have another key? Do you?'

Ally hoped she didn't look guilty. 'There is another key,' she said airily, 'but you said not to go in there so I haven't gone looking for it.'

Well, she thought to herself, *I* didn't *go looking for it because I knew exactly where it was.*

'I'd like to take another look up there now,' said Rigby, 'if that's all right with you?'

'Certainly.'

Rigby drained his tea and made his way upstairs, carrying a

large briefcase. She heard him moving around but couldn't decipher exactly what he might be doing. Had he found the drawer?

He reappeared after about ten minutes. 'That'll be all for now, Mrs McKinley,' he said, 'but if you hear or see anything which you consider may be in any way relevant to this case, will you please get in touch straight away?' He removed a card from his briefcase and handed it to her.

'Yes, sure,' Ally replied, knowing she should produce the hidden folder she'd found. She would produce it in due course but, in the meantime, she relished the thought of doing some research of her own.

'And thanks very much for the tea and shortbread,' he said with a smile as he made his way to the door.

When he'd gone, Ally emptied out the contents of the green folder onto the kitchen table: a dozen old photographs, a document and a ticket. The largest photograph was of a young woman, dressed in a cape and a long skirt, carrying a tiny baby. Like the others, it was faded and curling at the corners. The rest were mainly of a boy: an infant with well-brushed hair and a frilly collar on his jacket; one of a little boy staring intently into the camera; a tall young man in a formal suit and a stiff-collared shirt – this one with a background of high-rise buildings, almost certainly in the USA. There were photos of some groups of people, none of which tallied with the woman or the boy. There was a well-fingered, creased ticket for a one-way Atlantic crossing, Glasgow to New York, third class. It bore no name but was dated December 1851. Ally could only make out the detail with the help of Ken's old magnifying glass, smiling to herself as she imagined what he'd have thought of all this.

What got her even more thrilled was another much-folded and faded document of 'Entry of a Marriage'. After several attempts with the magnifying glass, and with increased lighting, she could just about decipher the name of one Jessie McPhee, who married a Robert somebody-or-other, the name even less decipherable. After moving the document around several times and adjusting the lights yet again, she thought she could make out the first letter of Robert's surname, which looked like an S. Ally felt her tummy turning over with excitement. Could that S stand for Sinclair?

Calm down, she told herself. *Don't jump the gun.*

She then photographed every single item, double-checking to ensure that they were all as clear as the originals, and replaced the originals in the folder.

Ally sat, deep in contemplation for a moment or two. Surely, she thought, there must be records going back a couple of hundred years in the local churches? But how did one find out? Perhaps it might be time to make contact with the local Church of Scotland minister. Ally was not a churchgoer, so she hadn't yet met the man, but now was surely the time to make his acquaintance. He must, at least, have some idea where the local church records might be stored.

She needed to find out who this Jessie McPhee had married and when. And could there be some connection between the woman, the baby and Carrington?

She'd hand the file in to Rigby and tell him she'd just found it. Surely he'd be delighted with such prospective information?

Ally had only seen the Reverend Donald Scott from a distance: a tall, gangly, angular man who, she'd been told, had enormous feet. 'Ye'll see them comin' round the corner long before ye see the rest of him,' Murdo had informed her.

The manse was a large Victorian house with an imposing oak front door, flanked by a stone tub of tiny geraniums on either side. Ally felt decidedly nervous as she tapped on his door, which was opened by a tiny, rather chubby lady with very blue eyes who was wearing at least four sweaters.

'I'm sorry to bother you,' Ally said hesitantly, 'but I wondered if I might have a brief word with the reverend?'

'Just a minute,' said the lady in the layers, 'and I'll see if my husband can spare you some time. Who shall I say is calling?'

'I'm Ally McKinley, and I've recently bought the malthouse a little way up the hill. The Auld Malthouse B&B,' she added.

'Oh yes. Wait here please.' The woman disappeared back into the house.

So this, thought Ally, *is* Mrs *Scott. Well, they do say that opposites attract.*

Mrs Scott reappeared. 'He can spare you just a few minutes,' she said, eyeing Ally up and down, 'so follow me, if you please.'

Ally followed her into a very chilly house, so no wonder Mrs Scott was swathed in sweaters. When she was shown into the tiny, book-lined room which served as the minister's office, there was a cold breeze coming in from a wide-open window. The man obviously liked plenty of fresh air, against which he was wearing a chunky cardigan over his black shirt and clerical collar.

He stood up and held out his hand. 'Good to meet you, Mrs McKinley, and what can I do for you?'

Ally tried to remember the speech she'd mentally composed but decided to get straight to the point. 'I wonder,' she asked, 'where I might be able to access old church records?' She cleared her throat. 'Births, deaths, marriages; that sort of thing?'

'You'd better sit down,' he said, indicating a green basket chair next to his own high-backed wooden one. 'Are you trying to trace some relatives?'

Ally shook her head. 'Um, no, not exactly. But I am trying to trace a marriage which would probably have taken place in the early 1850s.'

He settled his long frame in his chair again, and Ally let her gaze fall to his feet. Murdo was right – they were enormous, and they looked all the more so on the end of a skinny black-sock-clad ankle. 'Are we talking about Locharran Church?'

'Probably, but I suppose it could be any church in this area,' Ally replied.

The minister raised an eyebrow. 'Well, the church here is comparatively new, having been built in the 1870s, I believe, but we do have some old records somewhere.' He looked vague. 'I suppose my wife could check them when she has a moment. Have you some names?'

'I'm trying to trace the marriage of a Jessie McPhee,' Ally said, 'but I'm pretty sure it would have been earlier than that. Are there many other churches in this area?' She hoped he had a list, because she'd like to compare it with the one in the green folder.

'Oh, quite a few, but most of them are no longer used.' He sighed. 'Folk move away, you see, and communities fall into disrepair.'

'So, if the church was no longer used, what would happen to the records?'

The reverend stroked his long chin. 'I daresay the Church of Scotland will have them filed away somewhere. What was the name again?'

'Jessie McPhee.'

He scribbled the name down on a scrap of paper. 'And this is important to you? An ancestor perhaps?'

Ally nodded. 'Something like that.'

'Hmm.' He burrowed in a drawer for a minute or two before producing a piece of paper. 'These churches,' he said, jabbing at the paper with his forefinger, 'are neighbouring on this parish but are rarely used, if at all, these days. I can't let you have this because it's the only one I've got.'

Ally dug out her phone. 'Would you mind if I photographed it?'

'Help yourself.' He placed the piece of paper in front of her, then added, 'Perhaps we'll see you in church occasionally, Mrs McKinley?'

'Yes, perhaps,' Ally replied vaguely. 'And if you do find anything of interest, would you be kind enough to phone me?' She pulled out one of The Auld Malthouse B&B cards and laid it on his desk before getting up, eager to get away from the draughty window.

'Phone calls cost money, Mrs McKinley, so contact me in a week or two's time.' With that he handed her a card with a tiny drawing of the church, underneath which was printed *The Reverend Donald Pilkington Scott.*

'Yes, of course,' Ally said, making her way rapidly towards the door, not entirely satisfied with the visit.

The police now needed to see the green folder.

There wasn't normally a police station in Locharran, because there had never been any need for one. Until now. In light of recent events, the police had taken over a tiny self-catering cottage close to the Craigmonie Hotel. 'Temporary Police Station' the sign above the door proclaimed, further accentuated by two police cars outside.

Ally carried the green folder inside, where a uniformed policeman sat at a pine table which now served as a reception desk. He looked up from what appeared to be a blank piece of paper, which Ally hoped was not indicative of the progress they were making.

'Is Detective Inspector Rigby around?' she asked.

'He's with someone at the moment,' said the police officer.

'This is quite important. I really need to give him this file.'

'He has specifically asked not to be disturbed. Can I take your details and I'll ensure he gets this?'

Reluctantly, Ally obeyed and handed over the green folder.

. . .

The following day, at 10 a.m., Rigby was at her door. 'I won't come in,' he said before she could invite him, 'because I'm very busy, but I need to know where this folder came from.'

'I suddenly remembered,' Ally replied, 'that there was a secret drawer in the desk beside the window in Room One. I hope you don't mind, but I found a spare key and let myself in.'

Rigby did not look pleased. 'Did you not think to contact us? Furthermore, you were specifically instructed *not* to enter that room.'

'Yes, I thought about contacting you, but as it was late in the evening, I didn't think you'd appreciate that, so I brought it round next day.'

'Mrs McKinley,' Rigby said patiently, as if addressing a five-year-old, 'we are the *police*! We are open twenty-four hours a day for anything important. *Not*,' he added, 'that there's anything much in this folder that would appear to be particularly important.'

Ally stared at him, astounded. 'Don't you think it might contain something that might be able to prove or disprove Wilbur Carrington's ancestry?'

Rigby shrugged. 'Not so far as I can see.'

'Yes, but didn't you see the copy of the entry of marriage?'

'So you've studied the contents of this folder, have you?' Rigby asked, giving her a severe look before he continued. 'Yes, I did look at it, but as far as I can see, the marriage entry concerns one Jessie McPhee and an indecipherable man.'

'Yes, but if we could trace a copy, and the husband turned out to be a Sinclair, then that might go some way to prove Wilbur Carrington's claim?'

'But there's no indication whatsoever that he was a Sinclair,' Rigby said, looking genuinely puzzled, 'so we really have nothing to go on. This McPhee woman may be related to the

Carringtons in some way, particularly as they claim Scottish ancestry, but there's not enough here to give us any sort of lead. I'll keep it in my desk, just in case, but I don't think it's anything to get excited about.'

'Why then would he hide the folder in a secret drawer?' Ally asked.

Rigby looked at her for a moment. He hadn't seemed to have considered this. 'I suppose you're right,' he said. 'I'll give that some more thought but honestly, Mrs McKinley, it's not going to be my top priority.'

Ally sighed as she watched him leave. It wasn't the ringing endorsement she'd been hoping for, but it would have to do.

ELEVEN

Ally had decided that once a month she'd do a big supermarket haul in either Fort William or Inverness, and in between times she'd rely on Locharran Stores and the market, which took place on the green outside the village hall every Tuesday morning. There were stalls selling fresh vegetables, as well as fresh fish from Finlay McKinnon, who ran the boat-hire company – Fin's Fish – at the mouth of the river. Finlay also went to sea in his own boat, returning with hauls of pollock, haddock, mackerel and more. There was also a butcher and a baker, if not a candlestick maker, and they all sold fresh produce and newly laid eggs. As a result, Ally only visited Locharran Stores if she ran out of milk, bread or tinned goods.

With the prospect of Carrington's brother on the horizon, Ally decided to stock up on milk and bread so, shortly after Rigby's departure, she made her way down there, where she found Queenie deep in excited conversation with the earl's housekeeper, Mrs Fraser, which stopped abruptly the moment Ally came through the door. They both turned to look at her, guilt all over their faces.

'Have I interrupted something interesting?' Ally asked with a wicked grin.

'No, no!' said Queenie hastily. 'We were just talking about the weather. Very changeable.'

'Yes, the weather,' Mrs Fraser confirmed.

'Oh, indeed,' said Ally. 'Nice to see you again, Mrs Fraser.'

Mrs Fraser had now fully recovered her composure. 'Did you enjoy your visit to the castle on Sunday, Mrs McKinley?'

'Oh, I did indeed,' said Ally, 'and that was a delicious tea you produced. Wonderful baking!'

'Thank you,' said Mrs Fraser, batting her eyelashes modestly. 'Of course it's the cook who does the baking. The earl particularly likes the currant buns.'

'Yes, I'm sure he does,' said Ally, resisting the temptation to snort.

'Well, I'll be off then,' said Mrs Fraser, giving Queenie a knowing look.

Queenie straightened up. 'There's a special offer on Locharran whisky,' she said, 'and I thought you might be interested, Mrs McKinley.'

'Why is that, Queenie? I'm not a great whisky drinker.'

Ally had told most people in the village to call her Ally, but, for some reason, she'd hesitated to do so in Locharran Stores.

Queenie didn't flinch. 'Only because yourself and the earl enjoyed a tipple or two, I hear.'

Ally sighed. Mrs Fraser had wasted no time. 'I had one drink with the earl,' she said, 'and I'd greatly have preferred a glass of wine.' She looked Queenie in the eye. 'So, do you have a special offer on wine?'

'Well, no, but—'

'In that case, Queenie, I'll just have a couple of pints of milk and a loaf, please.'

'Did you hear that, Bessie?' Queenie hollered into the dark

depths of the back of the shop. 'Two pints of milk and a loaf for Mrs McKinley!'

She'd barely finished shouting out her orders when a stocky, middle-aged man came into the shop. 'Have you heard the latest?' he boomed at Queenie.

'I'm hearin' plenty,' said Queenie, giving Ally a knowing look.

'Rumour has it that the brother of that American is coming to Locharran. Now why would he be coming here?'

Ally was amazed that the news had spread so quickly, even in a small place like this.

'Have you heard that, Mrs McKinley?' Queenie asked.

Ally nodded. 'So the police have told me.'

'Well, hear *this*!' the man went on. 'That American was goin' to take over the *whole estate*! And now he's dead, I bet this brother's coming to stake his claim.'

'Oh, indeed?' said Queenie. She stretched back to her default position across the counter.

'Well, if it could be proved that the dead American was the real laird, then surely the brother would be the real laird now? And, who knows, he might have the same plans to make this estate into some sort of entertainment place, and if that happened, then we'd all lose not only our jobs but our homes as well.'

Queenie gave a little cough. 'This is Mrs McKinley, who's recently bought the malthouse.' She turned to Ally. 'And this, Mrs McKinley, is the earl's driver, Ian Grant.'

'Chauffeur,' corrected Ian Grant as he turned to look at Ally. 'I'm his *chauffeur*.'

'I'm sure your job and home are quite secure now,' Ally said, unsure of what else to say.

'Hmm,' said the chauffeur doubtfully. 'It might not affect the malthouse, but if that fellow had taken over the estate, he'd have made us all jobless and homeless. So it's no great surprise someone stuck a knife in his back.'

At this point, Bessie appeared with the milk and the loaf, and placed them on the counter. Ally wanted to get the transaction out of the way and make her exit as quickly as possible. 'Well, let's face it,' she said, 'the man is no longer a threat to any of us.'

'So long as the brother doesn't plan on carrying on where he left off,' said the chauffeur gloomily.

Ally decided that this was not a particularly good moment to make any mention of the brother's impending arrival at the malthouse.

'And I'll tell you this,' Ian Grant continued, 'Angus Morrison's goin' crazy, cos that bloody Yank was tellin' everyone that he'd bring *in his own gamekeeping team*! Angus is gettin' near retirin' age now, so who else would be wantin' an old gamekeeper?'

'He might have taken our shop out from under our very feet,' said Queenie, looking down at hers, 'and what would happen to me and Bessie then? Tell me *that*.'

As Ally got out her purse and placed a note on the counter, Ian Grant said, 'Not that the earl believed him, of course.'

'Well, Mrs McKinley would know all about that,' said Queenie, straightening up to put the money into the till, 'because *she* was invited up to the castle!'

The chauffeur turned round, taking a sudden interest in Ally. 'Were you now?'

'He only asked me up for afternoon tea,' said Ally defensively.

'And a whisky,' added Queenie.

'One small glass of whisky before I left,' said Ally, beginning to get annoyed. 'No big deal.'

'Aye, well he always liked the ladies,' said Ian, and Queenie nodded in agreement.

Ally pocketed her change, transferred the milk and bread to her bag, and said, 'The earl didn't appear to be particularly perturbed about any of this claim of Carrington's and, anyway, there seemed to be no definite proof.'

'Where that man went wrong,' said Ian as Ally made her way to the door, 'was tellin' everyone in the pub what he was plannin' to do. If he'd kept his big mouth shut, no one would've been tempted to stick a skean dhu in his back, would they?'

'Probably not,' said Ally, moving hastily towards the exit.

The following morning, Wednesday, while Ally was drinking her second cup of coffee and contemplating gloomily about how long she could survive without guests, a sleek dark-blue Jaguar pulled up at the gate. She watched as a man emerged from the driving seat and made his way up the path.

Ally opened the door to the man, who was an inch or two shorter than herself, probably in his late fifties, with crinkly grey eyes and a friendly smile.

'Mrs McKinley?' he asked in an American accent.

'Yes,' replied Ally, 'and you must be Mr Carrington's brother?'

'That's me – Tyler Carrington.' He held out his hand.

'I'm so sorry you've had to come here in such sad circumstances,' Ally said. 'It must have been a terrible shock.'

He didn't reply – just nodded and looked around. 'Nice place you've got here. The Auld Malthouse, eh? I guess the "auld" means "old"?'

'Yes, it does,' Ally replied. 'Welcome to The Auld Malthouse. Do you have luggage?'

'Yeah, in the car. I'll get that later.'

'Let me show you the room, Mr Carrington,' Ally said.

'Oh, please call me Tyler! You Brits can be so formal!'

'In which case, call me Ally.' She led him up the stairs and into Room 3. 'I hope this is all right?'

'It's just fine,' he replied, looking out of the window. 'Great views!'

'Yes, you can see right down to the river,' Ally told him, 'and if you look to the far right, you can just make out where it flows out to the sea.'

'Good fishing?' he asked. 'I'm keen on fishing and particularly rock climbing.'

'Very good for both, and there are boats for hire too. And, as you can see, we're surrounded by hills so I'm sure you'll find some rocks and crags to climb.' Ally wondered if and when he might be willing to talk about the reason he was here. She cleared her throat. 'Were you and your brother very close?'

He sighed. 'Actually, Wilbur and I weren't all that close, but I have to say I was absolutely shocked when I got that call telling me what had happened to him. Beyond *belief*!'

'It's affected us all,' said Ally, wondering if he had any idea just how controversial his brother's visit had turned out to be. 'Do you know how long you might be staying?'

'I guess that'll depend on how long it takes to find out what really happened. But don't worry, Ally, because I'll make sure you aren't out of pocket.'

Ally glanced at her watch. It was twenty-five past ten. 'Have you had breakfast, Tyler?'

'Yes, thanks, I had that in Inverness. I'd love some coffee, though.' She saw him cast an eye at the complimentary tea tray.

'That's just instant coffee on there,' Ally said, 'but if you come downstairs when you're ready, I'll make you some of the proper stuff.'

'Thank you so much. I'll bring my bags up and will be with you shortly.' He paused. 'I've got some climbing gear, ropes and stuff. Could I leave them downstairs someplace?'

'There's a cupboard in the hallway,' Ally said, 'if that's suitable?'

'That will be fine,' said Tyler cheerfully.

As Ally walked downstairs, she felt a sense of relief that this brother seemed normal and friendly because, in the back of her mind, she'd naturally thought he might be gloomy and judgemental.

On the contrary, when Tyler eventually came down and she showed him the sitting room and the dining room, he asked, 'Any chance you could join me for the coffee? I'd feel a little lonely sitting in here by myself.'

A few minutes later, they were both in the kitchen, one on either side of the log burner.

'Great coffee,' he said approvingly. Then, after a moment: 'Can you show me where Wilbur's body was found?'

'Yes, of course,' Ally replied, hoping he wouldn't ask about the bedroom.

'And have you put me in the same room that he was in?'

'No. The bedroom your brother occupied has been locked up by the police and no one's allowed in there, not even me,' Ally said firmly.

'And you don't have a spare key?'

Ally shook her head, wondering what was coming next. 'I'm afraid not. And even if I had, I've been forbidden to go in there, as I already told you.'

He gave her a sideways grin. 'But I bet you would have been *tempted* to go in there and have a look around, huh?'

Ally hoped he'd think her pink face was due to the heat of the log burner and not from guilt. 'I don't think there would have been much point, because the detective seems to have removed most of his things.' She endeavoured to change the subject. 'Do you have many relatives in Massachusetts?'

He shook his head. 'Not many. Wilbur has two ex-wives floating around somewhere but no kids. I got me just one ex-wife' – here he grinned – 'and a daughter who's married and living in California.'

'And you live in Massachusetts too?'

'Well, we hail from Barton Ridge, a small town about a hundred miles from Boston.'

'You must have had a massive shock when they phoned to tell you about your brother?'

'I did. But do you know what? Like I told you, we've never been very close, not like some brothers are. He was eight years older than me and let's just say he was none too pleased when an infant brother arrived on the scene. I guess he'd been pretty much spoiled until then. He was always aloof, and we've kinda gone in different directions. I have to say he was always a little crazy and got himself obsessed with certain ideas. Anyhow, enough about us – how about you?'

Ally gave him a brief account of her life leading up to her arrival in Locharran and converting the malthouse.

'Well, you've done a great job of doing up this place,' he said admiringly, looking around. Then, in a complete change of mood, he asked, 'Who do you think might have wanted to kill my brother?'

Ally was sorely tempted to reply 'probably half of the village' but restrained herself.

'I've no idea,' she replied, 'but I can only guess that he might have upset someone when he went out for a drink most evenings to the bar in the Craigmonie Hotel, down in the village.'

'Do you know why?'

Ally hesitated for a moment. 'I think he might have given them the idea that he thought *he* could be the rightful heir to the estate, and that he had some radical ideas for the place.'

'Really? How weird is that? Mind you, Wilbur's always

been a little crazy and gets these obsessions. What proof had he got? The whole thing's ridiculous! Well, he can't upset anyone now, and I'd be happy to reassure everyone that I got no part in his crazy ideas. So, do you think it would be a good idea if I was to visit that bar too and ask about what he said?'

'Just a thought. I really wouldn't know what else to suggest.'

'Hey, why don't you come with me? I need to know who's who!' Tyler drained his coffee. 'At some point, I guess, I'm going to have to fly back to the States with his body. Just at the moment, the police seem to be in no hurry to release it, although I don't know why they're hanging on to poor old Wilbur?' He scratched his head, which had close-cropped hair of a similar greying-red colour to his brother. 'Anyhow,' he added, 'as I said, I'm really keen on rock climbing, and it seems to me there'd be some great places round here, so it would be a shame to waste the opportunity.'

Ally decided that this might be a good time to clarify the catering arrangements. 'I don't do meals, Tyler, other than breakfast. It's not profitable for me when there are so many good eating places just a short distance away. It's only a few minutes' walk to the Craigmonie, which does great bar food and also has an extremely good restaurant, and to the fish and chip shop and to the bistro.'

'You know what I'm looking forward to, Ally? Wilbur and I ate deer meat from the time we were this high.' His hand wavered a few inches above the floor. 'And I've been hearing about what great venison they have up here, so I'm going to be sampling some of that for sure.'

'They do a lovely venison pie in the Craigmonie,' said Ally, deciding not to mention that Wilbur had chosen it for his last supper.

Surely this brother wouldn't suffer the same fate! Or might he?

TWELVE

When Ally arrived in Locharran she'd introduced herself to both Linda Peterson, who owned The Bistro, and to Luigi Concetti (who had a Highland accent you could cut with a knife) at the fish and chip shop. 'Och,' he'd said cheerfully, 'we'd be delighted if you sent us down a customer or two occasionally. And if we see anyone looking for a room, we'll send them right up to you.' He'd lowered his voice. 'The Craigmonie don't do us any favours, and they're bloody expensive.'

Linda Peterson had said more or less the same thing. 'You send them to me, and I'll send them to you!' Linda was English; she'd married a Scot who'd brought her up to Locharran and who had died from cancer some years previously.

Linda was a petite five foot two inches, as opposed to Ally's five foot ten, and referred to them as 'the long and the short of it all' when they were together. Linda had blonde hair cut in a sleek bob, large hazel eyes, a wicked sense of humour and a great talent for cooking. She and Ally had hit it off straight away, aware that they were both regarded pretty much as foreigners or, worse, *English*, who were referred to as 'Sassenachs' up here.

'They're very polite,' Linda had told Ally, 'but I can tell they regard me as a foreign species. There's still a deep-rooted hatred for the English amongst the older people, who still hold a grudge because of the greedy English landlords, the Highland clearances and all that.'

'I get the feeling they regard us lowland city dwellers in much the same way,' Ally had added.

After Tyler Carrington had been issued with his keys and breakfast times – 7 a.m. to 10 a.m. – Ally decided to walk down to the village and call in on her new friend, who she found peeling vegetables in her kitchen. 'Do you want a hand with those?' Ally asked.

'No, I'm fine thanks. Coffee?'

'No, thank you. I'm awash with it. I've been welcoming my new guest.'

Linda looked up from slicing green beans. 'What's he or she like?'

'He's Wilbur Carrington's brother, and he's nice enough,' Ally replied. 'Although he doesn't appear to be overly concerned about Wilbur. Does that seem entirely normal to you?'

'Depends how they got on, I suppose. I haven't got any siblings, so it's difficult for me to judge,' Linda said.

'Well, I have a brother, and I'd be gutted if anything happened to him,' Ally remarked. 'I wept buckets when he went to Australia years ago because I thought I might never see him again. Back then people didn't go backward and forward so much. He was there for years but decided to come home to Edinburgh for his retirement.'

'Did you ever visit him out there?'

'Yes, once. Ken and I went out for a month. Don lived near

Sydney, but he'd arranged for us to travel all over the place, and we had a wonderful time.'

'Lucky you!' Linda had begun to slice some courgettes. 'OK, so getting back to reality, what was Carrington really like – the murdered one, I mean?'

Ally thought for a moment. 'I liked him, although he wasn't as friendly and forthcoming as the brother who's just arrived. Wilbur was more intense, and definitely obsessed with everything to do with the earl and the castle. He seemed convinced that his ancestors had come from there and that he had some sort of right to it all.'

'Do you think he had any real proof?'

Ally shrugged. 'No idea.'

'So, presumably, if there was some sort of proof, the brother would be in line to inherit the earldom and the estate.'

'The brother – Tyler – reckons Wilbur was a little crazy and completely obsessed by it all, and that there was absolutely no proof of the claim. Now he wants to set the villagers' minds at rest by assuring them that what Wilbur said was rubbish. He plans to pay a visit to the Craigmonie Bar, which Wilbur frequented and where he'd publicised his claim, and he's suggested I accompany him.'

'Oh, wow, a *date*!' Linda teased. 'Will you go?'

'I might, only because I haven't been in there since I first arrived in Locharran, and I didn't know anyone then. I'm a little more savvy now!' Ally laughed. 'I expect everyone will think I'm cradle-snatching!'

'*Cradle-snatching*? How old is this Tyler then?'

'Probably in his fifties, late fifties maybe.'

Linda winked. 'I'd say that was ideal for you because you're young at heart!'

'For God's sake, Linda! I don't fancy him in the least, and I shouldn't think he's interested in me either. It's just that I can point out to him who's who.'

'Well,' said Linda, 'at least it'll give them something else to gossip about. And, incidentally, yes, this building is also part of the Sinclair estate, so I'm as keen as anyone to disprove Carrington's claim.'

'I'll have to see what I can do,' said Ally, laughing.

The next day, Tyler Carrington told Ally he was going for a long walk around the village and over the moors 'to get the feel of the place' and have a look for suitable crags to climb. He was planning to have a drink in the Craigmonie Bar in the evening, if Ally would care to accompany him? Ally agreed that she would.

The Craigmonie Hotel was a Victorian pinkish sandstone building, complete with turrets, its lawns backing onto the river, the venue of many a wedding reception. The Craigmonie Bar had been built on in the fifties as a one-storey afterthought. It was the nearest the village got to having a traditional-style pub, minus the history or the atmosphere. It did have a very comprehensive bar, stocking dozens of whiskies, most from small distilleries in the area. The walls were painted in an uninteresting off-white colour – probably magnolia – and the carpet was a bog-standard dark red with a small cream motif. Ally felt that it badly needed some updating: perhaps replacing the drab brown sofas with something lighter, adding a few ceiling beams or, at the very least, lowering the lights to produce some semblance of intimacy and cosiness.

There was also a Lithuanian bar manager called Ivan, who was also the bar's best customer. Ivan was a stocky young man in his thirties who, some fifteen years previously, had backpacked his way round Scotland with a girl called Marta. When Ivan had arrived in Locharran, he'd fallen in love not only with the place but with the whisky. He'd been studying hotel management in Edinburgh and, luckily for him, at that exact time, Callum Dalrymple had been trying to find a manager for the Craigmonie Bar. Thus, Marta made her way back alone to Edinburgh and Lithuania, and Ivan stayed in Locharran. No one could pronounce his surname, so he was known affectionately as Ivan the Terrible, a fact which didn't appear to bother him in the least.

Ivan could hold his drink well, probably due to all the practice he'd had. He had a few in the morning before opening time, and kept this level up nicely throughout the day, due mainly to everyone knowing of his penchant. 'Will ye have a wee dram yerself, Ivan?' they'd ask, and Ivan always did. As a result, he became more and more cheerful during the course of the day, and so, by the time Ally arrived with Tyler at half past seven, he was cock-a-hoop.

'Oh, good to see you, Mrs McKinley!' he greeted her with a beaming smile.

'Please call me Ally, will you, Ivan? And this is Tyler, Wilbur Carrington's brother.'

Ivan stopped in his tracks. 'He had a *brother*?'

'Just the one,' said Tyler calmly, 'and I'm making no claims round here. Just so you know.'

'Well,' said Ivan, 'that will be a big relief to many people.' He looked round at the cluster of regulars standing at the bar.

Tyler ordered a Scotch and water for himself, a wine for Ally and asked Ivan if he'd like one too. Ivan said he would most certainly like one, and, if they cared to sit down, he would bring their drinks over. Ally and Tyler sat down obediently on one of the drab sofas, aware that they were being watched by everyone in the bar. By the time Ivan delivered their drinks, their murmuring had reached a crescendo.

They were the 'regulars' of course: Ian Grant, the earl's chauffeur; Angus the gamekeeper; some of the workmen who'd helped to transform the malthouse; the earl's gardener; and, last but not least, Murdo the postman, husband of Morag.

First to approach was Ian Grant, who cleared his throat and introduced himself to Tyler. 'We all met your brother,' he said.

'So I believe,' Tyler said drily.

'Aye,' Ian agreed, 'we're all sorry about what happened to him, but he had us all bloody worried.'

Tyler took a slug of his drink. 'Well, you needn't be.'

'So is it true what Ivan says, and that *you're* not trying to claim the Locharran estate?'

'Absolutely true,' Tyler confirmed, 'not that *he* had much proof anyway. You can rest assured that the estate will always belong to the earls of Locharran.'

Ian nodded. 'Well, that's a relief. How long do you intend to stay around here, Mr Carrington?'

'As long as it takes to find out who killed my brother.'

Ian nodded. 'I wish you luck.'

As he moved back to join the others, Tyler asked, 'And who was that?'

'He's the earl's chauffeur.'

'And he's pigeon-toed,' Tyler remarked as he watched the chauffeur walk away, 'so I hope the car's an automatic.'

Ally smiled, but before she could come up with a reply, a big, white-haired man with a stoop, clad in breeches with a tweed jacket, approached. He had deep-brown eyes and an abundance of nostril hair. 'Angus Morrison,' he growled by way of introduction, 'and I've been the gamekeeper here for the past fifty years. Between us, the earl and myself keep everything the way it should be, as it has been for centuries. We do not want some passing tourist trying to undermine our way of life!' He glared angrily at Tyler.

'Be assured, Mr Morrison, that I am not my brother. I don't know where he got this crazy notion from, but it's of no interest to me. What does interest me is finding out who killed Wilbur.'

'Aye, well,' said Angus with a loud sniff, before turning away.

Tyler shook his head in disbelief. 'These folk are sure concerned about their jobs, Ally.'

'What you must realise,' Ally said, 'is that it's not just their jobs here that are at risk but their homes as well. Most of them live in tied houses.'

Tyler looked confused. 'What are tied houses?'

'A house that goes with a job. Almost everyone you see in here works for the estate and pays reduced rent to the earl for their homes. You can bet that most of them are second- or third-generation estate workers and would be very unlikely to have been employed in Wilbur's theme park. And so they wouldn't just be jobless; they'd be homeless as well.'

Tyler nodded and drained his Scotch. 'You ready for some more wine?'

Ally shook her head. 'No, I'm OK, thanks.'

'Well, I'm going to buy these guys a drink,' he said, getting up and heading towards the bar.

Ally watched as he made his way up to the group. Their suspicious looks rapidly turned to grins as he asked them what they were drinking, and it struck Ally that any one of these men could well have been his brother's killer, but probably best not to mention that.

However, when Tyler returned, he said, 'I guess any one of these guys had good reason to kill Wilbur.'

'Possibly,' Ally agreed. At the same time, her thoughts turned to the redoubtable Mrs Fraser. 'As did his housekeeper and cook,' she added. She'd never met the cook, but, according to rumour, she was another formidable woman who ruled the castle kitchen perhaps not with a rod of iron but definitely with a hefty rolling pin.

At that moment, Callum Dalrymple entered the bar and looked around. His eyes met Ally's, and he wandered over to where she was sitting.

'How are you?' he asked Ally, looking questioningly at Tyler.

'OK, thank you,' Ally replied, mesmerised by his blue Paul Newman-type eyes again. She introduced Tyler.

'I'm trying to reassure these guys that I've no interest in my brother's crazy claims,' he explained.

'That will be a great relief,' Callum agreed. 'We do need to find his killer, though. Your brother was murdered somewhere between here and the malthouse well over a week ago, and the police don't appear to be making much progress with the inquiry.' He turned to Ally. 'I reckon Inspector Rigby's in thrall to the earl – thinks he can do no wrong because of who he is.'

'You could be right,' Ally said, draining her wine. 'Anyway, I'm heading home now, but please don't feel you have to leave too, Tyler. It's only a short walk back, and I'm hoping that some guests might appear.'

'No, no,' protested Tyler, 'you're most definitely not walking up that hill on your own with a killer on the loose!'

They strolled up the hill towards the malthouse in silence for a few minutes, the semi-darkness only broken here and there by the lighted windows of the cottages that lined the lane and the occasional street lamp. A few lights twinkled on the surrounding hills and from the main part of the village below. It was calm, peaceful and quiet, aside from the odd distant hoot of an owl.

'It's hard to believe that anyone could be murdered in such a beautiful place,' Tyler remarked, stopping and looking around.

Ally nodded, having been thinking the same thing. 'I agree, but if your brother wasn't actually killed on this little lane, then it means he must have been waylaid, stabbed somewhere else and then taken to the malthouse. As far as I'm aware the police don't seem to have decided exactly where, or at what time,

Wilbur was killed. They seem to spend all of their time up at the castle.'

'I wonder why?' Tyler asked as they resumed walking. 'Although I guess the lord, the earl or whatever he is has to be their chief suspect, since Wilbur intended to usurp him. Is he a nice guy?'

'Well,' said Ally as they approached the malthouse door, 'he is rather fond of the ladies, but apart from that, he seems perfectly amenable.' She hesitated for a moment. 'I'm not entirely sure that he believed Wilbur anyway. He certainly didn't appear to be put out by the claim, and he made light of it when I spoke to him on the subject.'

'You know him well, Ally?'

'No, not well. But he invited me to tea at the castle and I asked a few pertinent questions.'

As they stood in the hallway, Tyler said, 'I guess then that I'm going to have my work cut out for me trying to get to the bottom of all this.' He headed towards the stairs. 'Thanks so much for accompanying me to the bar this evening. I enjoyed it, but I'm sure ready for sleep now!'

'Goodnight, Tyler,' Ally said with some relief. She'd been wondering if she should offer him coffee, although she didn't particularly want to, as she felt tired herself.

She waited for him to go upstairs and, as soon as she heard his door close, she headed for the kitchen and took down the painting from over the table. Her investigation into Wilbur's claim would start tomorrow, but before that, she needed to review her suspects for his murder.

Looking at her list of names, Ally realised that the first person she needed to consider was Ian Grant. He seemed like a nice man, but he was obviously proud of his position. He didn't like being referred to as the earl's driver; he was a *chauffeur*. And she'd heard on the grapevine that he had one of the nicest houses owned by the estate, so he would not be pleased at losing both his job and, probably, his home too. He was close to the earl, so might even have been selected to do the deed. Ian Grant joined the others on the back of Ally's picture at 11 o'clock, because he had probably as strong a motive as Mrs Jamieson and Mrs Fraser.

There was Linda and her bistro. No, no, no! But the land did belong to the estate, and Linda was a mere tenant. Had Linda got another house somewhere, or was she counting on having this property forever? She'd need to find out. Ally knew Linda wouldn't do such a thing, but, again, could she have been in league with someone? Ridiculous! Hesitantly, Ally wrote her name on a note and stuck it to the board. She put Linda at 6 o'clock and moved Angus up to 5 o'clock because Linda had to be her least likely suspect.

The Concetti family, with their little café and fish and chip business, also had to be considered. They did wonderful pizzas and pasta takeaways as well, and of all the suspects she'd listed so far, Ally felt sure they were one of the least likely to have committed the crime. Visitors, whether to a theme park or anywhere else, had to eat. The Concettis would be the most likely to survive such a turmoil. Still, if Linda was included, then they had to be too. The Concettis went up on the board next to Linda at 6 o'clock.

Ally looked at her board for one more moment, then hung it on the wall and made her way up to bed.

She needed her sleep before beginning her hunt for Jessie McPhee.

THIRTEEN

The next day, Ally decided it was high time she started visiting the churches on the minister's list. There were four of them, including Locharran where Donald Scott had said he'd have the records checked. But when? She'd rung up, as instructed, to be told by the reverend that his wife was very busy but he'd remind her and she should call back.

The other three were within a radius of about ten miles. One of them, at a village called Clachar, was in a seaside location not too far away. According to Morag, it had 'a nice wee beach'. She'd then asked, 'But why would you be wantin' to be goin' there?'

Why indeed? It was most likely to be a wild goose chase, but Ally had to start somewhere.

The day was bright and sunny so, after she'd served Tyler his breakfast, Ally made herself a packed lunch, got in her car and set off for Clachar. Like most roads in the area, this one was single track with passing places. As she drove across the heather-clad moorland, Ally met no one apart from one red Post Office van: *so* somebody *must live in Clachar*, she thought.

Finally, the road dipped down towards the coast, providing

a breathtaking view of the coastline with its stretch of white sand, presumably Morag's 'nice wee beach'. The sea was pure turquoise and the scene reminiscent of the Caribbean, provided you didn't venture into the icy water. Ally could see a cluster of cottages and the church, all a few yards back from the beach. Even if the church yielded nothing, at least it would be a delightful place to eat her lunch.

As she drove along past the cottages, it appeared that only a couple of them were occupied, with doors open and washing billowing on the clothesline. The others looked empty and forlorn, probably holiday rentals. *Must be very lonely down here in the winter*, she thought as she drove on towards the church. The church appeared to mark the end of the village, because the road stopped there.

Ally stepped out of the car, stretched and inhaled the wonderful aroma of the sea. It was a beautiful day. She made her way towards the large double doors of the church, its wood grey and splintering from the onslaught of Atlantic gales, its iron hinges rusted and flaking. She didn't really expect the door to open and had been fully resigned to walking around the outside in the faint hope of finding another entrance. But, much to her surprise, the huge door creaked open, and Ally found herself in a large, vaulted space, empty of pews or of any embellishment, the once beautiful stained-glass windows now shattered. Birds had flown in and were circling round the roof.

Ally felt incredibly sad. This must once have been a really beautiful church in a stunning location. How had it come to this? It was extremely unlikely she was going to find any kind of church records here.

Then the door opened behind her and an elderly man, leaning heavily on a stick, entered.

'Hello!' he said.

'Oh, hello,' Ally replied, startled. 'I trust it's OK me being in here? I was hoping that it was still in use and that there might be some old records somewhere.'

The old man smiled. 'Och, you're far too late, my dear. This kirk hasn't been used in thirty, forty years.'

'How sad,' Ally said. 'I don't suppose you know if there could be any records of births, deaths, marriages that might once have taken place here?'

The man shook his head slowly. 'No, I'm afraid not. There was a vault somewhere, if I remember rightly, but there's nothing now because of subsidence, and you'd need a digger to dredge it all up. But I can remember when this kirk was thriving, folks singing and praying together. I'm Alex Baird, and I used to look after the place.'

Ally shook his hand. 'I'm Ally McKinley. I live in Locharran, and I was hoping I might unearth some information.' Unearth was now an appropriate verb, she thought.

'Ah, Locharran! You've had that terrible murder there, have you not?' He sighed. 'That sort of thing just doesn't happen round here.'

'So I keep being told,' Ally said, smiling. She looked around at the empty church. 'This is very sad.'

'It is. Someone's stolen all the lead out of the roof, and someone's taken away all the beautiful pews. You'll probably find them for sale in some fancy shop somewhere.'

'You might well be right,' Ally said with a sigh as she followed him back out into the sunlight. 'It's been good meeting you, Alex.'

With a wave, he was gone.

Ally waited for a moment then decided to have a look round the graveyard. There just could be a McPhee here somewhere, yielding a clue, however small. The graves were overgrown with grass, thistles and, in some cases, nettles. How long had it been since anyone was buried here? And yet... there were two graves that were still cared for, the grass cut and some flowers – now dead – propped up against the stones. One was a McKenzie, aged ninety, and one was a Calder, aged three months. Ally stood sadly at baby Aisla Calder's tiny grave. She'd died twenty years previously, so that might have been about the time that the graveyard closed. Nevertheless, someone had visited the grave in the last few months, so maybe the mother or a relative lived somewhere near.

It took some time to clear away the overgrown greenery from the front of the other gravestones, but Ally couldn't find a single McPhee. How would she ever know for sure if Jessie McPhee had married her man here? Surely she'd have wanted to be married in the church she, and her family, attended? In which case wouldn't there be some relative buried in here?

She fetched her lunch box from the car and made her way down to the beach.

No sooner had she got back in the afternoon than Hamish Sinclair arrived at her door with a large salmon.

'I've had it cleaned and filleted,' he said as he handed it over, 'so it's all ready for you to cook and eat.'

Ally had heard that she should beware of Greeks bearing gifts, but there was no mention of Scottish earls. She thanked him profusely, noting how dapper he looked. He was wearing a different tartan kilt today, complete with sporran, but instead of the usual tweed jacket, he wore a white roll-neck jumper with a dark-green corduroy gilet on top. She noticed he'd trimmed his beard and had carefully parted and combed his hair.

'Come in,' she said, 'as I expect you'd like to see the changes I've made to the place.'

'I certainly would,' he said, giving her a coy smile, 'but that's not the only reason of course.'

Ally ignored his last remark, then showed him into the sitting room and the dining room before leading him upstairs.

Fortunately, Tyler had gone out, so she was able to let him have a brief look at Rooms 2 and 3, but not Room 1, of course.

Hamish was most impressed. 'I can't believe this is the old grain store,' he said. 'Never thought for a moment it could be so cleverly converted. You must have had a brilliant architect, Alison, and you've done a great job with the interiors. Are you a designer by any chance?'

Ally assured him she wasn't, although she'd done some research on the subject, and was thrilled by how much he liked it.

'And this is my kitchen,' she announced proudly at the end of the tour.

He looked around approvingly. 'I expect you spend most of your time in here?'

'Yes, I do,' Ally admitted. 'Now, what can I get you?' She thanked her lucky stars that she'd made some scones the previous afternoon and – somewhere – there was a box of short-bread. It hardly compared with Mrs Fraser's spread up at the castle, but it would have to do.

'I'd love some tea, Alison, but please don't offer me anything to eat because I really do have to watch my figure. When I have a lady friend, I'm much trimmer, because it gives me the incentive to keep in shape.' He looked at her with a glint in his eye.

'Do sit down,' Ally said, suppressing an eye-roll and indicating the chair by the wood burner. She tossed a couple of logs into the fire and then switched the kettle on, wondering if he would condescend to drink tea made with a humble teabag.

He sat down and cleared his throat. 'So, are there any men in your life at the moment, Alison?'

'Just my son, and my brother and all my male acquaintances,' Ally replied tersely, aware that he was studying her intently.

'But nobody to make your breakfast?'

Ally busied herself making the tea. She handed him a

pottery cup and saucer. 'Sorry, I haven't unpacked the bone china yet.'

'You haven't answered my question,' he persisted, giving her a wink.

Ally sat down opposite him. 'Hamish, let's get one thing straight. I am not, repeat, *not* looking for a lover! I'm perfectly happy on my own at this stage in my life. I've had a long, happy marriage, and, sad as I was when my husband died, I'm now enjoying a certain freedom that I didn't have before. I would like us to be friends, but that's as far as it goes. And' – she took a deep breath – 'if you continue to make suggestive remarks, you won't see my heels for dust!' She wondered if she'd overdone it. She liked the man, but she needed to make her feelings crystal clear.

Hamish put on a sad face. 'I suppose I can't win them all,' he said with a wry smile, 'but you're a fine-looking woman and I'd be a fool not to try!'

'Well, I'm very flattered, but this is as far as it goes – or will ever go. Isn't it possible just to be *friends*?'

He thought for a moment. 'Yes, I'd like us to be friends. I've a lot of hangers-on, Alison, but not that many friends.'

'You've got one now,' Ally said firmly, 'but *no* hanky-panky.' She stretched out her hand.

'No,' Hamish confirmed sadly, shaking her hand. 'No hanky-panky.'

An hour after he'd left, Ian Grant arrived at her door.

'Sorry to bother you,' he said, looking embarrassed, 'but the earl was wonderin' if he dropped his banker's card in your kitchen when he called on you today?'

'*Banker's card*?'

'Aye, he wondered if it had slipped out of his pocket.'

Ally hesitated for a moment and then said, 'Oh, do come in. I'll show you where he was sitting.'

As he followed her into the kitchen, Ally was beginning to feel embarrassed. Had the earl left his card behind on purpose? And if so, why would he send his chauffeur to collect it? And what if he'd dropped it elsewhere in the house when she'd been showing him around? How would *that* look?

Ally pointed to a chair. 'He sat there while he was having a cup of tea.'

Ian ran his hand down the sides of the chair and finally came up with what looked like a credit card from a well-known bank. 'Got it!' he said.

'How on earth did it get down there?' Ally asked, mystified.

'I wouldn't put it past him to have done that on purpose,' Ian Grant said with a grin. 'And now you're going to ask me why he didn't come to pick it up himself, aren't you?'

'Well, yes,' Ally replied. 'Why would he do that?'

'Because normally it gives him an excuse to come back.' He grinned again. 'Perhaps he thought he hadn't been persuasive enough.'

'Does he do this sort of thing often?'

'All the time,' said Ian Grant cheerfully. 'I suppose he sent me because he's had his cousin and his wife, his nearest relatives, arrive from London unannounced, and he can't get away.'

Ally shook her head slowly. 'This is ridiculous!'

'He *is* a bit ridiculous. I've worked for him for twenty-nine years, and he's always been the same.'

Ally sighed. 'Do sit down, and would you like a cup of tea? I'm Ally, by the way.'

'And I'm Ian. No, I won't wait for tea, but it's kind of you to offer. We met in the shop, didn't we?'

'Yes, we did,' Ally said. 'And you can tell that boss of yours that even if he had been able to come back and collect the card himself, my answer would still have been no and that our relationship would be strictly platonic.'

'I believe you,' he replied, 'but millions wouldn't! Particularly round here. Don't let it get to you.'

'I won't,' Ally said. Then she remembered something. 'I understand you had the job of ferrying Wilbur Carrington around?'

Ian rolled his eyes. 'Bit of a thankless task. He wanted to go to all these old churches and graveyards looking for God knows what. "His ancestry" he said.'

'Do you think he found anything?'

'I'm not sure. I've been racking my brain to try to remember what he said. Didn't think it was important at the time, but it obviously would be now.'

'It certainly could be,' Ally agreed as she accompanied him to the door.

As he drove away, she thought how much she liked the man and was particularly impressed by his candour.

Nevertheless, it hadn't been a very productive day.

FOURTEEN

'I believe the laird paid you a visit yesterday,' said Queenie casually on Saturday morning when Ally arrived in the shop to buy some bread.

'Yes, he was interested to see how the malthouse had been converted,' Ally replied equally casually.

'Mrs Fraser says that Mrs Jamieson had to prepare a *salmon* for him to take with him! A salmon, no less! And after you having *tea* with him last Sunday,' Queenie added, nodding in her sister's direction. 'She was in here this morning, wasn't she, Bessie?'

Bessie, wiping down the counter, nodded obediently.

I bet she was in here, Ally thought. *I bet she couldn't wait to spread the news.*

Bessie muttered something.

'Oh yes,' said Queenie. 'Bessie's just reminded me that you were in the Craigmonie Bar the other night with the American's brother.'

'I get around,' Ally replied drily.

'Well, we haven't had a femme fatale around here for a while, have we, Bessie?' She pronounced it 'fem-fatal' so it took a couple of moments for Ally to get the gist of the conversation.

Bessie nodded and stopped wiping for a moment to study Ally's reaction.

'You *still* haven't got a *femme fatale* round here,' Ally retorted. 'I'm merely getting to know the local people, and I'm trying to help Mr Carrington's brother to do the same.'

'The brother says he's not going to make a claim, but who knows?' Queenie shook her head and looked up at the dark-beamed ceiling, perhaps hoping for some divine intervention from above.

'I very much doubt he's got any interest whatsoever in making a claim,' Ally said. 'The man has flown in from *Massachusetts*,' she pronounced it carefully for Queenie's benefit, 'to identify his brother's body, to visit where he was killed and to try to convince the local people that he's not interested in any claim. He happens to be staying in my guest house and I feel sorry for him, OK? Just a seeded loaf, please.'

With a loud sniff, Queenie turned to Bessie. 'Can we have a loaf for Mrs McKinley, please?'

Bessie, acquiescent as ever, did as she was told.

Outside the shop, Ally took a deep breath and wondered at her sanity at coming to this remote place where everyone seemed to know everyone else's business. But as she approached the malthouse, which was looking majestic in the morning sun, Ally decided that, yes, she had made a great choice. She was still a novelty, but things would settle down eventually, she felt sure.

'Anyone home?' trilled a high, female voice.

Ally laid down her mug of coffee and switched off her laptop, on which she'd been replying to emails, and made her way towards the front door. And there, resplendent in head-to-

toe pink, alongside a mountain of pink luggage, stood a little lady. She was as wide as she was tall, and she was wearing a pink floral smock over pink cut-off trousers on her chubby little legs, the outfit topped by a red baseball cap perched jauntily on her wayward white hair.

'Hi! The lady at The Bistro said you might have a spare room to let?'

Another American accent! Apart from anything else, Ally thought, this woman must be frozen! Summer had not yet reached the Western Highlands, so this lady was a little ahead of the season. When she looked more closely, she thought she could see that the woman might have been crying.

'I do have a room,' Ally replied, 'but it's really a double. Queen-size bed. I'm afraid I'd have to charge you double room rates.'

'That's not a problem,' said the visitor as she picked up a pink suitcase in each hand.

'Great!' said Ally, with some relief, as she picked up the third case. 'Follow me.'

As she made her way upstairs, Ally contemplated the coincidence of yet another American guest. Could she be a relative of the Carringtons? Never mind her pedigree, Room 2 would finally be occupied again.

'My name's Ally McKinley,' she said, leading her pink visitor into the room.

'I'm Mamie! Mamie Van Nuyen.' She looked around. 'Great room!'

'Well, welcome to Locharran, Mamie. Any idea how long you might be staying?'

Mamie laid down her luggage and shook her head wearily. 'A few weeks probably. I have to tell you that I came to find out who killed my fiancé, Wilbur Carrington.'

'Your *fiancé*?'

'Yeah, we were going to be married this coming fall. I cannot believe what's happened.'

'Oh, Mamie, I'm so very sorry. How awful for you! If there's anything I can do...'

Mamie took a deep breath and gave Ally a watery little smile. 'I keep having these little weeps, but I must stay strong because I know he'd have wanted me to.' She took a shuddery breath. 'Let's not talk about it for the minute.'

Ally nodded. 'OK.' She showed her guest the en-suite bathroom, explained the TV, Wi-Fi facilities and breakfast times. She fervently hoped there'd be no wailing from Willie and was pleased to see that Mamie appeared to be happy with everything. She hesitated for a moment. 'I have to tell you that his brother, Tyler, is also staying here. I guess you know him?'

Mamie shook her head. 'No, I don't. I've heard Wilbur mention him, but I live in California, and we've never met when I've been to the east coast.' She unzipped her suitcase and began to unpack.

'I'll leave you to it then,' Ally said, 'but if you need or want anything, just come down and let me know. I'll be downstairs somewhere, or in the garden.'

'I will,' said Mamie, who'd paused in the unpacking to look out of the window. 'What a great view!'

'There are lots of brochures on the hall table with details of interesting places to visit,' Ally added as she was about to leave the room. Then she had another thought. 'I assume you have a car?'

'Oh, sure,' Mamie replied. 'I picked up this cute little Ford at the airport.'

Ally made her way downstairs, relieved that she could finally put up a 'No Vacancies' sign.

Mamie wasn't the only one in the pink.

'She had a huge lunch,' Linda said later as Ally joined her in the tiny, sheltered garden behind The Bistro. The pots were filled with tiny geraniums, and the wisteria – now the love of Linda's life – was in bud. 'Then she asked if I had any rooms to let, and I said no, but my friend at The Auld Malthouse had!'

'Thanks so much for that,' Ally said, dipping a ginger biscuit into her tea. 'So now I have a houseful.'

'I didn't tell her about our local murder,' Linda said with a grin, 'because I thought I'd leave that to you!'

'She knew all about it actually,' said Ally, 'because Wilbur Carrington was her *fiancé*!'

'You are *kidding* me! So why is she here? Is she trying to find out who killed him too?'

'So she says. And she's never met Tyler, so that'll be interesting if they both come down to breakfast at the same time.'

'I take it that the brother isn't married?'

'Divorced apparently,' Ally replied.

'More tea?' Linda held up the teapot.

'Yes, please.'

After she'd refilled the cup, Linda asked casually, 'How did the afternoon tea go up at the castle? I forgot to ask you the other day.'

'Lovely tea. They know how to bake.'

Linda giggled. 'You *know* what I mean!'

'Oh, *that*?' Ally took a sip of tea. 'I got the impression he thought he might get lucky. Particularly as he appeared at the malthouse yesterday with an enormous salmon as a gift. Ostensibly he'd come to see how the place had been converted, but he was still on the same old track. Still, as I say, he did bring me a salmon.' Ally related their conversation. 'I hope I've convinced him to be a platonic friend because, strange as it may seem, I really liked the man – but not like *that*!'

'Good luck then,' said Linda doubtfully, 'because that would be a first.'

'Did he ever try it on with you?'

Linda nodded. 'My poor Jim was hardly cold in his grave when your *platonic* friend came sniffing around.'

'How did you deal with it?'

'I lifted up his kilt, had a look and said, "Not up to my standard, I'm afraid"! He didn't hang around to argue!'

'Did I tell you,' said Mamie the next morning at breakfast, balancing some scrambled egg on top of some bacon and some black pudding, 'that my father's side was Dutch, but my mom was half a McKenzie. I've always wanted to come to Scotland, but not like this...' Her eyes welled.

'*Half* a McKenzie?' Ally asked as she laid the cafetière of coffee on the table.

'See, *her* mother was a McKenzie.' Mamie was into the mushrooms now. Grief did not appear to have diminished her appetite.

At that very moment, Tyler appeared, and Ally was none too sure how she should handle this.

'Mamie, this is Tyler Carrington. And, Tyler, this is Mamie Van Nuyen, who was your brother's fiancée. I gather you haven't met before? Now, would you be happy sharing a table, or would you prefer your usual table by the window, Tyler?'

Tyler and Mamie stared at each other in total amazement for a moment. 'Oh, I'm fine with sharing, if Mamie doesn't mind,' he replied.

'Good to meet you, Tyler,' said Mamie, giving her mouth a quick wipe. 'I've heard Wilbur talk about you, but...'

Ally left them to it, but from what she could hear from the kitchen, they seemed to be getting along reasonably well.

. . .

When Ally entered the dining room half an hour later, she found Mamie on her own, polishing off the croissants.

'I can't believe I've finally met him, and in such *awful* circumstances!' She poked butter into the final croissant and took a bite. 'Do you know what's even crazier? I write crime mysteries, as a kind of hobby, you know? And it's almost as if fate has sent me here to solve what happened to my wonderful Wilbur.' She blinked a tear away.

As Ally cleared some of the empty plates, it occurred to her that while she was a little doubtful of Rigby's likelihood of finding the killer, perhaps this Mamie might.

'Will you be needin' Morag again soon?' asked Murdo a little later as he delivered the post.

Ally nodded. 'Yes, I could do with her help. There may only be a couple of bedrooms occupied, but it's still a big house, and by the time I get round it all, it doesn't leave much time for anything else.'

'I'll tell her,' Murdo said.

In truth, Ally missed Morag's company. As well as being a good cleaner, Morag was also a mine of information about what was going on in the village, and she had a quirky sense of humour.

Although she did enjoy her new-found independence, Ally wondered if she might be beginning to feel a little lonely at times. She'd just about got used to being without Ken, but she missed her family and – occasionally – the buzz of city living. Thank goodness she had her investigation to keep her occupied, she thought.

FIFTEEN

As both her guests were out, Ally decided to mow the lawn. She'd almost finished when Tyler returned to pick up his sunglasses. 'It's gotten kinda warm,' he said. Then he cleared his throat. 'I can't quite figure out why that Mamie Van Nuyen is here.'

'Same reason as you, I expect,' Ally replied. 'To try to find out who killed your brother.'

'Sure,' he said, sounding doubtful, 'but it's not as if they were related because she hadn't actually *married* Wilbur.'

'They were *going* to be married, though.'

He raised an eyebrow. 'We only have her word for that. How come she was living way over in California and not with Wilbur? Three thousand miles apart?'

Ally shrugged. 'Perhaps you should ask *her* that?'

'I will,' Tyler said, 'if she stops eating for long enough to talk. Thing is, she could be putting herself in danger, Ally, because for sure there's a killer out there somewhere. It's no place for any woman to be snooping around.'

As he made his way upstairs, Ally began to feel sorry for Mamie. Why shouldn't she try to find out who had killed her fiancé? And surely where she lived was her business? Did Tyler's chauvinistic attitude stem from the fact that he alone wanted to find the killer and didn't want any competition? Particularly from a mere woman?

'Do you know,' said Mamie, helping herself to a chocolate biscuit, 'there's a lot of real nice people in this village?'

Keen for a break from gardening, Ally had asked her in for a cup of tea when she returned mid-afternoon.

'Yes, there are,' Ally agreed, 'and it's impossible to think of any of them as killers. Tyler seems determined to find out, though.'

Mamie demolished her biscuit. 'Well, he wasn't at all close to his brother, not like I was. And I'm equally determined to find out who could do such a terrible thing to my poor Wilbur.' Her eyes misted.

'You said you were a writer?' Ally asked casually.

'Yeah, I'm really interested in crime. I like water-colouring too and incorporating little sketches into my novels, which I self-publish. There's some wonderful scenery around here which I'm looking forward to sketch-ing. What about you? Have you always run a guest house?'

'Oh, goodness, no! This is my first guest house, and I've only been open a couple of months,' Ally replied. 'I'm from Edin-burgh, and before I retired, I was a television researcher, which meant I had to get all the details right of whatever the company was working on.'

'That sounds really interesting.' Mamie drained her tea.

Ally nodded. 'Sometimes it was, but, like any job, some-times it was a bit boring. I liked the artistic side of it, when I worked alongside costume or props, but when it came to researching a politician's background or something, it could become very tedious – unless I found a nice, juicy scandal from years back!'

'I can imagine!' Mamie said. 'But maybe it's stood you in good stead to do some research around here to see what you can find out about my poor Wilbur.'

'Perhaps I should try,' Ally said, smiling and thinking of her board on the kitchen wall, as she refilled Mamie's mug of tea. Milk and three sugars. She herself sincerely hoped that *somebody* would solve this thing before long, because she had no idea when she was going to be able to let out these three rooms again, and summer was on the way.

'Perhaps,' Ally said hesitantly, 'we should form a threesome to try to solve this, and to try to help the police. There's safety in numbers.'

'Absolutely!' said Mamie, helping herself to a piece of shortbread. 'I think that's a terrific idea.'

'Come and join me for a drink this evening,' Ally said, 'around six thirty maybe? I'll ask Tyler too.'

'Hey, that's so kind of you!' Tyler exclaimed a couple of hours later when he came back from his daily scrambling up rocks.

'I'm not really into cocktails, but I can do spirits, wine and beer,' Ally added.

'I'd be honoured,' said Tyler.

Three hours later, Ally poured a hefty Scotch for Tyler, along with a jug of water, and a white wine for Mamie. She poured herself a glass of Malbec, and hoped that this get-together might iron out any wrinkles in the relationship between Tyler and Mamie, and unite them in their common goal: to find out who had killed Wilbur Carrington.

'There are a number of people in this village who might

have had good reason to kill Wilbur,' Ally said, when they all had a drink in their hands and had exchanged pleasantries.

'Agreed,' said Tyler, raising his glass before taking a large swig of his drink. 'Starting with the Earl of Locharran.'

'Oh, surely not!' Mamie exclaimed, helping herself to some cashew nuts.

'Because,' Tyler continued, 'he would have been the biggest loser, wouldn't he? His title, his castle, his estate, his *everything* – if Wilbur had proved himself to be the rightful heir.'

'He wasn't the only one, though,' Ally put in, 'because most of his employees would have been affected. And some villagers rent their homes, very cheaply, from the estate. I can't imagine any of that would continue in some sort of theme park!'

'I'm sure Wilbur would have been very kind to them,' Mamie interjected, dabbing her eyes with a lace-edged handkerchief. 'He was a good man. And, after all, it was a historical Scottish theme park that he had in mind, with lots of clan battles being re-enacted, that sort of thing.'

'A good man!' Tyler exclaimed. 'Wilbur was only concerned with being good to himself.'

Ally could sense trouble brewing. 'Look,' she said hastily, 'we're not here to argue about Wilbur's intentions; we're here to try to find out who killed him.'

'Well, I have an appointment with the earl, Hamish Sinclair, tomorrow,' said Tyler, 'and I'm damned sure I'll know if he's lying.'

'Perhaps I could go with you?' Mamie asked hesitantly.

Tyler sighed loudly. 'Well, I—'

'That's a good idea,' Ally interrupted, 'because Mamie might pick up on things that you wouldn't, Tyler. Women's intuition and all that.'

Tyler did not look convinced but said, 'Fine. I'll call the castle and ask if my brother's fiancée can come too.' He regarded Mamie with something approaching distaste.

Ally sipped her wine. 'Look, we're all in this together. Both of you want to find the killer for personal reasons, and much as I enjoy having you both here, I need to have some idea when you might be leaving so I can take some bookings for the summer. The tourist information office in Fort William has already been in touch asking when my rooms will be free.'

'Oh, we'll have this thing worked out well before summer,' said Tyler confidently. Then, as an afterthought: 'When exactly *does* summer arrive here?'

'Usually around June, or so I'm told,' Ally replied, 'so another four or five weeks. Anyway, let's get together again in a couple of days and see what you've come up with.'

'Sure will,' agreed Mamie, polishing off the remainder of the nuts.

After they'd both gone out, Ally sat out on her newly mown lawn with a second glass of wine. She was not entirely convinced that these two, Tyler and Mamie – with the best will in the world – would be able to find out much. Apart from their bickering, she was aware that these incomers would be regarded with some suspicion. Not only were they foreigners, but they were connected to the man who'd come to take over their village and would probably have made them homeless to boot. And who was to say that Tyler Carrington might not be planning to carry on where his brother had left off?

Ally decided it was high time to do some sleuthing, but could she find the killer? She sighed, remembering that never in her whole life had she been able to guess who the villain was in any book or film that she'd ever seen. Perhaps she didn't have a gift for detecting, but there was always a first time.

She'd begin with Morag and Murdo, a casual chat.

. . .

Morag arrived mid-morning the following day.

'I thought ye might be needin' some polishin' done,' she said, pulling on her Marigold rubber gloves.

'Yes, good,' said Ally distractedly. Then: 'Have either Murdo or yourself got any idea who might have killed Wilbur Carrington? I mean, you're local and know everyone here better than I do.'

'I haven't a clue,' Morag replied. 'But that man managed to make plenty of enemies in the short time he was here. You'd be spoiled for choice.'

'But,' Ally persisted, 'who would *you* suspect?'

Morag sucked her teeth and picked up a tin of furniture polish. 'Well, it wisnae Murdo or me,' she replied with a grin, 'but I wouldnae be surprised if it turned out to be Ian Grant, the laird's chauffeur. At least that's what he calls himself, but he's been known to drive the van at times, and once he had to drive the tractor when poor old Jim got the flu.' She nudged Ally. 'And he's got the nicest house on the estate, right close to the castle, with a nice view and all, and a snooty wife who thinks she's better than the rest of us.' Morag sniffed loudly. 'Stuck-up madam, she is. She was in my class in school and told us all she was goin' to be a *secretary* and travel the world. Well, she got as far as the secretarial school in Inverness and got that homesick that she had to come back to Locharran!'

Ally began to wonder if the snooty wife could also be a suspect.

'What's the earl's cook like?' she asked casually. 'Mrs Jamieson, isn't it?'

Morag pulled a face. 'You wouldnae want to get on the wrong side of her! Big woman, she is, and she's been lordin' it in the castle kitchen for as long as I can remember.'

'I never see her around the village,' Ally remarked.

'She doesnae often leave the castle, but she sometimes goes

to church on a Sunday. She wears a purple felt hat that she was wearin' forty years ago. Not much trendy fashion there!'

The trouble with suspecting *everyone*, Ally discovered, was exactly that: you had to doubt even people you liked and would normally trust. She'd got her suspects up on her makeshift board, but now she had to try to imagine them doing the deed. Again, she imagined Murdo, lunging at Wilbur Carrington with the skean dhu, then hauling him up to the malthouse and instructing Morag to act surprised when she found him. Or Queenie, wielding a dagger in the middle of the night, terrified of losing her shop. Would these two women have skean dhus? Why not – they were readily available? What about Angus, the old gamekeeper? Surely he would have a selection of tools for killing and dissecting animals: guns, rifles, knives. Hamish, of course, may well have felt that the time had come to put one of his skean dhus to good use, to annihilate this American pretender. Mrs Jamieson would most likely have worried about her job, but she would undoubtedly have used one of her razor-sharp kitchen knives. Then again, if she and Mrs Fraser had access to most parts of the castle, it would be comparatively easy for either of them to borrow one of his lordship's daggers.

Ally was vacuuming downstairs, deep in thought. She made her way into the dining room, where she found Morag clearing the side table and brandishing the bread knife. Ally jumped.

'Did ye think I was goin' to skewer ye?' Morag asked cheerfully.

Skewer? Was Morag in the habit of *skewering*?

'I'll tell ye somethin' else,' Morag continued.

Ally switched off the cleaner. 'And what would that be?'

'That Callum Dalrymple at the Craigmonie is a likely suspect.' She narrowed her eyes as she looked at Ally. 'I bet he was up here before Carrington was cold to tell you that he was killed somewhere between the Craigmonie and here?'

'Well, yes, he was.'

'There ye are then,' said Morag.

'Meaning what?'

'Meaning he had a right old row with Carrington in the bar that night. The American was drunk apparently, and Dalrymple ordered him to leave. There was a bit of an argument, and do you know what the American said?'

Ally shook her head.

'He said, "I've got your number and you're gonna be the first to go when I take over this estate."'

For a moment, Ally was speechless. Then: 'But that doesn't necessarily make Dalrymple a killer though.'

'And,' added Morag, plainly enjoying imparting this information, 'Dalrymple had a drawerful of skean dhus! Debbie, who's the cleaner there, told me that he has masses of kilts and costumes, and he likes to dress up for special events at the hotel. And let me tell you, there's loads of special events at the hotel: weddings, parties, birthdays, you name it!'

'OK then,' said Ally, wiping her brow. 'Is there a skean dhu *missing*?'

Morag gave an exaggerated shrug. 'No idea! Debbie says she never counted them, so she wouldn't know.'

Ally tried to visualise Callum Dalrymple with his Paul Newman eyes and found it difficult to imagine him as a killer. But Paul Newman eyes or not, she had to admit that he was a likely suspect. What a pity that Debbie had never counted the daggers in his drawer. And surely the police would be able to trace the origin of the weapon? Why hadn't she considered Callum as a suspect, and where would he fit in on her board?

SIXTEEN

'I think I'll get a dog,' she said casually to Morag the following morning as she drank her mug of tea before setting out to do the bedrooms. Ally had always wanted another dog. They'd had a Labrador when the children were small but, later, it wouldn't have been fair to have a dog in a flat when she was out so much of the time. But now the timing was perfect. Furthermore, dogs needed walks, and Ally needed the perfect excuse to explore the area, to 'bump' into people and get chatting.

'Aye, well a wee dog might be nice,' said Morag.

'I thought of a bigger dog actually, a Labrador perhaps.'

'They're awful greedy,' Morag said, draining her mug and standing up. 'And they need a lot of walkin'. How about a nice wee Westie?'

Ally shook her head. 'No, I'd prefer a Labrador. We had one when the kids were young, and I've always loved them.'

'Och well, ye'd better have a word with Angus, the game-keeper, up at the kennels. He's got a kennel full of Labs and one of them just might be in pup.'

'I'll do that,' said Ally, deciding to visit the kennels the very next day.

. . .

The kennels housed around a dozen Labradors, all black, in a concrete building with a door leading out into a yard, from where all of them indulged in a frenzy of barking, tail-wagging and leaning up against the fence if anyone approached. It was one of several outbuildings a couple of hundred yards down the hill from the castle and, as Ally approached, Angus emerged from one of the old stone-built sheds. Ally could decipher a ride-on mower in its murky depths. It was a warm spring day, but Angus was wearing his usual uniform, a shabby Harris Tweed plus-four suit, his sturdy legs encased in brown woollen stockings and his feet in brown leather boots. He was a shaggy man; shaggy white hair, shaggy white eyebrows and a shaggy white moustache.

'Aye,' he said by way of greeting.

'Hello! I'm Alison McKinley from The Auld Malthouse.'

'Och aye,' he said, nodding sagely, 'I know that. You were in the Craigmonie with *that American*.'

'Yes, well...' Ally hesitated. 'I was wondering if any of the dogs might be expecting? I'm after a Labrador puppy.'

'Aye, I know that too,' replied Angus, squinting up at the sun.

'You do?'

'Aye, I was talkin' to Murdo McConnachie in the bar last night. Male or female?'

'What, Murdo?'

He looked at her as if she was some kind of halfwit. 'The dog,' he said patiently.

'I haven't really given it much thought, but probably a bitch would be best,' Ally replied, feeling foolish.

He continued studying her from underneath his bushy eyebrows. 'Aye, that would likely be best.' He straightened up. 'Ye could breed her, but we'd be wantin' a percentage.'

'I wouldn't want to breed her,' Ally said. 'I just want a dog for company.'

Angus snorted. 'Aye, well, his lordship will be chargin' ye a small fortune, because them dogs have pedigrees as long as Loch Ness.'

'But, Angus, do you or do you not have a pregnant Labrador?'

'Oh aye,' said Angus, fingering his moustache, 'we do indeed.'

'And when will she give birth?'

'Oh, maybe in a month, give or take a few days.' Angus closed the door of the building behind him.

'Oh, OK.' Ally sounded slightly despondent.

'Or ye could have one of Bella's,' said Angus.

'Bella?'

'Aye, Bella pupped a wee while ago. But they'll no' be ready to leave their mother for another week or two.'

'Oh, Angus!' Ally beamed. 'I'd love one of Bella's! Did she have girls? Could I see them?'

'Aye, she had three of each, so you can take your pick of the lassies.' He reopened the door behind him and indicated to Ally that she should follow him.

'Oh!' Ally exclaimed as he indicated the bed of straw where Bella and her brood were nestling; six beautiful tiny black puppies and their proud mum. As she bent over the little nursery, one little pup kept trying to climb up her arm. She turned to Angus. 'Is that a girl?'

'Oh aye,' said Angus, turning the pup over, 'that's a girl, all right.'

'Can I have her?'

'Aye, soon.' He dug in his pocket and found a sheet of coloured stickers. 'This is yours then,' he said, sticking a green one on the pup's back. 'Ye'll need to come back soon. With your cheque book.'

'I will. Now,' said Ally, determined not to waste this visit, 'before I go, who do *you* think stuck that dagger in the American's back?'

'Well,' said Angus, squinting at the sky again, 'it wisnae me. I wis stayin' with ma sister in Strathpeffer while all this was goin' on.'

'So you weren't here the night the American was killed?'

Angus shook his head, still looking at the sky. 'No, Mrs Malthouse, I wisnae here.'

Ally smiled inwardly at his change to her name. 'You were definitely in Strathpeffer?'

He was now regarding her as if looking at an imbecile. 'I just told ye that.'

Ally walked home via the shop, because she'd decided that perhaps she needed some sort of notebook in which to write down her thoughts. She got all sorts of ideas as she was wandering around, and then usually forgot them. She could keep a little notebook in her pocket.

Queenie was leaning across the counter as usual, but there was no sign of Bessie.

'Will ye be needin' milk?' asked Queenie, reluctantly tearing her eyes away from a couple of schoolchildren who were studying the sweets.

'No, I'm OK for milk at the moment,' Ally replied, 'but I'm looking for a small notebook of some kind.'

'They'll be on my *stationery* counter,' said Queenie importantly, indicating a shelf laden with pens, pencils, crayons, painting boxes and drawing pads. After a minute, she added, 'Will ye be wantin' lines?'

'Lines?'

'Aye, for writin' on. To keep yer writin' straight. The ones with lines is next to thae magazines, but don't ye go lookin' at that top shelf because them magazines isnae suitable for a lady such as yersel'.'

Since Ally was the same height as the top shelf, she could hardly avoid the covers of young ladies in various shades of undress before she finally found a notebook with lines.

'That'll keep your writin' nice and straight,' Queenie repeated approvingly. Then, as Ally withdrew her purse from her shoulder bag: 'Yer guests were in here a wee while ago.'

'Oh?' Ally placed her purse on the counter.

'Aye. On their way to the castle, they said. Bought a box of chocolates for the laird, the ones with whisky and stuff inside them.'

'Chocolate liqueurs?' Ally suggested.

'Aye. Now why would they want to be goin' to see *him*?'

'I don't know, Queenie. I don't ask my guests where they're going or why.'

Queenie wasn't finished yet. 'So who was that woman then? Is she the brother's wife?'

'No, she's the fiancée of the murder victim.'

'*Away* with ye!' Queenie clutched her chest. 'That *old woman*?'

'Well, Wilbur Carrington loved her, and he was in his sixties anyway,' Ally said, keen to pay and get away.

'A fiancée! Fancy that!' Queenie was plainly fascinated by this information. '*Bessie!*' she hollered as Ally paid for the notebook. Bessie appeared from somewhere in the dark depths of the storeroom at the back of the shop. 'Bessie! That old woman in pink was the *fiancée* of the man who got murdered!'

Bessie contemplated this for a moment. 'There's hope for us all then.'

Queenie scowled at her sister as she handed Ally her change. 'Dinna be daft!'

. . .

Ally opened her notebook and studied the pristine white page with its horizontal blue lines, and wondered where to start. Morag had gone home so she turned the painting round and replaced Angus's Post-it with one marked 'Callum' before hanging it up again. One suspect removed, another one added. She looked at her bevy of Post-it notes.

She honestly did not think that Hamish Sinclair was likely to be a killer, other than of pheasants and deer.

Angus the gamekeeper she'd now ruled out altogether, unless he'd nipped back from Strathpeffer in the dead of night on a flying murderous mission. Unlikely, but she had a feeling that Morag was related to Angus in some way and might be able to confirm this.

The chauffeur then; she'd come to rather like Ian Grant, but he certainly had an incentive as he and the snooty wife seemingly had the 'nicest house'.

More surprising was Callum Dalrymple, who'd apparently had a row with Wilbur in the bar and, if Wilbur's claim was genuine, Callum would almost certainly be out of a job. Ally reminded herself that she must not be influenced by his sexy blue eyes because he, too, was a likely suspect. She pressed his newly written note more securely on the board.

She hoped her friend, Linda, would never see this board. She, along with the Concetti family, had to be included only because they leased properties from the estate.

Finally, there was Murdo and Morag. To suspect them still seemed preposterous, but they too could be evicted. Since Murdo drank in the Craigmonie Bar most nights, he might well have been involved in the tussle.

Ally sighed. Where to start? And where was the proof that Wilbur Carrington was indeed the rightful laird? Did Rigby have any kind of proof? It was time to have a chat with the police inspector again. And why had she bought this stupid notebook because she hadn't written down a word? She'd use it for her shopping lists.

Just at that moment, she heard her guests returning. Ally decided to find out how they had got on so went out into the hallway. Tyler was already three-quarters of the way upstairs, but Mamie was still taking off her shoes and placing them neatly underneath her pink jacket in the hall cupboard.

'How did it go, Mamie?'

Mamie gave a little sigh. 'That Tyler is like a bull in a china shop! Straight in and asking questions, whereas I'd have used a more subtle approach. Know what I mean?'

'I do. Did you find out anything interesting?'

'Not really. The earl could not have been more charming, but he plainly did not take Wilbur's claims seriously. I'd have liked to ask a little more about his history, to see if it tallied with more of Wilbur's ideas, which, I have to admit, do seem a little far-fetched now.'

'But, Mamie, if they were so far-fetched, then why was he murdered?'

Mamie shrugged, looking confused. 'Maybe he just happened to be in the wrong place at the wrong time?'

'There's no denying that. But there's never been any murders round here, so isn't it just too much of a coincidence?'

'Well, let's hope the police are on the ball!'

There was something about Mamie which fascinated Ally. Apart from her living some three thousand miles away from her fiancé (what was to stop her moving to Boston?), she always seemed cheerful and resilient. 'Would you care for a cup of tea, Mamie?'

Mamie would. 'I really like the way you make tea over here,' she said as she entered the kitchen and sat down by the log burner. 'It tastes different back home, and I prefer iced tea in the States.'

'We don't go in much for iced tea over here,' Ally remarked.

'Guess you don't get warm enough weather,' Mamie said, grinning.

'Oh, we do get hot weather occasionally,' Ally replied, handing her tea, in a cup, with a saucer. 'Anyway, I meant to ask you how your writing is going, and if you've written anything since you've been here?'

Mamie sipped her tea and sighed. 'I don't seem to be able to concentrate. I guess my mind is all taken up with thinking about poor Wilbur. But do you know what I really enjoy doing to take my mind off things?'

Ally shook her head. 'Tell me.'

'I adore doing jigsaw puzzles!'

'Isn't that a coincidence!' Ally was genuinely surprised. 'I love doing them too!' She was thinking of the thousand-piece puzzle of the Trevi Fountain on the board up in her bedroom, which she'd neglected of late. The pieces were small, the fountain was intricate and it was going to take some time to complete it.

'And do you know what?' Mamie said. 'I bought one in your village shop only yesterday! It's a beautiful picture of Locharran Castle, but God only knows why I bought it because it's going to take forever to put together! And heaven knows where I'm going to lay it all out.'

Ally thought for a moment. 'Why not use the coffee table in the sitting room? Would that be big enough, do you think?'

Mamie considered. 'Yeah, I reckon it would. Thanks so much! I'll get started on it this very evening!' She drained her tea. 'That was delicious,' she added as she got up to go.

Ally thought she'd enjoy watching Mamie putting the puzzle together, and it might even encourage her to get going again on the Trevi Fountain!

In the meantime, the bigger puzzle remained unsolved.

· · ·

As if on cue, DI Rigby appeared on the doorstep the following morning, just after her guests had finished breakfast and gone off on their separate ways: Mamie in her car, Tyler on foot. Where did they go? She had no idea. Mamie said she was driving around to do some sketching, and Tyler said he liked walking on the hills.

Rigby cleared his throat. 'We've come,' he said, indicating the young constable behind him, 'to make a final clear-out of the room that was occupied by Wilbur Carrington.' He produced the room key from his pocket and waved it in the air.

'Come in then,' Ally said.

'We'll clear it all out today,' said Rigby, 'and then we won't need to bother you again.'

'Meaning I can let it?' Ally asked hopefully.

'Meaning you can let it,' the DI confirmed as he made his way upstairs, followed by the constable.

They were upstairs for the best part of half an hour before the young policeman came down carrying two large boxes and made his way out to the police car. Five minutes later, Rigby appeared carrying a full set of bedding, including the mattress cover.

'I'm afraid you've got some laundry to do now,' he said with the glimmer of a smile.

'Can I assume then that you still haven't got any promising leads?' Ally asked, desperate to get some information before he disappeared.

'Unfortunately not,' Rigby confirmed with a sigh, 'but the earl's chauffeur seems to think he knows something so I've made an appointment to meet with him. Tyler Carrington is becoming very impatient; thinks we should have it all wrapped up by now so that he can head home with his brother's body.' He paused. 'And then we have this Miss Van Nuyen...'

'She was the victim's fiancée.'

'Yes, we are aware of that. Don't quite know why she's

appeared on the scene, though. Nothing she can do. At least she doesn't ask questions all the time, like the brother does.'

'Surely he only wants to find out who killed Wilbur?'

'Hmm.' Rigby looked unconvinced.

'No prints on the skean dhu?'

He shook his head.

'And do you have any definite proof that Wilbur Carrington was the rightful heir to the estate?'

'There *are* some documents missing,' said Rigby somewhat grudgingly, 'but it looks increasingly possible.'

'So what's missing?'

Rigby pursed his lips. 'I'm not at liberty to say, Mrs McKinley.'

'No, I don't suppose you are,' Ally said sadly, looking at the pile of washing on the floor and thinking of his rather dismissive attitude towards the green folder.

'Suffice to say we are continuing with a full-scale investigation,' he said, getting ready to leave.

As she waved him goodbye, Ally thought about the painting hanging over her kitchen table. Rigby was careful not to share too much information with her, but she couldn't help but wonder how her suspect list compared to his...

SEVENTEEN

The earl rang up the following morning. 'Shall we meet for a lunchtime drink and snack?'

Ally was dumbstruck for a moment.

'I know it's short notice,' he said, 'and I promise I'm not going to compromise you in any way, but I would like an outing and some *friendly* female company.'

'Well, thank you,' Ally replied. 'Where did you have in mind?'

'Not Locharran,' Hamish Sinclair said firmly, 'but there's a nice wee inn about five miles away on the side of Loch Trioch. Do you know it?'

'No, I don't,' Ally replied, 'but it sounds lovely.'

'I'll pick you up at noon then,' he said.

He arrived in his dark-green Jaguar on the dot of twelve. Ally had spent half the morning trying to decide what to wear. Would he remember the cashmere sweater she'd worn for afternoon tea at the castle? Hopefully not, and she decided to wear it again with her cream jeans, adding a long navy-and-cream scarf which she wound loosely round her neck in a carefully careless style.

As she sank into the sumptuous leather passenger seat, Ally wondered how many local eyes were focussed on them. Although she wasn't overlooked, there was always someone around, and both the earl and the car were instantly recognisable. *What the hell?* she thought. *Let them think what they like!* She decided not to mention the credit card.

The 'nice wee inn' was called The Bothy, because that was exactly what it had once been, no doubt providing overnight shelter to many a shepherd or a walker who might have got lost on the moors in the mists, in the days before the road was built when there were no mobile phones. In fact, the road seemed to finish there, although it appeared to then continue as a rough track round the loch. The original old stone bothy had been extended sympathetically to three times its original size, Hamish informed her, and now housed a bar and restaurant complete with tartan carpets and thirty-something varieties of whisky – just in case you were unaware you were in Scotland.

The staff all knew perfectly well who he was. 'Good afternoon, sir,' they all chanted, and Ally was aware of being scrutinised from every angle. How many women had the old lothario brought here, for goodness' sake?

'They do an amazing venison casserole,' said Hamish when they were shown to a table with panoramic views of the loch and the sheep on the hillside behind. 'Or would you prefer some fish? They have excellent sea bass here.'

'I'd love to try the venison casserole,' Ally replied, now realising that she was here for lunch and not just for a snack.

'Two venisons,' Hamish said to the hovering waiter, 'and a bottle of decent claret.'

'Hamish,' Ally said, 'you fascinate me. You and your castle, and being the earl and everything.'

'Oh, don't give it a thought! It's just how it is!'

'I've no doubt it is. But if anything should happen to you, who would be your heir?'

'I have a cousin,' he said, pulling a face, 'who I don't much like. Not that he likes me much either, but he'd like to be the earl. I have no children, you see.'

'You've never married?'

'Yes, I was once. She was very beautiful.' He looked sadly down at his plate. 'We'd been married less than a year and she was only twenty-two when she died.'

'Oh, Hamish, I am so sorry. I had no idea.' Ally began to feel much more sympathetic towards him. Perhaps his womanising was on account of his sad past?

'I've had lots of lady friends, as I've no doubt you've been told, but she was my one true love. Still, one mustn't dwell on the past. Let's talk about something else, shall we?'

They made small talk while they waited for the wine, and Ally told him she was buying one of his Labrador puppies.

'Good idea. Everyone should have a dog,' he said, 'and please have it with my compliments.'

'No, Hamish,' Ally said firmly. 'If I can't pay you, then I'll go elsewhere. It's a very generous offer, but I won't accept it.'

'You are such an independent lady! Perhaps you'd accept a wee discount then?'

'Only a very wee one,' she replied with a smile before adding, 'Any further information on the Wilbur Carrington claim, or the murder?'

Hamish shook his head. 'Not that I'm aware of.' He sighed. 'Stands to reason I'm the chief suspect with everything to lose if he'd proved his claim. But, Alison, I assure you that I did *not* kill that man. I felt like it sometimes because he was such a damn nuisance, but I didn't.'

For no good reason, Ally believed him.

'Not that Rigby believes me,' he added. 'He and his team are up at the castle, asking questions and examining everything, every other day, and driving us all mad.' He paused for a moment. 'Carrington's biggest mistake was telling everyone in the village who he thought he was and what he planned to do. He should have kept his mouth shut.'

'Agreed,' Ally said.

He leaned across the table when they'd finished eating the delicious casserole. 'You really are a very attractive lady.' Then, seeing her face, he added quickly, 'I know, I *know*, we're just *good friends*!'

'Yes, we are, and so I'd like to pay for my own lunch today, please,' Ally said, to emphasise the point.

'Definitely *not*!' the earl exclaimed. 'Surely I can treat you to lunch without any strings attached! Now, how about a dessert? The treacle tart is out of this world.'

Ally resisted the treacle tart and settled for a Celtic coffee, made with local whisky and local cream. They chatted about the village, his family, her family and the nosy locals. 'I've long since learned to ignore them,' he said, 'although I suppose I've given them plenty of cause for gossip over the years!'

When he'd driven her home, he said, 'We must do this again soon. I've really enjoyed your company.'

'And I've enjoyed yours,' Ally replied truthfully.

There were no messages on her mobile or her landline, so no one was interested in booking Room 1 yet.

Ally decided to take a walk down to Fin's Fish and buy some seafood for later in the week. The fish seller, Finlay McKinnon, was a small, wiry man with a weather-beaten face and a full head of curly white hair who went out in his boat every morning early and almost always came back with a considerable haul, which he sold throughout the day. In the summer, when he sold his catch by the afternoon, he'd shut up his little hut and take tourists out fishing into the sea loch.

'Ach, ye're a bit late for the prawns, Mrs McKinley, but I've a lovely couple of bass here,' he informed her, looking up at the sky. 'Looks like it's goin' to rain any minute.'

As Ally paid for her fish, the heavens opened. She sheltered in Finlay's hut for a few minutes, wondering how to get home without being soaked.

'Looks like it's on for the night,' Finlay said cheerfully.

Just then, a man's voice said, 'You want a lift back up to the malthouse, Ally?'

Ally looked round to see Ian Grant, the earl's chauffeur, picking up a bag of fish from the front of Finlay's hut. He was standing in the rain wielding a large umbrella.

'Oh, I definitely would,' Ally said.

'Come on then,' he said, holding the umbrella over her. 'I'm just round the corner.'

Round the corner was the earl's mud-splattered old Land Rover, and Ally climbed gratefully into the passenger seat.

'Just been pickin' up his lordship's fish,' he explained, chucking the parcel onto the seat behind.

'Thanks so much,' Ally said, fastening her seat belt. As he started up the motor, she asked, 'How are things up at the castle?'

Ian Grant snorted. 'Much as usual, police snoopin' around all over the place, and no nearer findin' the murderer. But maybe not for much longer, though.'

Ally felt a little frisson of excitement. Did he *know* something? 'Really? Why? Have you heard something? Seen something? I mean, Carrington's body was found outside my back door, so I'm naturally anxious.'

'Can't say just at the moment,' he said as they began the climb up the hill, 'but I have an appointment to chat with Rigby soon.'

They'd arrived at the malthouse. As he pulled on the hand-brake, he asked, 'Do ye need the umbrella?'

'No, no,' Ally replied. 'I'll make a run for it. Thanks so much for the lift.' She hesitated for a moment. 'Would you like to come in for a drink?'

Ian glanced at his watch. 'Just for a moment maybe. I don't think his lordship's likely to want to go anywhere in this storm.'

They both made a dash for the malthouse door, almost colliding with Mamie, who was also running for shelter from where she'd parked her little Ford. Mamie, as always, was clad in pink – from what seemed to be an inexhaustible supply of outfits – apart from the white trainers on her tiny little feet.

'Oh my!' she exclaimed breathlessly. 'I guess I got back just in time!' She looked enquiringly at Ian Grant as she peeled off her pastel-pink jacket to reveal a deep-pink sweater underneath.

'This is the earl's chauffeur,' Ally explained. 'Ian Grant. Ian, this is Mamie Van Nuyen, who was the fiancée of Wilbur Carrington.'

Ian stared at her for a moment, then nodded. 'Yeah,' he said as Ally led him into the kitchen and Mamie headed upstairs. 'I saw her in the shop the other day, buying a load of chocolate bars.'

'That sounds like Mamie!' Ally exclaimed, laughing.

Ian opted for 'a wee Scotch, as I've only to drive up the hill'.

'I'm really interested to find out what you want to chat to Rigby about!' She looked at him hopefully as she poured some whisky for him and some wine for herself.

'It's called "shootin' yourself in the foot",' Ian replied drily, 'but I'm willin' to risk it.' He raised his glass. '*Slàinte mhath!*'

'*Slàinte mhath!*' Ally clinked her glass against his. 'Shooting yourself in the foot?'

'Aye, well, if what I've worked out is true, then I'd likely be losing my job and my home.'

'Oh my God!' She looked at him in astonishment. 'Can't you give me some idea—'

'Best not to,' he said, tossing back his drink in one, 'because you do *not* want to get involved in this.'

'So you must have worked out that Wilbur Carrington *was* the real heir?'

He shook his head. 'I shouldn't have said anything. All I can say is, "Watch this space!"'

'I certainly will,' Ally agreed.

'I'd best be on my way,' he said, standing up. 'Thanks so much for the drink.'

'You're very welcome,' Ally said, accompanying him to the door. 'Thanks for the lift!'

In the morning, while she was serving Mamie her breakfast, Ally wondered if she should tell Mamie what Ian Grant had said. She decided she would. 'The chauffeur said he had something of interest to tell the police,' she said, 'but added that he'd be shooting himself in the foot. Which was intriguing.'

Mamie, a large piece of bacon halfway to her mouth, looked mystified. 'Meaning?'

'Meaning the information he's about to impart would not necessarily benefit himself.'

Mamie looked confused. 'In what way?'

'Ian's house, like some of the others, goes with the job, so if the job goes...'

'That's interesting,' said Mamie, spearing some sausage. 'I wonder what he knows?'

'Yes, it is interesting,' agreed Ally, 'but he wasn't about to tell me.'

'Probably guesswork,' Mamie said dismissively.

'I wouldn't be too sure,' said Ally.

. . .

It was around noon when Ally was bringing in her washing from the clothes line and was about to begin folding sheets in readiness for ironing, when she heard sirens wailing somewhere nearby. Police? Accident?

As she placed the sheet back in the laundry basket and went towards the front door, she encountered Tyler, who was just coming in.

'What's going on out there?' Ally asked.

Tyler shrugged. 'No idea. I tried to walk up to have a look, but there's police everywhere cordoning off the road up to the castle. I spoke to one policeman who just said, "Accident," so it could be anything.'

The road up to the castle! Ally felt her blood run cold; surely not the earl?

As Tyler made his way upstairs, Ally went back to her laundry basket wondering what on earth had happened and, more importantly, if anyone was involved or injured. There seemed little point in taking a walk up the hill if the area was cordoned off. She sighed, knowing she'd find out soon enough. There were unwary tourists around now, and the road to and from the castle had a couple of sharp bends. As Murdo put it: 'They're that busy lookin' at the scenery that they're never lookin' at where they're goin'.' As the earl and his staff had looked at the scenery countless times, hopefully this did not involve them.

Ally's phone rang.

'Hi, it's Linda. Why not come down for a drink if you're not doing anything better? Bit of excitement up the road, as you probably know. I'll try to find out what's going on.'

This seemed like an excellent idea. She hadn't seen Linda for several days, and there was more chance of finding out what was happening if she was down in the village.

As she was about to leave, Ally glanced into the sitting room. Mamie had laid her jigsaw puzzle out on the table and had begun to piece together the frame. But there was still a long way to go. Ally couldn't help herself; she found two pieces which she slotted into place.

'Is it too early for a nice glass of chilled Prosecco?' Linda asked, glancing at her watch.

'Somewhere on earth it's exactly the right time,' Ally replied, laughing. 'Never too early!'

'I've got bookings for dinner later,' Linda said, 'and I find that a couple of glasses of this puts me in the right frame of mind to tackle work. I never drink at all while I'm working, because I just don't have the time.'

'Well, I only have to toddle up the hill,' Ally reminded her.

They clinked glasses. 'Here's to a successful season for us both,' Linda said.

'Well, the good news is that I've finally got Room One free for letting again,' Ally said, 'although I'm not too sure anyone might want to stay in a village where a killer is, presumably, still on the loose, and when they discover that my other guests are relatives of the victim.'

'And then you've got Wailing Willie for good measure!' Linda added, with a grin.

Ally rolled her eyes. 'Don't talk to me about—'

She was interrupted by the continuous buzzing of a doorbell.

Linda placed her glass down on the table. 'No peace for the wicked!'

Ally could hear women's voices, with a great deal of exclaiming going on, before Linda returned, sat down, picked up her glass and downed the lot.

'What's up?' Ally asked tentatively.

'That was Laura, my waitress. She can't come to work tonight because her husband, who's a policeman, can't stay home with the kids as he usually does. He's going to have to be at the police station until late, due to the "incident".'

'*Incident*? You mean up the hill? Not an accident?' Ally didn't like the sound of that.

Linda nodded. 'Incident. It was the earl's Land Rover, apparently, which came off the road at the first bend and crashed down below. But the earl wasn't in it. The only person in it was the driver,' Linda replied.

'Driver? You mean... chauffeur?' Ally asked.

Linda nodded grimly. 'The chauffeur. Certified dead at the scene.'

EIGHTEEN

Ally, shocked to the core, couldn't bring herself to speak for a moment. 'Ian Grant?' she managed eventually.

'That's him,' Linda confirmed sadly.

'Oh my God!' Ally could scarcely believe what she was hearing. 'Only yesterday he gave me a lift in the Land Rover when I got caught in the rain down at Fin's Fish.'

'Just thank your lucky stars you weren't in it today,' Linda remarked, looking equally shocked.

'Oh, Linda!' Ally exclaimed. 'It's not that I *knew* him, of course, because I've only met him a couple of times, but he seemed a nice man. This is just awful! Surely he must have known that road like the back of his hand? How could he miss the bend or whatever?'

'He's been more than twenty years with the earl, I believe, so he'd know every stone on the road,' Linda said thoughtfully. She sipped her drink. 'Perhaps there was a fault with the Land Rover? Or maybe he had a heart attack?'

Ally thought for a moment. 'He said he was going to speak to Rigby about something, something important.' She shivered. 'Perhaps someone knew that?'

'*Who* would know?'

'I've no idea but, if he told me, then there's a good chance he told someone else.'

Linda grimaced. 'Like his boss? The earl?'

'I can't believe the earl has any part in this. Anyway, we don't know exactly what happened, and it's entirely possible that Ian Grant had a heart attack or something.'

'But why *wouldn't* the earl be a suspect again? Are you sure you're not a bit biased? Aren't you a little bit interested in him?'

'Not even the tiniest bit!' Ally spoke truthfully, but she realised how it might look to other people. 'He's become a *friend*, Linda, and nothing more.'

Linda shrugged. 'I believe you, but the gossipmongers round here won't.'

'Let them gossip!' Ally said, draining her Prosecco. 'They'll have plenty to talk about now anyway. Thanks for the drink. Time I went home.'

Ally arrived home in a state of shock. There was no sign of either Tyler or Mamie, which was a relief because she really didn't feel like talking to anyone. How could an experienced driver like Ian Grant miscalculate a bend that he'd driven round for years? It had to be that he'd suffered a heart attack or some sort of blackout and lost control. Or had he? She was still haunted by what he'd said. What exactly had he wanted to talk to Rigby about?

She spent a quiet evening watching TV, with no phone calls. She went to bed early but knew it might be difficult to get to sleep. It was past midnight before she finally dropped off, when she drifted into a fitful sleep, culminating in a dream in which she was a passenger in the back of a Land Rover which was being driven at speed by someone who, from the rear, looked exactly like Ian Grant. When the driver turned round, the face was that of Mrs Fraser. 'Where would you like to go?' she asked Ally. 'We've made some lovely scones for tea.'

Ally could see the bend in the road rapidly approaching, but Mrs Fraser still had her head turned around, looking at Ally. 'Or we could have some lovely pancakes...'

'*Look out!*' yelled Ally. 'Watch where you're going!'

She'd obviously woken herself up and was struggling to get out of bed. She lay back and looked at the clock: 5 a.m. Ally was not confident about getting back to sleep as the events of the previous day infiltrated her consciousness. After ten minutes, she gave up, got up, had a shower, got dressed and made herself some coffee. She switched on the news, just in case, but there was no mention of any incident in Locharran, so perhaps it was being treated as just a local accident and not worthy of the national news.

Ally set the table for her guests' breakfasts and set about getting food ready, just as Morag arrived.

'Ye couldnae make it up!' she exclaimed as she took off her coat. 'Our wee village is bloody *damned. Doomed.* Have ye heard the news?'

'Oh yes, I've heard,' Ally replied, 'and I still can't believe it. Surely Ian Grant had a heart attack or something?'

'Well,' said Morag, tying her apron round her ample waist, 'they've taken the body away to be examined, and they've taken the car away to be examined, too, down at Gordon's Garage.' She sighed theatrically. 'The whole place is crawlin' with police!' She, like many of the villagers, pronounced it as 'polis'.

Just then, Ally heard someone enter the dining room next door and she began to brew a cafetière of coffee. She'd already set out fruit, juice, cereals, yoghurts, milk and honey on the side table in there so that guests could help themselves, although occasionally Tyler fancied porridge. And it would almost certainly *be* Tyler, as he liked to be up and about early, unlike his almost-sister-in-law, who was not an early riser.

Ally carried the coffee into the dining room. 'Good morning, Tyler! Did you sleep well?'

'Good morning, Ally. Yeah, I slept quite well, thanks. I decided to have an early night.'

'Have you heard the news?'

'News?' he asked, helping himself to muesli and yoghurt.

'Apparently the reason for the road to the castle being blocked yesterday was because the earl's Land Rover was involved in an accident, and his chauffeur was killed.'

'Oh my God!' Tyler looked horrified. 'Do you know what happened? Was there some sort of collision?'

Ally shrugged. 'Not that I know of. So far as I'm aware, the Land Rover missed the bend or something and somersaulted onto the road beneath.'

Tyler sat down with his bowl of muesli, looking quite shaken. 'Surely there was some other vehicle involved because the chauffeur must have driven down that road millions of times?'

'That's exactly what I thought,' Ally concurred.

'Guess he had a stroke or heart attack or something then.'

'I expect we'll find out sooner or later.'

'I think perhaps we should get together for a chat again this evening.' Tyler hesitated. 'With Mamie, I guess. Perhaps one of us might have unwittingly seen or heard something? I'll bring some whisky and some wine, if you could provide the glasses.'

'Good idea,' Ally agreed.

When she returned to the kitchen, Murdo's little red van pulled up outside and, after his usual perfunctory knock on the back door, he rushed into the kitchen in a state of high excitement.

'I've just been down to Gordon's Garage,' he said, depositing a couple of envelopes on the table, 'and ye'll *never* guess what?'

Both women looked at him expectantly.

'Well, there's *polis* swarmin' around everywhere, but I went in and had a word with Billy Gordon, who was havin' a cup of tea, and he told me – under his breath – that them brakes had been *cut!*' Murdo looked triumphantly at them both, plainly delighted to be the bearer of such awful tidings. Then, to emphasise the point, he added loudly, 'Some bugger had *cut the brakes!*'

There was a horrified silence for a moment before Morag said, '*What?*'

'Cut!' repeated Murdo. 'Cut *deliberately!*'

Ally's worst fears had materialised. She sat down and asked, 'There could be no mistake?'

'No mistake! Billy Gordon's been a mechanic for forty years and he saw straight away what had been done!'

'Oh my God,' said Ally.

By mid-morning the entire village knew. Ally had decided not to mention this to Tyler, but would tell him and Mamie later, if they hadn't already heard by then.

She ventured only as far as the village shop because she needed to buy some eggs and found the building full of people, all talking excitedly.

'Ah, Mrs McKinley,' said Queenie, who was obviously having a field day listening to all the gossip, 'ye'll have heard about poor, *poor* Ian?'

'I have indeed,' Ally replied.

'Who would want to be killin' our Ian?' Queenie asked, shaking her head slowly from side to side.

'I've no idea,' Ally said sadly, 'and I still can't believe it.' She cleared her throat. 'I'd like a dozen eggs when you have a moment, please, Queenie.'

Queenie remained in her default across-the-counter position. 'Ye see, Mrs McKinley, it's one thing when some foreigner or other gets himself killed round here, but it's somethin' else altogether when it's one of our *own*.' She shook her head some more. 'I've known him since the day he was born,' she added with a sigh.

Looking around, Ally could see that everyone had that look of disbelief on their faces. A thin woman with thin lips, who Ally had never seen before, emerged from the frozen-food section and placed her basket on the counter in front of Queenie.

'Myrtle's that upset!' exclaimed the woman. 'She's lost her dear husband, her provider and, more than likely, her *home* as well.'

Ally assumed the woman was referring to the snooty wife.

'Aye,' said Queenie, 'and now they'll be needin' a new driver, won't they? And if she's still in that house, where's the new driver goin' to be stayin'?'

'But the earl would never throw her out, would he?' the woman asked.

'Ye can never tell,' Queenie replied. 'After all, he's gentry, and *he's* never going to be homeless now, is he?'

'No, Queenie, he is not. But surely he wouldnae be that cruel to poor Myrtle?'

'Time will tell,' said Queenie sagely, pursing her lips and narrowing her eyes. Then, as if remembering she had another customer, she turned to Ally. 'What was it ye were wantin'?'

Ally's guests had gravitated towards the kitchen, as did most people who visited The Auld Malthouse.

Mamie, attired in a pink T-shirt with Minnie Mouse on the front said, as she sat down, 'I meant to say to you, Ally, that the night before last, I heard some kinda funny noises coming from my bathroom, but I guess it must have been the wind or something.' She crossed one fuchsia-coloured leg over the other, sipped some wine and took a large handful of pretzels.

'It hasn't been particularly windy,' Tyler said, frowning at her.

'Then I guess it must have been the heating or something,' said Mamie.

'I'll have it checked,' Ally said quickly, praying that neither of her guests had heard anything about Wailing Willie. On top of everything else that was taking place around them, it would probably freak Mamie out.

Tyler had appeared in the kitchen with a bottle of Scotch, a bottle of red wine and a bottle of white wine. He poured some white for Mamie, some red for Ally and a hefty measure of Scotch for himself.

'I got some great photos of Ben Nevis today,' Mamie said. 'I decided to go all the way to Fort William because there wasn't a cloud in the sky, and I wanted to see the top of the mountain for once.'

'I went further afield today too,' Tyler said. 'I decided to walk to Murchan, which must be a good five miles each way.' He took a gulp of his drink. 'There's some great climbing over there. I guess it might have been a bit gloomy round here? Have you heard any more about the chauffeur's untimely death, Ally?'

Ally took a deep breath. 'I have. Apparently, the Land Rover's brakes had been cut.'

'*Cut?*' they asked in unison, both looking utterly shocked.

'So,' Tyler said, laying down his drink, 'that must mean that *somebody* wanted him gone?'

Ally nodded. 'He gave me a lift back from Fin's Fish, in the Land Rover, the evening before last when I got caught in the rain. He insinuated that he knew something, because he said he needed to see the detective inspector. Well, it would seem that he never got the chance.'

Tyler let out a long whistle. 'I guess this has to be tied up with Wilbur.'

'Obviously, because they don't go killing each other round here any more, Tyler,' Ally said with a faint smile. 'The clan fights that fascinated your brother are long gone. Now we have two murders within a couple of weeks! *Of course* they're connected!'

'So the chauffeur plainly knew something important about Wilbur's murder, like you said, Ally, and that's why he was killed,' stated Mamie.

'Before he could tell anyone,' Ally added. 'I did ask him to tell me what he knew, but he wouldn't.'

'Poor guy,' said Tyler. 'Which means that Wilbur's killer is still roaming around and prepared to kill anyone else who might have a clue as to his identity. I hope the police are on the ball.'

Ally hoped so too but wasn't overconfident. She strongly suspected that Rigby might be having a major headache. Probably wished he'd stayed in Birmingham.

'What we've got to do now,' Tyler said, downing a large gulp of Scotch, 'is check out every person in the village who might have some reason to kill Wilbur or this Ian Grant. I guess, from what you've said, Ally, that it could be anyone who works for the earl.'

'Or their wives,' added Mamie. 'After all, these ladies don't want to lose their homes, do they?'

'No, they don't,' Ally agreed, 'but I don't quite see how you're going to be able to do this checking.'

'I guess I'm going to have to knock on every door and ask questions,' said Tyler.

'Well,' said Mamie, 'nobody's going to invite you in and tell you they did the killings, are they?'

Tyler rolled his eyes. 'Why are you always so negative?'

'I'm just being realistic,' Mamie snapped.

Ally decided they were getting nowhere. 'Look,' she said,

'let's all just keep our eyes and ears open and talk to *anyone* who might be helpful, and we'll get together again in a couple of nights and discuss anything that might come up in the meantime.'

With some relief, they drained their drinks and headed upstairs, leaving Ally wondering why on earth they bickered so much when they surely had the same aim – to discover Wilbur's killer. That was what mattered, wasn't it?

NINETEEN

Ally didn't sleep well. She kept imagining Ian Grant in his Land Rover, out of control as he approached the bend, knowing he wasn't going to make it. He must have had a few moments of sheer terror. The village was shell-shocked, and both Tyler and Mamie were uncharacteristically quiet at breakfast the following morning. Tyler said he planned to walk around the village and try to talk to people. Ally was none too sure that this was a good idea but didn't say so. It was a nice day and Mamie asked if she could sit in the garden and perhaps do some sketching. 'I guess it's best to keep out of the way,' she said, and Ally could only agree.

As she tidied up the bedrooms, Ally tried to think of something else besides this awful incident. When she came downstairs to join Morag in the kitchen, she said, 'I think I need to cheer us all up and get some watercolours or something for the bedroom walls.' She'd been aware for some time that she needed some more artwork. The few pictures she'd brought from Edinburgh had been hung in the downstairs rooms, but the staircase, landing and bedrooms were still unadorned, apart from mirrors.

It was Morag who suggested Desdemona Morton. 'She's

awfy weird,' Morag informed her, 'very arty-crafty.' She lowered her voice although there was no one around. 'She had a thing with your pal, the earl, years ago. They're still quite friendly.'

'A thing?'

'Aye, a bit of hanky-panky was goin' on back then, before the earl went and married her *sister*! Desdemona was not well pleased.'

This was news to Ally.

'No, I don't suppose she was. Where does this Desdemona live?'

'Och, she's got an old place out in the wilds, on the side of Loch Trioch. She drives an ancient truck and occasionally comes down to the village.' She lowered her voice conspiratorially. 'She's *English*!'

'I wonder what brought her up here?' Ally mused.

'It was the parents that came here, lookin' to "get away from it all", and they certainly managed that! They were ever so posh and gave their two girls them funny names. I mean, Desdemona, for God's sake, who would believe *that*!'

'Don't tell me the sister was called *Ophelia*?' Ally asked, laughing.

Morag looked astounded. 'How did you *know*? Well, anyway, the parents made this big walled garden and grew all sorts of stuff. I seem to remember that he wrote books about plants and things and they taught the girls at *home*. They weren't goin' to have *them* mixin' with the hoi polloi at the village school! And,' she added, 'the mother was supposed to be an actress or somethin'.' She sniffed loudly. 'Couldn't have been much of an actress if she ended up on the side of Loch Trioch, now could she? Not a lot of drama goin' on around there, unless she helped a ewe with lambin' or somethin'!'

Ally was fascinated. 'And it was this Desdemona's sister, Ophelia, who actually *married* the earl?'

'Oh aye, that she did. Desdemona had been romancin' with him, but he had his eye on the younger sister. Ye *know* what thae men are like, suckers for a pretty face. Anyway, she died, and they hadnae even been married a year.'

'That's so awful!' Ally recalled the conversation with the earl when they went out to lunch.

'Anyway, the parents died years ago, and this Desdemona lives out there all by hersel'.'

'What are Desdemona's paintings like?' Ally asked, still trying to digest this news.

Morag shrugged. 'All right, I suppose, if you like that sort of thing. They've got some in the Craigmonie, and she sells them to galleries and that.'

Ally knew, from her brief visit to Morag and Murdo's abode, that they had a large picture of a green-faced Chinese lady in pride of place above their fireplace, and that every other inch of wall space was taken up with photographs of their family and countless grandchildren. Perhaps Morag was not the best person to offer artistic advice, but nevertheless Ally was curious. And she badly needed some sort of diversion from the village's misery.

'The place where she lives is right isolated,' Morag went on, 'back of beyond. Way up, miles past The Bothy.'

Morag's navigation skills left something to be desired and so Ally only had a vague idea where she was going when she set out from the malthouse. As there was no formal address, there was no point referring to the satnav, and all she knew was that Desdemona lived 'further up the loch from The Bothy'.

She could remember the way to The Bothy from when Hamish had taken her there, and she was pretty sure that the road hadn't gone on much further.

She was right; it didn't. It became little more than a farm

track, a rough, rutted road with a grass ridge in the middle. Driving slowly, with some consideration for her silver Golf's suspension, Ally continued for almost a couple of miles before finding, on her right and by the lochside, a large grey stone house, with an assortment of outbuildings, and a high-walled garden. This had to be it, particularly as there was an ancient truck parked outside.

Ally pulled in and parked on the grass verge before making her way to the front door of the house. The door had been red at one time, judging by the peeling paint that remained. Desdemona's painting expertise plainly did not include anything as mundane as Dulux.

There was a cacophony of barking from one of the outbuildings as four dogs of varying types and sizes came crashing towards her. Two of the smaller ones, who both looked like some sort of Jack Russell mix, were yapping round her heels, but the larger two – one resembled a Gordon setter and one an Irish wolfhound – were studying her, barking furiously, and Ally felt a frisson of fear. Just then, a woman emerged from one of the outbuildings. She had a tangled mass of shoulder-length, greying black hair, black beady eyes in a tanned, wrinkled face, and was wearing a conglomeration of sweaters and a long, Indian-style, patterned skirt, beneath which could be seen some sturdy lace-up boots.

Ally, disconcerted for a moment by her beady stare and the barking dogs, asked, 'Are you Desdemona Morton?'

'What if I am?' asked the woman, pulling the two larger dogs back by their collars. 'What do you want?'

Ally cleared her throat nervously. 'I understand you sell watercolour paintings of the local area?'

The woman continued to stare. 'What if I do?'

'Well, I wondered if I might have a look at some of them. I'm looking to buy some.'

Desdemona looked her up and down. 'You'd better come in

then,' she said ungraciously. She then shouted at the dogs, and they slunk away behind the building.

Inside was what had to be Desdemona's studio and gallery. The walls were rough stone, there was a slate floor and there were skylights at regular intervals across the roof, casting sunlight down on some of the loveliest watercolour paintings Ally had ever seen.

'These are beautiful!'

Desdemona gave a ghost of a smile. 'Yes.'

Ally made her way round the walls, against which the paintings were propped up on a wooden shelf. There were pictures of the mountains, lochs, beaches and even a village which looked very much like Locharran. And every single one featured a tiny, lone, Lowry-like figure in the foreground. 'Who's that?' she asked, pointing to one of them.

Desdemona shrugged. 'Whoever you want it to be.'

'They are absolutely beautiful,' Ally said. 'Are they all available?'

'Yes.' The woman gave no indication of being in any way interested in making a sale.

'I'd like to buy several,' Ally said, 'but it would depend on the price.'

The woman looked at Ally before narrowing her eyes and quoting a price which was beyond Ally's limited budget.

'How about if I bought a couple?' Ally asked hopefully.

'Then maybe we could come to an arrangement.' She sniffed again. 'You buy one of these in the gallery at Fort William and it'll cost you a whole lot more.'

Ally had no doubt she was right, and she really wanted the pictures of the loch and the village. 'I've come to live in Locharran,' she said. 'I'm on my own and I've bought the old malthouse, which I've had converted into a bed and breakfast. I'd really like these for the bedrooms, and I think they would definitely encourage guests to buy your paintings.'

'Hmm,' said the woman, 'the malthouse. Is Willie still wailing away?'

Ally laughed. 'Not sure about that.'

Desdemona leaned forward slightly. 'What on earth's going on in Locharran, anyway? I hear there's been a *second* murder.'

'I'm afraid there has, and the whole village is really in shock.'

'I daresay it is,' she said. Then, narrowing her eyes again: 'Has Hamish had his wicked way with you yet?'

Taken aback, Ally was dumbfounded for a moment. 'No,' she replied. 'He certainly has not.'

'So, he's tried then.' Desdemona nodded, rolling her eyes. 'He doesn't change. And I should know because he's my brother-in-law. Now do you want these two pictures or not?'

'How much?'

'Ach, I'll give you a good price now I know that you're on your own and why you're buying them.'

The price was just about affordable, and Ally nodded. Desdemona wrapped the two paintings in some bubble wrap and tape before adding, 'These murders. The killer will be whoever you suspect the least. That's always the way.' She helped Ally carry them out to the car, yelling again at the dogs.

As Ally loaded her purchases into the back of her car, she could still see the tiny figure silhouetted in the forefront of the picture of the loch, through the bubble wrap, and she wondered if it was meant to be the earl.

'I've not introduced myself,' Ally said, holding out her hand. 'I'm Ally McKinley.'

The woman took her hand cautiously. 'Desdemona Morton,' she said.

'Good to meet you, Desdemona,' Ally said.

'Would you like to see the garden? Did you know I sell seasonal stuff to some of the regular businesses? I could provide you with some of your herbs and vegetables.'

'I'd be very interested to see what you had to offer.' Ally was fascinated by this strange woman, not to mention her background, as described by Morag. She followed her through a wooden gate, built into the wall, into the large walled garden, half of which appeared to be overgrown.

'I haven't time to cultivate it all,' said Desdemona by way of explanation. 'You should have seen it when my parents were alive.'

The half that wasn't overgrown was carefully cultivated with rows of carrots, swedes, potatoes, Desdemona explained, and some leaves that Ally couldn't identify. But what was most impressive were the herbs: rosemary, coriander, bay leaf, sage, basil, parsley, oregano, mint and thyme were the only ones Ally could identify, and there were lots and lots more. She didn't really want to show her ignorance, so she said, 'I had no idea you could have such a prolific garden in this part of Scotland.'

Desdemona shrugged. 'You can grow anything in a walled garden if you look after it. The Gulf Stream is usually kind to us, and we get more rain than frost. You want angelica, alligator pepper, aniseed, borage, cumin, ginger, lovage leaves, sorrel, yarrow, *anything*, you come here!'

'I certainly will,' Ally said, impressed.

'I think she thought she might be the next Countess of Locharran,' Morag said drily the following morning when Ally described her visit.

'She did?'

'For sure. Herself and the earl were together for a fair time, maybe a year or two. But, like I told ye, before he met the sister.'

'Ophelia?'

'The very same. Now the sister was bonnier than Desdemona, and the earl hadn't met her because she'd been away somewhere-or-other, but when she got back, he was all over her like a rash!'

'Poor Desdemona!' Ally exclaimed, fascinated.

'Aye. It was a while ago now. And Desdemona never spoke to her sister again! Didn't even go to the funeral!'

'I knew that the earl was a widower, but I'd no idea about all this,' Ally said. 'How did Ophelia die?'

Morag scratched her head. 'I seem to remember she'd eaten something she shouldn't have, because she had some sort of allergy or somethin'.'

'Oh, how awful! The poor earl!' Ally exclaimed.

Morag looked less sympathetic. 'Aye, but it didn't take him too long to recover. It wasn't much more than a year before he was on the lookout for other women.'

TWENTY

The earl phoned the following morning. 'I cannot believe what's happened to poor Ian. We are all in mourning up here, although I daresay Rigby will be suspecting me again. Poor Myrtle – that's his widow – is beside herself with grief.'

'I am so sorry,' Ally said. 'He seemed such a nice man.'

'He was. He wouldn't hurt a fly. I can't begin to think who would have wanted to kill him.'

'He very kindly gave me a lift the evening before he was killed, and he told me that he had some important information for Rigby. He wouldn't say what it was, but I guess it might have cost him his life if someone knew about it.'

'The same someone who killed Carrington,' Hamish said. 'Anyway, I really phoned to give you some more cheerful news. Angus tells me your Labrador pup is almost ready to be collected, and I'd really like you to have her as a "Welcome to Locharran" present.'

'No, no!' Ally protested. 'That's very generous of you, but I absolutely insist on paying.'

'Why?' asked Hamish. 'Do you think I'm going to be

wanting favours in return? I thought we'd sorted all that out and that our relationship was to be platonic?'

'*Of course* I didn't think you'd want favours in return!' replied Ally, who'd actually been thinking exactly that.

'In which case, why can't you accept this wee dog as a gift?' Hamish sounded a little put out. 'I've already told Angus that there's to be no charge.'

'Hamish, this is so kind of you, but I really can't—'

'Yes, you can. It's a gift from a friend, just a *friend*, and it will be really hurtful if you refuse. Now, you'll need to give Angus a call to let him know when you're likely to be ready to pick the puppy up.'

With that he replaced the receiver, leaving Ally groaning inwardly. It would shortly be all around the village that the earl had now given *that woman at the malthouse a puppy! A* pedigree puppy, *no less! Would you believe it?* Everyone would, of course, believe it, and for all the wrong reasons.

However, the first thing she had to do was to get organised, and to let Angus know when she planned to pick the puppy up. She'd need to visit the vet, down by the river, to find out about inoculations and stuff, and also to buy some of the necessities, such as a collar and lead, a basket and, naturally, food.

Ally phoned the kennels.

'Aye?' said a gruff voice.

'Is that you, Angus? I wondered when I could pick up my puppy?'

There followed a grunt. 'Saturday afternoon, three o'clock,' he said firmly.

She wouldn't dare argue. 'OK, Angus, I'll be there.'

Ally had forgotten just how much palaver there was when you took on an animal. Apart from all the jabs, there were shelves groaning with pills and potions for just about any canine ailment, then the leads, and the baskets, and the toys.

'How big is your dog?' the pretty girl behind the counter in the vet's asked. 'What is it?'

'It's a Labrador,' Ally replied.

'You'll need a big basket then, and maybe a cage to start off with. And they eat a lot.' The girl thought for a moment. 'And they get very dirty because they love rolling around in all sorts of *awful things*!' She laughed heartily. 'You'll need some shampoo, and doggie towels...'

'I've got plenty of old towels,' Ally said, mentally counting the cost of all these recommendations. 'Let's just see how we get on, and I can always come back for any extras.'

As she lugged the large basket, the cage and the bag of necessities into the boot of her car, Ally wondered about a name. What on earth should she call this little dog? It was important to use a name from day one, because the puppy needed to respond to it. Why hadn't she thought about all this earlier? Probably because she had so much else on her mind. She closed the boot and wandered back into the reception area.

'What's your name?' she asked the girl at the desk.

The girl looked startled for a moment. 'Are you going to report me for something?'

'Oh *no*, not at all! You've been very helpful. I'm trying to decide on a name for the puppy and I thought I might use yours, if it's suitable and you don't mind?'

The girl laughed. 'I'm Flora,' she said, 'and I get teased a lot because my surname is MacDonald!'

Ally laughed. 'I suppose you do! But Flora is such a pretty name, and I think that is exactly what I'm going to call my little puppy.'

'I'm really flattered – thank you!'

Flora was a good choice, Ally thought, as she left the vet's. It had been the name of her grandmother, who she'd often visited in her little home near Fort Augustus as a child. She could still smell the peat fires Granny Flora burned in every room. Yes, Flora was a really good choice.

When she got home, she found Rigby on her doorstep again.

He watched in fascination as she unloaded her purchases. 'Are you getting a dog?'

Ally nodded. 'Next week. To what do I owe the honour of this visit, Inspector? Have you discovered who Jessie McPhee's husband was?'

He looked at her in amazement. 'Jessie McPhee?' Then he seemed to remember. 'No, no,' he replied, 'nothing further there.'

I don't suppose there is, she thought, *because you won't have done a damn thing about it.*

'You'll be aware,' he continued, 'that Ian Grant's death was not accidental?'

She nodded. 'I believe the brakes were tampered with?'

Rigby sighed. 'They were. Now I believe, from what Finlay McKinnon says, that Grant gave you a lift the night before he was killed?'

Ally wondered what this was leading to. Did he think that she had some part in the poor man's demise? 'Yes, he did,' she replied, 'because it was raining heavily.'

'And did he give you any indication that perhaps he was nervous, or was being watched, or did he appear to be in any way worried?'

Ally shook her head. 'What he did say was that he had something he wanted to tell you the next time he saw you.'

'Do you have any idea what that might have been?'

'None at all,' Ally replied. 'He flatly refused to tell me.'

Rigby had a faraway look in his eyes. 'I wonder who else he might have told?'

'I don't know, but it looks as if he might have told someone. Do you want a cup of tea?'

He looked at his watch. 'Thanks – I've just got time for a quick one.'

As Ally was filling the kettle he asked, 'What's this Mamie Van Nuyen like?'

'She's OK,' Ally replied. 'I rather like her.'

'You don't think it's a bit strange that she seems so keen on investigating Carrington's death?'

Ally shrugged. 'She was going to be married to Wilbur later this year.'

'So I believe. She's come into the station a few times to find out how we're progressing.'

'She has?' Ally had no idea about Mamie's visits to the station. 'She's obviously very concerned.'

'Hmm. And what about the brother, Tyler Carrington? What do you reckon on him?'

'Honestly,' Ally said, pouring tea into a mug, 'I really don't have any thoughts about either of my guests. They're plainly here because of Wilbur's murder and want to see the thing solved.' *And don't we all*, she thought privately. She handed him the mug.

'You trust him?' Rigby asked.

'Who? Tyler?'

'Yes.'

'Yes, I think so.' Ally wondered where all this questioning was leading. 'Why wouldn't I?'

'And you've noticed nothing unusual round here?'

'Not since I discovered a corpse outside my back door,' Ally replied drily.

'And do Tyler Carrington and Mamie Van Nuyen get on OK with each other?' Rigby asked, taking a big gulp of tea.

Ally thought for a moment. 'I think so. Maybe they're a little suspicious of each other.'

'Why do you say that? Surely they knew each other in the States?'

'Apparently not. Mamie and Wilbur had a long-distance relationship, because he lived on the east coast and she lived on the west coast, and, she told me, when she visited him in Massachusetts, Tyler was never around. So they'd never met before.'

'Seems a bit strange to me,' said Rigby, draining his cup. 'Something odd's going on around here, and I need to get to the bottom of it.'

Indeed you do, thought Ally, wondering if he was any closer to solving the mystery than she was.

'Well, I'll be off,' he said, carrying his mug across to the sink. 'I may come back to have a word with both your guests again, though.' He sighed as he made his way towards the door. 'There are times,' he added, 'when I wish I'd stayed in Birmingham.'

After she'd closed the door, Ally peeked into the sitting room. Mamie had added a few pieces to her jigsaw puzzle. Ally studied it for a moment, then added one other.

After Rigby had gone, Ally decided she should get Mamie and Tyler together again, to see if Tyler's door-to-door questioning had come up with anything at all. Her conversation with Rigby had not convinced her that the police were close to making an arrest, and, for the first time, Ally felt a little afraid. Without doubt someone in the village was the killer and was still roaming around freely.

She decided she'd do a supper for her guests, something easy, like lasagne. And she needed to do it before she collected the puppy because, although no doubt it would be an adorable distraction, house-training and supper parties were unlikely to mix well.

Both had been receptive to the idea when she asked them at breakfast the next morning, Tyler at 8 a.m. and Mamie at 9.30

a.m. Ally had no intention of mentioning anything about the green folder because she was beginning to doubt her own fascination with the subject, particularly in view of Rigby's apparent disinterest. The minister hadn't come back to her either, so was the wife still poking around in the archives, or had they forgotten about the whole thing? If she wanted any further research on the subject, then she'd have to do it herself.

Supper was a success. The lasagne was followed by a lime-and-ginger cheesecake, which had Mamie gobbling up a second helping. They'd drank lots of wine and appeared very relaxed, so Ally thought it was a good time to get back to the subject of the crimes.

'How did your door-to-door questioning go?' she asked Tyler.

He gave a deep sigh. 'Can't say it was any too successful,' he admitted.

'I don't think they trusted you,' Mamie put in.

'That's ridiculous!' Tyler barked. '*Of course* they trusted me! I've reassured them that I'm not in any way interested in continuing along the same lines as my brother. I hate goddamn theme parks anyway, and I don't want any part of his claim.'

Mamie licked her spoon and reluctantly set it down on the plate. 'I don't think that knocking on doors and telling these guys all over again that you aren't about to claim one inch of Locharran and, in the same breath, asking if you can have a word with their wives, was a particularly brilliant idea.' She turned to Ally. 'I decided to accompany him.'

'Did *you* get a chance to talk to any of the women?' Ally asked Mamie.

'No, I didn't,' snapped Mamie, 'because he antagonised the guys so much that they just went right back inside and slammed the doors behind them.'

'I'm sure you both meant very well,' Ally interjected hurriedly in an effort to defuse the situation, 'but the villagers are suspicious of outsiders at the best of times and probably don't even trust each other at the moment.'

'That poor chauffeur!' said Mamie. 'What on earth did *he* have to do with anything?'

'Well,' said Tyler with a scowl, 'didn't you tell me something about him having information for the police or something?'

Mamie scowled back. 'Yes, that was after Ally told me he'd given her a lift home. What a night of rain that was!'

'Rigby's been asking me if I had any idea what the information might be,' Ally said, 'but I've no idea. Nevertheless someone, somewhere, must have got wind of it.'

'Well,' said Tyler, stifling a yawn, 'I'm not certain my brother had all the proof he needed anyway.'

'Why do you say that?' Mamie asked.

'Because, if he had, what was to stop him just laying claim to everything straight away, via a lawyer? Why was he chasing around the village telling everyone what he planned and perhaps hoping to find out something while he was at it?'

There was some truth in that, Ally thought, thinking of the green folder again. 'So you think that Wilbur wasn't entirely sure of his claim?' she asked as she produced the cheeseboard.

'First and foremost,' Tyler said, helping himself to some Stilton, 'Wilbur was a dreamer.'

'Rubbish!' exclaimed Mamie. 'He was a very practical man.' She took a chunk of Brie.

Tyler rolled his eyes. 'So did *you* know what he was planning then?' he asked Mamie.

'He was a very private man,' Mamie replied primly, buttering a cracker.

'So he didn't tell you, *his fiancée*?' Tyler arched an eyebrow. 'I find that hard to believe. Didn't you fancy the idea of being a *countess*, Mamie?'

Ally was realising that her attempt to reconcile these two was not working very well and she needed to change the subject. 'What do you think about Rigby?' she asked.

'Not a lot,' said Tyler. 'What's the guy doing, for God's sake?'

'He's a nice man, though,' Mamie said, attacking the cheddar, 'but I guess he doesn't appear to be very efficient. I've gone into the police station a few times with suggestions, but he seems to have his own method of doing things.'

Tyler glared at her. 'What sort of suggestions?'

'Oh, just thoughts I've come up with,' Mamie replied vaguely. 'I guess he needs a push.'

'Well, he ain't going to want *you* pushing him,' Tyler said, shaking his head in despair.

'Let's at least all agree that we don't think Rigby's got very far in this investigation,' Ally said, desperate for agreement on something.

'He wouldn't last five minutes in Boston,' said Tyler.

'He wouldn't last *two* minutes in Burbank,' Mamie said triumphantly.

'Then perhaps you should send some of your super-sleuths over here,' Ally suggested. 'Anyone for coffee?'

The evening had ended amicably enough, but Ally was relieved when they both returned to their rooms, and she had the quiet kitchen to herself as she loaded the dishwasher. Her attempt at improving relations between Mamie and Tyler hadn't really worked out. What *was* it with these two? Why were they so suspicious of each other? Surely they had one common aim, and that was to find out who killed Wilbur? Why did they keep sniping at each other as if it was some sort of competition? Perhaps that was it; Tyler, as the brother, felt that he should be the one to find the killer, instead of Mamie, the mere fiancée. Ally liked them both, particularly Mamie.

Ally finished clearing the kitchen and headed up to bed. Not for the first time she wondered if she were wise to be getting mixed up in all this. But with the police appearing to be at an impasse, she felt compelled to continue with her detection work.

TWENTY-ONE

Solving crime took a back seat when Ally went to collect her puppy.

Angus had a list of instructions. 'Ye'll need a cage for the wee thing,' he said, 'so you know where she is, until she gets the lie of the land.'

Ally was grateful Flora had told her this and she was already prepared.

'And she'll need four wee meals a day for four months,' Angus continued, looking doubtfully at Ally. 'Ye'll need to take her to the vet, and she canna mix with other dogs until she's fully vaccinated. He's been up to give her her first shot, but she'll need a booster.'

'Yes, I'm beginning to remember everything now,' Ally said, 'although it's years since I've had a puppy.'

Flora was a delightful little dog; affectionate, playful and curious, although she didn't like being hauled outside at regular intervals to do what she was quite happy to do on the kitchen floor. She had pawed away the newspapers Ally had laid everywhere, because she much preferred to do her business on the slate floor beneath. She also howled for most of the first night, in spite of Ally bringing the cage into her bedroom and placing a warm hot-water bottle inside, in a futile attempt to emulate the mother. Flora missed her mother and her siblings, and she wanted Ally to be aware of this.

After several sleepless hours, Ally was very aware of it.

She began to wonder if she'd made some terrible mistake. Shouldn't she have got a puppy in the wintertime when there was plenty of time to house-train it before any guests arrived? Fortunately, both Mamie and Tyler were as charmed with the little animal as she was, and didn't seem to mind when she escaped from the kitchen a couple of times to climb over their feet beneath the dining-room table.

'Isn't she just the cutest thing!' Mamie exclaimed, completely besotted.

Ally knew that the next big event would be to take Flora to the vet. Will Patterson was a typical country vet and a well-respected character in the village, unfazed by the size or shape of his patients, which ranged from hamsters and gerbils to sheep and cattle. He was also the father of five daughters, which caused much mirth in the village and caused many chauvinistic remarks such as, 'Keep tryin', Will – ye'll hit the jackpot next time!'

In the meantime, Flora was rapidly getting the hang of being taken outside at regular intervals and being rewarded with a treat if she did what she was supposed to do. She'd also stopped howling at night and seemed to be adapting to her new surroundings well. It was now time to visit Will Patterson.

Flora MacDonald was behind the desk again as Ally arrived with Flora in her cage.

'Oh, isn't she just gorgeous!' the girl cooed, peering into the cage where her namesake was struggling to get out, tail wagging furiously. After a five-minute wait, Ally and Flora were told, 'Mr Patterson will see you now!'

Prepared to meet the Will Patterson of five-daughters fame, Ally was taken aback to be greeted by a tall, attractive man about her own age, with grey hair and very nice blue eyes.

'Oh, hello!' he said, washing his hands. 'And who do we have here?'

'This is Flora,' Ally replied, placing the cage on the table.

'Well, good to meet you, Flora!' The man opened the cage and picked up the squirming puppy with expertise. 'I believe you're from one of Angus's bitches?'

'Yes, she is,' Ally confirmed, wondering who this man was and how he knew of Flora's origin, 'and I've only had her a couple of days.'

'So I hear.' The man smiled, causing his eyes to wrinkle and twinkle in a most attractive way. 'I'm sure you've been here long enough to know that word gets round very quickly.' He'd already rolled Flora over and was examining her thoroughly. 'I'm Ross Patterson by the way, father of Will, who's up to his eyes in lambing and calving at the moment.'

Ally returned his smile. 'Well, I'm Ally McKinley, and I've recently bought the malthouse.'

'Yes, I know who you are.' He gave her a further disarming smile. 'I'm not supposed to be working any more, but Will's been so busy that they've had to dust me off and drag me out of retirement. I don't mind really, particularly when I get to meet lovely little ladies like this!' As he spoke, he was examining Flora's nether regions, which she seemed to be enjoying, as she licked him with enthusiasm.

There was something very attractive about his eyes, Ally thought. They were kind, and friendly, and very blue. Nicer, actually, than Callum's, although not quite so Paul Newman-ish. He knew who she was and he knew that Flora was from the earl's kennels. She suddenly thought that he might well think that Flora was the result of services rendered and, for some reason, she didn't want him to think that.

Ally cleared her throat. 'Doubtless yourself, and everyone round here, thinks that this is a gift for services rendered, but it isn't, I assure you. And I don't know what I have to do to convince everyone otherwise.' To her shame, Ally felt her eyes prickle with tears.

He looked up from examining Flora. 'I believe you, Mrs McKinley, but don't you go worrying about what people think. They thrive on supposition and gossip round here.'

Ally felt a rush of gratitude. 'Thank you for being so understanding, Mr Patterson.'

He smiled again. 'Ross – call me Ross. Everyone does.'

'OK, Ross, I'm Ally.'

'Well, don't let them get to you, Ally. I came up here from Glasgow nearly forty years ago and was regarded with great suspicion. But don't worry because they'll find someone new to gossip about soon.' He'd given Flora her booster and was now persuading the puppy back into her cage. 'You've got a fine wee dog there, Ally.'

'I think so too,' said Ally, picking up the cage and hoping that Ross Patterson would be on duty again next time she needed to call.

'How did you get on at the vet's?' Morag asked next morning as she stacked the dishwasher with breakfast plates.

'Oh, fine,' Ally replied. 'Flora was very well behaved and didn't seem to mind being examined and inoculated.' She paused. 'Incidentally, I didn't see Will Patterson, but I did see his father, who, I believe, has been dragged out of retirement because Will is so busy.'

Morag nodded. 'Aye, a nice man. I remember when he first

came up here from Glasgow. He had a nice wife too. Will and his brother were just wee bairns at the time.'

'I rather liked him,' Ally said, thinking of the kind blue eyes.

Morag gave her a sideways look. 'He's had his share of grief, though. There were two boys: Will, who also became a vet and runs the practice, and then there was Alan.' She shook her head.

'What happened to Alan?' Ally asked, filling the kettle.

'Och, awful tragedy that was. He got in with all the wrong crowd, got into drugs and died of an overdose.'

'Oh, that's *dreadful*! I can't believe that sort of thing goes on around here!' Ally exclaimed.

'Aye, well, it does,' Morag said. 'It happens everywhere.'

'How heartbreaking!'

'Aye,' Morag sighed, 'and then, shortly after that, his wife had a heart attack.' She shook her head in despair.

'Hopefully she survived?' Ally asked.

'No, she did not,' Morag replied. 'He's been a widower for many a year. Funny, isn't it, how some folk seem to get all the bad luck? By the way, did you know they've taken Callum Dalrymple in for questioning?'

'*What?*' Ally, shocked, froze between the sink and the door.

'Callum Dalrymple's been *arrested*,' Morag repeated.

'Why on earth would they suspect *him*?' Ally asked, astounded.

Morag shrugged. 'Well, he did have a blazing row with Carrington in the bar the night before he was murdered. I hear that Callum's DNA was all over the body.'

'Well, it would be, wouldn't it, if they'd had a row and it got a bit physical?' Ally said.

Morag shooed Flora away from where she was trying to climb into the dishwasher. 'I'll tell you what I think, for what it's worth.' She narrowed her eyes and pursed her mouth. 'I reckon that that Rigby thinks he's got to be seen to be doin' somethin' because, God only knows, he's not done much so far.' She sniffed loudly. 'All he's been doin' is ask the same folk the same old questions, day after day after day.'

Ally could hardly disagree with that. 'But surely they must have *something* on him if they've taken him in?'

'They're not goin' to be tellin' us, are they?' Morag retorted, slamming the dishwasher door shut now that Flora had moved away to investigate Ally's shoes by the back door.

'Probably not,' Ally agreed, thinking of Callum with his Paul Newman eyes, languishing in a cell. Should she move him further up the board, towards twelve o'clock? Maybe Morag was right. Two killings had taken place, the weeks were flying by, and what had Rigby got to show for it so far? Furthermore, Morag had confirmed that Angus had indeed been in Strathpeffer on the night of Wilbur's murder so she had at least been able to eliminate him.

'It stands to reason that whoever killed Carrington must also have killed poor Ian Grant,' Morag said. 'And Ian was very friendly with Callum, so that doesn't make sense, does it?'

'No, it doesn't.' Ally sighed.

She checked her to-do list for the morning. She needed some butter from the shop, so she'd have to walk down the hill now while Morag was here to keep an eye on Flora.

Queenie was in a high state of excitement when Ally arrived at the shop. Before Ally could open her mouth, Queenie burst out with, 'They've arrested somebody at last!'

'So I believe,' muttered Ally.

'And not before time!' Queenie continued. 'I havenae been feeling safe in my bed since all them murders took place. And neither has Bessie. Have ye, Bessie?'

'Have I what?' asked Bessie, emerging from the storeroom behind with an armful of toilet rolls.

'Ye've not had a wink of sleep, have ye, since all them murders?'

Bessie looked slightly bewildered but shook her head obediently.

'Thank God that *polisman's* finally found someone to arrest,' Queenie said, turning her attention back to Ally. 'He might as well have stayed down there in Bradford for all the good he is.'

'Birmingham,' corrected Ally.

'What's Birmingham got to do with it?'

'Birmingham is where Rigby comes from, Queenie.'

'Ach well, it's all the same down there in *England*,' Queenie retorted with some disdain. 'When are they ever goin' to find out who killed poor Ian?' Then, as if suddenly remembering: 'I hear ye've been given a wee dog?'

'Yes, and I've named her Flora,' Ally replied. 'Now, could I have some butter, please?'

Queenie didn't move. 'Angus was telling us about the earl's *very* generous gift,' she said.

Here we go again, thought Ally. 'It was a very generous gesture on his part,' she replied, 'although I would have much preferred to pay.'

'Aye,' said Queenie, nodding, 'and Angus was saying that ye would likely have had to pay nearly a thousand pounds for a wee pedigree pup like that. A *thousand pounds!*'

Ally had had enough. She took a deep breath. 'Queenie, can I tell you something? I'm very fond of the earl, and he's become a good friend. His love life is *his* business and has nothing whatsoever to do with me. This puppy is a "Welcome to Locharran" gift and that's it. I need you to know that I am not having it off with the earl, with Tyler Carrington or with anybody else. *Have I made myself clear?* And now, can I have my butter, please?'

Queenie appeared speechless, and Bessie, who'd been

standing behind with her mouth hanging open, turned on her heel. 'I'll get that for you straight away, Mrs McKinley,' she said.

TWENTY-TWO

When Ally got home, her phone was ringing.

'Hi,' said Linda, 'I'm closing the bistro tonight because there are no bookings and, anyway, I'm knackered! I did wonder if you wanted to come down for some supper and a drink?'

'But why would you want to do any cooking at all?' Ally asked. 'How about you coming up here for a change, and why don't we have a takeaway?'

'Great idea,' said Linda, 'so let's just have some fish and chips. I'll have a word with Luigi Concetti and he'll do us some nice ones. I'll bring them up with me.'

'You're a star!' said Ally.

She decided to take Flora, who was trying to climb up her leg, for a short walk round the garden on her lead and, as they set off, she met Tyler coming in the gate.

'Have you *heard*?' he asked, sounding excited.

'Heard what?' asked Ally.

'They've found the murderer of my brother!' Tyler's voice rose dramatically. 'They've got Callum what's-his-name from the Craigmonie Hotel in custody!'

'Yes, I had heard,' Ally replied, 'but I find it hard to believe that he's a killer.'

Tyler looked at her in astonishment. 'What do you mean? That guy's DNA was all over Wilbur's clothing! What more proof do you need?'

Ally shrugged. 'I still don't think it's him. I'll be very surprised if it is.'

'Hey, you probably like the guy and so you can't believe it, but do you know something? The majority of killers are very likeable! Nobody can ever believe that they could kill. They say stuff like "he was always such a gentleman", "he was always so polite" – blah, blah, blah! On and on they go! These guys are great actors, you know – should be up for Oscars!'

'I'm sure you're right,' Ally said, bending down to untwist Flora's lead from round her legs, 'but I still don't think Callum did it.'

'He had a very strong motive,' Tyler said. 'Apparently Wilbur had told him that, when he claimed his inheritance as the Earl of Locharran, Dalrymple would be the first to go.'

Ally wasn't so sure. 'That was when Callum was trying to persuade Wilbur to leave the bar, but Wilbur refused and then got nasty.'

'Come on, Ally! They had some sort of fight, and Dalrymple's DNA was all over Wilbur's clothes. There's little doubt it was him! The trouble with you is that you think the best of everyone, but you know what? Life just ain't like that!'

With that, he wandered away, leaving Ally puzzling a little about how convinced he was that Callum Dalrymple was the killer. And she wasn't at all sure that she *did* think the best of everyone, but she did get gut feelings about things, and these feelings hadn't let her down so far. Of course, there was always a first time.

. . .

'My God,' said Linda, 'have you heard the latest?'

She'd arrived with the fish and chips, and the delicious aroma was making Ally's mouth water.

'Do you mean about Callum?'

'What else? He's been taken in for questioning apparently?'

'Yes,' said Ally with a sigh, 'and Tyler seems convinced he's guilty.'

'I don't,' Linda said firmly, 'but I suppose they have to start somewhere.'

Linda was completely won over by Flora. 'Oh, she's just adorable!' she exclaimed as the little dog licked her hands enthusiastically. 'Have you taken her to the vet yet?'

'As a matter of fact, I took her yesterday.' She wondered if she should mention the retired vet with the lovely blue eyes, then decided she would. 'And, believe it or not, instead of seeing Will, I saw his father.' She placed the fish and chips onto plates and put them in the oven to reheat.

'Oh, you mean Ross?' asked Linda casually.

'Yes, he introduced himself. I thought he was rather nice.'

'You wouldn't be the only one,' said Linda. 'He's a widower, you know.'

'Yes, so Morag told me. And she told me about the other son, who got into drugs.'

'That was before my time here, but very sad,' Linda agreed. 'But let me tell you, there's a lot of old girls in this village who'd be more than happy to welcome Ross Patterson under their duvets!'

Ally grinned. 'Including you?'

Linda looked coy. 'Well, I did have a drink with him once,' she admitted.

'Oh, really?' Ally wondered where these sudden waves of envy had come from.

'It wasn't exactly a date,' Linda admitted, 'but I ran into him at the Craigmonie and he invited me to join him for a drink. So I did.'

'And...?'

'And nothing!' Linda sighed. 'He didn't suggest a further meeting. Shame.'

'Would you have liked to see him again?'

'Well, he is very handsome.'

'Interesting!' Ally busied herself checking the booze cupboard. 'How about a nice Merlot with your fish and chips? Or I've got lots of Pinot Grigio in the fridge.'

'Pinot's fine,' Linda said.

'So, where does he live?' Ally asked, trying to sound disinterested as she struggled to open the bottle.

'He's converted an old barn out on the lochside, near the sea. I believe it's beautiful, and he's also converted a load of outbuildings into holiday lets. I've heard that they're full for most of the year, so that must give him a nice little income. Though vets aren't exactly on the breadline to begin with, are they?'

'I don't know many vets,' Ally replied, fascinated, pouring them both some wine.

'So he'd be a good catch,' said Linda, grinning at Ally over the top of her glass.

'Why are you looking at me like that? I'm not after catching anyone!' Ally retorted.

'Just saying!' Linda lifted up her glass. 'Let's drink to good catches!'

In spite of herself, Ally laughed. 'You're incorrigible!'

'And, Ally, do bear in mind that widowers are *very* thin on the ground. A rare species indeed! And there's an awful lot of widows around, us included, so he'd be spoiled for choice if he ever wanted to find a lady friend.'

Ally sipped her wine. 'Well, I'm not looking for a man friend, so let's change the subject! Shall we eat?'

. . .

The following morning, after she'd served breakfast to both of her guests and tidied up, Ally decided it was time to visit another church. She'd never know if any record of Jessie McPhee existed beneath the subsiding church at Clachar, but at least she'd established that there were no McPhees in the graveyard.

The next church on her list was Brodale which was, according to her map, about eight miles inland and on the moors. She looked at Flora, who was chasing one of her toys round the kitchen floor and would not be happy at being left on her own, even if Morag was here for some of the time. Flora, and the cage, would have to be transported to Brodale, too, where Ally could give her a good walk around before the drive home. The puppy had become quite used to her cage but was less happy at being driven anywhere, and howled on the short distances she'd had to endure so far. Ally knew that the dog had to get used to being transported around, and this would be a good opportunity.

Ally set off for Brodale with Flora howling in the cage in the back. After about five miles, the noise stopped and, at the destination, she found her puppy was fast asleep.

Immediately, Ally could see that this trip was probably wasted as well, because the church, which was on its own on the moors in the middle of nowhere, was nothing more than a ruin. A complete ruin, without a roof, and with only two of its original four walls still standing. She sighed. There was no chance of finding anything here, but Flora needed a walk so she'd have a wander round the ruin and the adjoining cemetery.

There was no sunshine today, only a stiff breeze which rippled across the surrounding bracken. Ally attached the lead to the collar of a sleepy Flora and set off to have a look around. In the absence of any windows, a roof and some walls, the floor of the church had become a bed of weeds, nettles and dandelions. It was difficult to imagine that people must, at one time, have worshipped here – and where had they come from? She'd passed a few remote crofts on the way, but the inhabitants would have had to walk several miles to get here. Still, Highlanders were a hardy breed and would probably have thought little of it.

Flora was now fully awake, on a long retractable lead, and sniffing at every stone. It was unlikely she'd find any interesting canine smells round this place, but perhaps she could detect foxes, deer or even wildcats. Wildcats still survived in the Highlands although they were rarely seen.

After they'd walked round what remained of the walls, Ally headed towards the overgrown churchyard. She'd thought Clachar graveyard had been sadly neglected, but it was nothing compared to this. Even after she'd pulled away enough grasses to decipher the writing on the stones, they were so damaged by years of wind and rain as to be illegible. She could make out some McLeods with difficulty, but little else. It was as well that she had Flora on a lead in this jungle because otherwise she'd never be found.

It was when Flora began barking that Ally turned round to see a tall woman with long grey hair leaning on the graveyard wall and staring at them. Ally picked up Flora and carried her towards the woman. 'Do you live round here?' she asked, slightly disconcerted by the woman's pale green eyes.

The woman kept staring but said nothing. She was wearing a strange combination of jackets and coats over a long skirt, underneath which appeared to be trousers.

Feeling uncomfortable, Ally said, 'I was hoping to find out if any McPhees lived in this area?'

The woman continued to stare. 'McPhees,' she said.

'Yes, McPhees. Just wondered if you knew—'

'McPhees,' the woman interrupted. 'Are you American?'

Startled, Ally replied, 'No, I'm not. Why do you ask?'

The woman gazed up at the sky for a minute. 'The American wanted to know about the McPhees.'

'Really?' Ally felt excited. 'When was that?'

The woman shrugged. 'Before yesterday.'

Ally knew she had to tread carefully. 'Can you remember how long before yesterday? A week? Two weeks?'

'Before yesterday.'

'Try to remember. This could be quite important.'

'American. He was American. Never met an American before.'

'Do you think it might have been weeks ago?' Ally persisted.

The woman looked at her as if she was deranged. 'I *told* you! Before yesterday!' With that, she turned on her heel and set off, in a strange loping way, across the moor.

Ally set the dog down again. 'Oh, Flora! What am I to make of that? Was it Wilbur, or was it Tyler? And were they looking for the same information as I am?' She watched as the strange woman disappeared into the distance, going to goodness knows where. Ally walked Flora round the churchyard again and then said, 'I don't think there's much point in staying up here, Flora, so let's call it a day.'

As she drove away, Ally couldn't believe it could have been Tyler. Why would Tyler be roaming around looking for clues to his ancestry if he wasn't the slightest bit interested in the earldom? No. It must have been Wilbur.

TWENTY-THREE

It was shortly after she got home that Flora was violently sick. At first Ally thought it might just be some belated car sickness, as it was the longest drive the puppy had experienced so far. But as the evening progressed and Flora continued to be ill, Ally began to panic. She'd only had the dog for five minutes, and already the poor little thing must have eaten something that upset her! There was nothing for it but to phone the vet.

'We're just about to close, Mrs McKinley,' said Flora, the receptionist. 'But if you could bring her down straight away, perhaps Mr Patterson could have a look at her before he goes home.'

Ally was so concerned about the puppy that she didn't even consider, or care, about which Mr Patterson it might be. She popped the sad-looking Flora back into her cage and into the car, and sped down the hill to the vet's. Five minutes later, she was ushered into the surgery and came face to face with Ross Patterson again.

'She's been really sick,' Ally said, placing the cage on the table, from which a sad-eyed Flora looked up mournfully.

'Oh dear,' said Ross Patterson, opening the door and lifting out the puppy, who gave a feeble wag of her tail. 'And what have *you* been eating, Flora?'

Ally shook her head. 'Honestly, I've just been giving her the recommended puppy food, and I've no idea how it could suddenly disagree with her.'

He studied Flora for a moment. 'Has she been anywhere she could have eaten something unsavoury? Has she been outside?'

'Well, yes,' Ally replied, charmed again by the vet's kindly blue eyes. 'We went to Brodale Church today, but she was on a lead the whole time I was looking round the church and the gravestones.' She wondered briefly if she was coming across as a bit odd. 'I was looking for some names,' she added hurriedly.

'Ancestors perhaps?' He popped Flora back into her cage.

'Well, yes, but not mine,' Ally said, feeling a little embarrassed.

'I shouldn't think you'd be able to decipher many names up on those old stones,' he said. 'The whole place has been deserted for years.'

'You're right – I couldn't,' Ally admitted.

'So, perhaps Flora might have picked up something in the long grass up there?' He seemed to be studying her, and Ally felt her face flushing.

'I was watching her most of the time,' she said defensively.

'But not when you were trying to read the headstones?'

'Probably not,' Ally admitted, 'but there was only grass and bracken round there.'

'In which,' he said, smiling, 'there could well have been a tiny dead bird, fox dirt or all manner of nasties. Labradors will eat almost anything.'

Ally wanted to hang her head in shame.

'When was she sick last?' he asked.

'About an hour ago,' Ally said, glancing at her watch.

'Whatever it was she ate, she's probably got rid of it now,' he said, 'and I see no need to distress her further with any medicine. If she's ill again, ring up straight away.'

Feeling increasingly guilty, Ally asked, 'I thought you were about to close?'

'Yes, but I shall be on the end of the phone for any emergencies.'

'I'm really sorry to have bothered you,' Ally said.

'It's no bother at all. I'm pretty sure she'll be OK now, but don't give her anything else to eat this evening. Just make sure she has plenty of water and I'm sure she'll be fine by the morning.' He paused. 'Not many people visit Brodale these days.'

Ally wondered if he'd be able to shed any light on her odd encounter. 'I did meet a strange woman up there while I was looking at the stones.'

'Oh, that'll likely be Delia. She lives not far from the church. She's a little confused but harmless.' The vet fondled Flora's head before shutting the cage. 'So, did you find what you were looking for?'

Ally shook her head. 'No, I didn't. I was trying to find some McPhees.'

'Who *aren't* your relatives,' he stated.

He must think I'm nutty as a fruitcake, Ally thought. 'I know it sounds crazy, but I think that there may be some connection between a Jessie McPhee and the man whose body was found outside my back door. Not only that, I've got his brother and fiancée staying with me now.'

Ross Patterson stared at her in amazement. 'I'd heard that the American's body was found at the back of the malthouse, and I'd heard rumour that there was a brother around. But a fiancée as well? All in the malthouse?'

'Yes, a fiancée as well.' Ally suddenly wanted to get the whole thing off her chest. 'They both want it solved, and so do I.'

'And you're up there alone with them, in that big place?'

'Yes, but they're both very nice.'

He frowned. 'What about the police? *Rigby*, isn't it?'

Ally nodded. 'Yes, but he doesn't appear to be making much progress yet. That's why I thought I might take matters into my own hands.'

'So, where do these McPhees come into all this?' he asked.

She took a deep breath, now desperately wanting to share her suspicions with someone. 'It's quite a long story.'

'I'm sure it must be, and I'd rather like to hear it,' he said.

'You'd need to come up to the malthouse,' she said, smiling.

'Is that an invitation?'

Ally took a deep breath. 'Yes.'

Driving back with a now sleeping puppy, Ally felt nervous. Why on earth had she invited a man she hardly knew to the malthouse? Would he think her promiscuous, or just a bit crazy?

Then again, he didn't *need* to come, did he? And what did it matter what he might think because she was unlikely to see him again anyway. And what should she offer him? A cup of tea? Something to eat?

As she parked at the side of the malthouse, she turned to see a large black Mercedes pull up behind her, and out got Ross Patterson. Well, there was no going back now!

'Let me carry that,' he said as Ally lifted Flora and the cage out from the back of her car. He followed her inside, into the kitchen, and laid the cage down beside the Aga. 'Wow!' he exclaimed, looking around. 'You've certainly made a change to this old place!'

Ally felt ridiculously pleased. 'I had a great architect.'

'But you also have good taste,' he said, giving her that dazzling, disarming smile of his.

For the first time in years, Ally felt herself blushing. 'Do sit down,' she said, 'and what can I get you? I do feel guilty at having waylaid you from going home after a busy day.'

'I don't mind one bit being waylaid,' he said, sitting down beside the log burner, 'and a cup of tea would be just the thing. Milk but no sugar please.'

Ally filled the kettle and got out a couple of mugs. She really fancied a glass of wine after the day she'd had, but she shouldn't offer him that when he was driving. She'd make do with tea until he was gone. Flora was still sleeping peacefully in her cage.

'You know, don't you, that this Carrington who was murdered was telling everyone in the village that he was the rightful owner to the earldom and the estate?' she said.

He nodded. 'That's all everyone's been talking about. That and Ian Grant's death, of course.'

She handed him his tea, sat down opposite with hers, and took a sip.

'So,' he said, 'what's with the McPhees?'

Ally took another sip. 'Well, after Rigby had examined Carrington's room and locked it up, I found the room's spare key because I suddenly remembered that there was a secret drawer in the antique desk. I'd pointed it out to Carrington when he first arrived, although I didn't think for one moment that he'd actually use it. And that's where I found a folder.'

'Interesting. And did you have a peek inside?'

Ally nodded. 'I photographed everything before I handed the folder to Rigby.'

'And that's where you found the McPhees?'

'Just one McPhee – Jessie.'

'Ah,' he said, drinking some tea.

'Would you like a biscuit, or a scone, or—'

He waved his hand. 'No, thank you. Tell me about this Jessie.'

Ally hesitated for a moment, then said, 'Would you like to see the photographs I took?'

'Yes, I would.'

'I've locked them away in my little office,' she said, laying down her mug and standing up. She returned a minute later with the envelope containing everything, which she spread across the kitchen table.

Ross picked up his mug of tea and moved across to the table, where he sat down and began to study Ally's photographs of the folder's contents. He picked up and studied a couple of them. 'So,' he said, 'did this Carrington have any proof of his claim?'

'I don't think he could have had all the proof he needed because otherwise, surely, he'd just hire a lawyer to go straight ahead and sort it all out. I think he must still have been looking for something.' Ally placed the photo of the entry of marriage in front of him. 'It seems that this Jessie McPhee may have married someone with an S at the beginning of their surname. Now, if this happened to be a Sinclair, then we might have something to go on. Unravel some history.'

He sighed deeply. 'So, do you think she might be buried at Brodale?'

Ally shook her head. 'I think it's more likely she's buried somewhere in America. I'm trying to find old church records of marriages in this area, so trying to discover what was her family church, but without success. After all, it's always traditional for marriages to take place in the bride's family church.' She proceeded to tell him of her visit to the minister and then to the churches at Clachar and Brodale. 'I didn't expect to find Jessie's grave, but I thought I might be able to narrow down my search if there were McPhees in the area.' She handed him Ken's magnifying glass.

'Definitely an S,' he confirmed, taking a sip of his tea. 'Look, I'll have a word with Donald Scott, the minister, because I know him quite well, and I'll ask him to get a move on with checking the records.' He sighed. 'I believe he was recently diagnosed with the beginnings of dementia, so he's become increasingly forgetful and probably forgotten all about it.'

'I'd be really grateful if you would,' Ally said. Then, hesitatingly: 'I'd offer you a glass of wine if you weren't driving...'

He gave her another of those crinkly, almost mischievous smiles, which set her off blushing again.

'I reckon I can get away with half a glass,' he said, 'as I've only a mile or so to go.'

'Oh, good,' she said. 'Um, red, rosé, white?'

'Red preferably, but I really don't mind. This is very kind of you!'

Ally dug out a bottle of the best Shiraz she had, along with two glasses, filling one just over the halfway mark and the other nearer to the brim.

He was studying the folder's contents again. 'Thank you, Ally. Now, these were almost certainly taken across the pond,' he said, pointing to one of the black-and-white photographs, 'and the woman with the baby just might be your Jessie McPhee.'

'That's what I thought, but it's just that I'm getting nowhere fast,' Ally said morosely.

'OK, so let me have a word with both the minister and Rigby,' he said, pushing aside his mug and sipping his wine. 'They just might reveal more to me than to you, if only because of their dated attitude to women up here.' He rolled his eyes and sipped again. 'This is a nice wine.'

Ally thanked her lucky stars that she'd bought that Shiraz on special offer, when it had gone down to half price for all of three days.

'You must let me reciprocate,' he added. 'Perhaps I can take you out to dinner and drinks sometime next week?'

'Oh, don't feel you have to...' Ally began hastily.

'I don't feel I *have* to do anything,' Ross said firmly, 'but I'd really enjoy your company.'

'Then I'd love to!' Ally tried not to gulp down her wine too quickly. 'I feel I should be offering you something to eat.'

He shook his head. 'No, I must be getting home because Ebony, my *grown-up* black Labrador, is shut in the kitchen. When I'm working, my daughter-in-law takes her out for a walk in the afternoons and then shuts her in again.' He looked across at the still-sleeping Flora. 'She should be all right now, but keep an eye on her. Now,' he added, withdrawing his phone from his pocket, 'may I have your phone number, please?' He drained his glass of wine.

Ally gave him the number, and he tapped it into his phone, before replacing his glass on the table and standing up. 'I'll call you to arrange a date,' he said.

'I'll look forward to it,' Ally said truthfully as they made their way towards the main door.

'And so shall I,' he said.

As Ally closed the door behind him, she smiled to herself. What a nice man he was! Perhaps she was on the verge of something new...

TWENTY-FOUR

After he'd gone, Ally felt happier than she had in days. It was a terrific relief to be able to share her worries with someone. Although Linda had become a good friend, she was inclined to make light of the situation and seemed to enjoy the resulting local gossip. Linda was also enjoying Mamie's repeated custom, particularly for afternoon cream teas.

There was one further church on her list, at Murchan. She probably wouldn't find any McPhees there either, but she *had* to look. And she'd keep Flora on a short lead this time, so she could keep a better eye on her. In fact, Ross had been right; the puppy had fully recovered by the next day and was her normal lively self again. Like all babies, she was quick to become poorly and equally quick to recover.

Murchan, some five miles inland from Locharran, was a proper village with a pub, a shop, a church and even a hairdresser, Ally noted as she drove along the main street. There was also a proper, free parking area at the church, and a neatly painted notice on the gate asking visitors not to let their dogs foul the graveyard. Ally looked dubiously at the fully recovered and excited Flora, and was glad that she'd remembered to put some poo bags in her pocket.

Ally was impressed as she looked around. The grass had been cut, there were some comparatively fresh flowers on some of the graves, and there was even a waste bin next to the wall. It was all so orderly that Ally had the irrational feeling that she wasn't likely to find a single McPhee here.

But she was wrong.

She began examining the stones nearest to the gate, where there was a plethora of Robertsons and Baxters, but not a single McPhee. Unsurprised, but undeterred, Ally worked her way round the stones, keeping a watchful eye on Flora. Then, slowly, she gravitated towards the oldest part of the graveyard, where the stones were lichen covered, almost indecipherable, and many were leaning at peculiar angles. And there she found them: five McPhees, dating back to the early 1800s. There was Donald McPhee sharing a grave with his beloved wife, Annie. Then there was Margaret McPhee, Kenneth McPhee and Mary McPhee, all having died in the 1860s and 1870s, and with separate graves. There was no sign of a Jessie, but Ally felt sure that Donald and Annie might well have been Jessie's parents, and the other three could even be siblings. She photographed every stone and tried to do some mental arithmetic. If the married McPhees had been born in 1801 and 1803 respectively, they could have married around 1820 or 1822, and Jessie could have been born any time in the following decade, which would tie in with her marriage to the mysterious S in 1851.

As she headed towards the gate, Ally found the total silence somewhat disconcerting. There were no strange ladies staring at her from over the wall, and no old boy to tell her the history of the church. No one at all, and it all seemed a bit eerie. Ally was relieved to get back into her car, and pleased that Flora had refrained from eating or doing anything she shouldn't in the graveyard.

When, fifteen minutes later, she parked back at the malt-house, Ally was astonished to find none other than Callum Dalrymple on her doorstep.

'Callum!' she exclaimed as she locked the car.

He grinned. 'Did you think I'd be swinging from the gallows by now?'

'No! Come in and tell me all!' Ally opened the door, and he followed her inside. 'When did they release you?'

'Yesterday evening,' he replied, 'and now the whole village is in a dither because they don't know who to suspect next!'

'I'm really glad you're out of there,' Ally said. 'And neither Linda nor I thought you had anything to do with it.'

'Well, that's reassuring,' Callum said. 'And don't get me *started* on Rigby...'

'Let me get you a drink. What would you like?'

'Tea's fine,' he said, 'because I've got to get back to work shortly. I just wanted to have a word with you.'

'Oh?' Ally filled the kettle. 'I imagine that you're not DI Rigby's greatest fan at the moment.'

Callum shook his head. 'No, I am *not*. I think he needed a token suspect, particularly as they found my DNA on Carrington – which *of course* they did, because I had to manhandle him out of the bloody bar that night! I've never known such an aggressive, nasty piece of work. He'd had far too much to drink, upset just about everyone in the bar with his bloody awful vision of "his" future Locharran and was refusing to leave.'

'I'm staggered,' Ally said truthfully, 'because he was really mild-mannered while he was here. I remember you saying he got a bit belligerent, but I didn't realise your run-in was so serious, and that he was so aggressive.'

'And,' added Callum, 'the reason I'm here is because I'm a bit worried about this brother of his who, I believe, is staying here?'

Ally nodded as she made two mugs of tea and handed one to Callum. 'Yes, his name's Tyler.'

'Well, if he's anything like his brother, you need to be careful,' Callum said, sipping his tea.

'Tyler's nice,' Ally said defensively.

'With all due respect, you thought Wilbur was very nice, didn't you?' Callum said. 'And he wasn't. So, all I'm saying is to be careful, because he might not be what he seems.'

'From what he told me, he only wants to see the killer found so he can fly back to the States with Wilbur's body.'

'I hope you're right.' Callum looked worried. 'Are you here on your own with him?'

'No, because Wilbur's fiancée arrived from the States shortly after he did, so she's staying here too.'

'*Fiancée*? What the hell is *she* doing here?' He gulped more tea, studying Ally over the rim of his mug.

'Same as Tyler, I think. She wants to find the killer. In fact, they don't seem to get on all that well.'

Callum scoffed. 'We all want to find the damn killer, for God's sake! What makes her think she can do better than the police? Wait a minute, forget that, she probably can! Anyway, just be wary of this brother.'

'Oh, I will.'

Callum then told her about his arrest, about Rigby's interrogation and his night in the cells. 'I suppose he has to be seen to be doing something,' he said bitterly, 'but anyone in the bar that night would probably gladly have stuck a knife in Carrington's back.'

'Have you any thoughts about who it might be?'

'You'd be spoiled for choice!' Callum replied cheerfully, draining his tea.

'Now, where have I heard *that* before?' Ally said as she escorted him to the door.

'What I can't get my head round is why Ian Grant was

murdered? It's really sent shock waves through the village. I'm bloody sure he had nothing to do with any of this.'

'I feel the same,' Ally admitted.

'Thanks for the tea. I must get back before it gets busy. But, Ally, just be *aware*.'

'I will,' Ally replied.

When Ally had waved him goodbye and returned to the kitchen, she reckoned that Callum had given her a lot to think about.

She took down the oranges-and-lemons painting and turned it over, checking that all the Post-it notes were still in position. Not for one moment did Ally think that Tyler was anything like his brother. She believed him when he said he wasn't interested in the earl or the estate. But if he was lying, and he didn't actually like Wilbur, then of course he should be a major suspect. Yet she'd never suspected him because he'd been in America at the time of his brother's murder. She still didn't really suspect him, but what were the possibilities that he'd managed to get in and out of the country without being detected? She tore off another Post-it, scribbled 'Tyler' on it and stuck it on her dial at eleven o'clock.

With the excitement at finally finding some McPhees, Ally had almost, but not quite, forgotten about Ross Patterson. And so, when he phoned, she couldn't quite make out who he was for a brief moment.

'How about that dinner I suggested?' he asked, and she could tell that he was smiling from the way he spoke.

She came quickly to her senses. 'That would be lovely.'

'Tomorrow evening?'

Ally looked at the weeks of empty, dateless evenings on her wall calendar. 'Um, yes, why not?'

'Good,' he said, 'and I'll pick you up about seven, if that's OK?'

That was very much OK. 'I'll be ready,' she said.

No sooner had she come off the phone than she started worrying about what to wear. Where might they be going? Should she dig out the navy cashmere again? But in the last few days, the weather had turned a whole lot warmer. It might only be May, but the Gulf Stream was in the right place for once, and warm weather was being forecast for the immediate future. She had a nice new silk shirt which she'd never worn, and perhaps white trousers and her trusty blazer. Would he take her to The Bothy perhaps? She was unaware of any other smart restaurants in the area, but Ross would certainly know his way around.

It suddenly struck her that, during her seven years of widowhood in Edinburgh, the only men who'd ever asked her out were a couple of lecherous ones at the TV studios. And now, here she was, in this so-called godforsaken place, having been out for a meal with an earl no less, an American (Tyler had, after all, invited her out for that drink) and now a very dishy semi-retired vet! Wouldn't Queenie have a field day if she found out! Still, somebody had to keep the gossip going.

Clad in her navy-and-white striped shirt, white trousers and navy blazer, Ally studied herself in the bedroom mirror. Not too bad, she thought. Though she could surely do with a little more walking, which she would, of course, when Flora was a little older.

Morag had offered to puppy-sit Flora for the evening, because Murdo had invited some mates round to shift a few beers while they watched Celtic playing somebody-or-other on TV, and Morag wanted to watch her serial and a popular quiz show.

'You look right glamorous,' she told Ally when she arrived. 'Are you goin' to tell me who's the lucky bloke? Is it the earl?'

Ally shook her head, smiling. She was fully aware that Morag would be at the window the moment she went out of the door and would most likely recognise Ross's car, if not Ross himself.

Ross, in his black Mercedes, drew up outside The Auld Malthouse at one minute past seven.

'You look very chic,' he said approvingly, gallantly getting out and dashing round to open the passenger door.

'Thank you,' she murmured, thinking that he looked pretty good himself. The blue shirt he wore with his cream slacks exactly matched the colour of his eyes. Was that on purpose? she wondered.

As Ally settled herself comfortably in the front seat, he asked, 'Have you been to Seascape before?'

She shook her head. 'No, I've not heard of it.'

'Well,' he said, 'I hope you'll like it. Do you like fish and seafood? I guess I should have asked you that before I booked the table!'

'I'm very happy with fish and seafood,' Ally replied, wondering where this Seascape place was.

It turned out to be a half-hour drive, on the main road out beyond the loch to where it opened out into the sea. Ross drove up a winding road, arriving at a long, low, modern building, which was situated on the top of a cliff and afforded panoramic views. Ally remembered Morag telling her that Ross lived out here somewhere.

'Wow, this view is spectacular!' Ally exclaimed as she got out of the car. It was quite windy up here, and she hoped it wasn't about to wreck the hairdo she'd spent half the afternoon trying to style with her collection of brushes.

'The table I booked should give us this view without the force eight gale,' he said, taking her elbow as he led her in.

He was right. The entire long far wall of the restaurant was glass, and their table was in a prime position. Ally was entranced. She looked around at the amazing view, at the white walls, wooden flooring, crisp white tablecloths and dark-blue napkins. The waiting staff – both sexes – wore dark-blue-and-white-striped butcher-style aprons over crisp white shirts. Ally was very aware of blending in perfectly with her surroundings. If he noticed at all, Ross was far too polite to comment.

Ross ordered wine. 'Chablis all right?' he asked.

Chablis was very much all right, as was her scallops starter. She ordered sea bass for her main because not only did she love it, she didn't fancy wrestling with seafood shells and doubtless adorning the front of her new silk shirt with splashes of sauce.

Ross's main course was some sort of zarzuela, a Spanish seafood speciality, which did involve a fair amount of shell removal, a task he managed with far greater skill than she would have. As they ate, he wanted to know all about her life in Edinburgh, about her late husband, about her children. Ally opened up to him and found herself chattering easily and feeling relaxed in his company. Then she began to worry that she'd been talking far too much. Should she now ask him about his family, knowing about the tragedy involved?

'I've been chatting far too long,' she told him, 'and now it's your turn!'

He told her about his late wife and the great sadness he'd suffered for a couple of years after her death. He spoke about Will and how proud he was of his son's dedication to the veterinary profession, about Will's wife and the five daughters. Then he told her about Alan.

'For a long time,' he said sadly, 'I blamed myself. You see, I thought that by coming here, away from the city and all its temptations, I was doing the right thing for the boys. But Alan died of a drug overdose, right here in Locharran. Why, in God's name, was I not savvy enough to know that drugs, dealers and pushers are *everywhere*? Why was I working such long hours, unaware that Alan had gone from occasional recreational drug use to full-blown heroin? What sort of father was I?'

'A normal, loving father, I would have thought,' Ally said truthfully. 'You couldn't have been everywhere and known everything that was going on. I mean, I've got a son, and I hadn't a clue what he was up to half the time.'

Ross shook his head sadly. 'That's what really killed Barbara, my wife, you know. She couldn't face life when we lost Alan, and I discovered later that she'd stopped taking her medication. It was an awful time. Awful.'

'It must have been.' Ally badly wanted to stroke his hand, to comfort him somehow.

But before she could find a suitable comment, he said, 'Look, we haven't come here to wallow in doom and gloom! Tell me, have you found any of these McPhees yet?'

'As a matter of fact, I have,' she replied. She then proceeded to tell him about her trip to Murchan and about finding the gravestones. Ally told him about the births and deaths of a family that could well have been Jessie's. 'I really need to see the records for Murchan Church. I don't suppose you've had a chance to speak to the reverend yet, have you?'

'I was going to speak to you about that actually. I thought it might be worth us going to see him together,' he suggested, 'if Donald's got these records... In the meantime, how about dessert?'

'I won't, thank you,' Ally replied, recalling her reflection in the mirror. 'But don't let me stop you ordering something.'

He shook his head. 'No, Ally. I'm not a great one for desserts, but I could murder a Celtic coffee!'

'A wonderful idea!' said Ally, feeling quite squiffy because she'd drunk most of the wine in view of him having to drive.

They chatted on about this and that; about food, about travel, about Scottish politics. The evening passed in a flash, and when he delivered her back to the malthouse, he kissed her gently on the cheek and said, 'I've so enjoyed this evening. And I'll phone you just as soon as I can get an appointment with our exalted minister!'

As she got ready for bed, Ally felt a frisson of excitement, and not just because a handsome man had just kissed her. Perhaps, with Ross's help, she might finally be able to find out something about the elusive Jessie McPhee...

TWENTY-FIVE

Ross phoned the very next morning.

'Donald will see us at two o'clock this afternoon – *precisely*! He's a stickler for times so we'd better not be late. How about I get to the malthouse for a quarter to two, and we stroll down to the manse from there? It can't be more than a ten-minute walk, but if it's wet, I'll drive us down.'

'That's fine by me,' Ally replied, comforted to know that somebody was on her side and willing to help her to find this crucial information. That wasn't the only reason, however, because Ally was becoming increasingly fond of the vet. She couldn't wait to tell Linda! Perhaps Linda had already heard because someone *must* have seen them driving out of the village on their way to Seascape. If they hadn't, they'd most certainly be noticed today walking through the village on their way to the manse.

Ross duly arrived at quarter to two and, in bright sunshine, they set off together with an excited Flora on her lead, down the hill and through the village, towards the church and the manse next door.

He chuckled. 'This'll get them all gossiping!'

'Who cares?' Ally realised, as she spoke, that she really didn't.

'I don't,' he said. 'Do you?'

'No,' she replied, laughing.

'I'd like to hold your hand,' he said, 'but I fear it would be too much for them all.'

Ally would have very much liked him to hold her hand but knew he was right.

'The last time I was here it was freezing inside,' Ally told him, 'and not least because his window was wide open.'

'There's no central heating, of course, and it's a big, draughty house. And he's very canny with his money, so you're unlikely to get a warm welcome,' Ross said. 'Not only that, but I know that Donald likes to have a crafty cigarette now and then, although Janet – that's his wife – strongly disapproves. That might explain the open window.' He consulted his watch. 'One minute to two. Do you think it's safe to ring the bell?'

They decided it was. Ally picked up the puppy, noting that the geraniums in the tubs had doubled in size from when she was here last.

The woman in the layers – one less today – opened the door.

'Good to see you, Ross,' she said. 'Come on in.' She didn't give Ally as much as a glance as she led them to the minister's tiny office, where, once again, the window was wide open. In spite of his precautions, Ally could still detect a faint smell of cigarette smoke.

'Sit down! Sit down!' Donald had got to his feet, a little flustered. 'Oh, you've got a wee dog!'

'I hope it's OK,' Ally said hesitantly. 'I don't want to have to leave her outside.'

'Well, I suppose so. I trust she's house-trained?'

'She'll be fine,' Ross cut in, sounding a little impatient.

Donald nodded. 'Go get another chair then, Janet.'

Janet, tight-lipped, did as she was told and returned with a small, wooden kitchen chair, looking pointedly at Ally.

'I'll take that one,' said Ross gallantly, steering Ally towards the more comfortable green basket chair.

Janet sniffed and made an exit. Ally was aware that she wasn't greatly approved of by Mrs Scott. Was it because she didn't go to church, or was there another reason?

Ross came straight to the point. 'Mrs McKinley here visited you a while back with regard to looking up historical births, deaths and marriages from the churches in this area.'

Donald Scott squinted at Ally. 'So you did.'

'We are particularly interested in the records of Murchan Church,' Ross continued, 'which may contain the entry of the marriage of one Jessie McPhee, around 1851.'

The minister sniffed. 'That rings a bell,' he said vaguely, gazing out of the window.

'And so,' Ross continued, 'we'd like to be able to access that information. Is there any way you might be able to borrow this from the church headquarters or wherever?'

'Well,' said Donald, sniffing again, 'we probably have it here somewhere.'

'You *do*?' Ally and Ross chorused together.

'I don't think we sent it back after the American came looking for that same information.'

'The *American*?' Ally asked as she and Ross looked at each other in stunned silence for a brief moment.

'Hmm.' The minister seemed blissfully unaware of the importance of what he'd said. He pulled out a couple of drawers and shook his head. 'I think Janet must have stashed it away somewhere; it's a great big thing, you know.' He looked disapprovingly at Flora, who was wriggling in Ally's arms.

'*What* American?' Ross asked.

'Can't remember his name, but he got killed shortly afterwards.'

'Do you mean Wilbur Carrington?' Ally asked, scarcely able to believe what she was hearing; why on earth could he not have told her that last time?

'That's him.'

'And you still have the church records here?' Ross asked.

'Unless Janet sent them back.' He looked vague, then swivelled round in his chair, pulled the door open and bellowed, '*Janet!*'

There followed some grunting and shuffling as Janet finally reappeared. 'Yes, dear?'

'The Murchan Church records. Have we still got them?'

'Aye. You told me to put it in the bottom of the wardrobe, because it was too big to fit in any of the drawers. Don't you remember?'

'Did I?'

'Yes, Donald, you did.'

'Well, well,' said Donald dreamily, 'my memory's not what it was.'

All that Ally could think was that if he had only produced these records when she'd been here before, it would have saved trailing round three graveyards. She set Flora down on the floor and prayed she wouldn't soil the minister's threadbare carpet.

'Do you think you could bring it in then, Janet?' Ross asked politely. 'If it's very heavy, I'd be happy to carry it for you.'

'I'd really appreciate that,' said Janet, giving him a flirtatious little smile.

Ross followed Janet out through the door, and Ally could hear their footsteps resounding across the hallway and then up the stairs, which creaked loudly.

'Fancy me forgetting that big book!' the minister mused. 'Just as well Janet hadn't got round to sending it back.' Then, as if remembering that he had a visitor, he added, 'I don't recall seeing you in the kirk, Mrs McKinley?'

'I'm afraid that having guests is a seven-day-a-week occupation,' Ally replied. 'Breakfasts don't normally finish until nearly eleven, and then I have to service the rooms.'

'Hmm.' He frowned. 'We do have evensong occasionally.'

'I'll bear that in mind,' Ally said, relieved to hear Ross approaching.

He came in with a large, dusty tome, its ancient leather cover mended and patched many times by the look of it, and laid it on the desk.

'That's it,' the minister confirmed, somewhat unnecessarily. 'Now, be careful with these pages.' He gently turned over the yellowed sheets of paper. 'I've got back to 1821 here. Is that anywhere near what you're looking for?'

'May we look?' Ross asked.

The minister shrugged. 'Just be careful with it. I forget what dates the American was looking for, but he seemed to find it.' He paused. 'Not that it did him a lot of good.'

Murchan Parish Records was the Holy Grail, as far as Ally was concerned. And if Wilbur had found what he was looking for, then so must they. She gently turned the pages until she found McPhee featured again. There was Donald McPhee and Annie Thompson, who married on 3 June 1822. This tallied with the gravestone she'd found in Murchan. They'd had five children, Jessie being the youngest, born in April 1831. Her fingers trembling, Ally turned the pages and found the marriages of Jessie's siblings, and then that of Jessie herself.

Jessie had married Robert Sinclair, fifth earl of Locharran, on 19 June 1851.

To prove anything conclusively, there then had to have been a birth. There was no further mention of Jessie. Ally knew that to get the further information she needed, she had to visit Hamish Sinclair again.

They both thanked the minister profusely and made their exit. Ally was already planning her next step – and looking forward to getting back to her cosy kitchen!

TWENTY-SIX

There was no time for any 'chance' meeting, and Ally knew that if she was to be able to talk to Hamish, she'd need to phone. For the umpteenth time, she cursed herself for not having got his mobile number. She decided against calling Mrs Fraser and instead tried the landline number she had for the castle. To her great surprise, he answered the phone himself.

'Really sorry to bother you, Hamish, but I do need to speak to you quite urgently.'

'Shall I come down to the malthouse?'

'Could I please come up to the castle? And' – she paused, worried that he might think she suspected him – 'do you have any old records, family records, births, deaths, marriages, that sort of thing?'

'Well, yes, of course. I already dug those out, you know, for Carrington – Wilbur Carrington.'

'Would you mind digging them out again?' Ally asked. 'Just one little detail I want to check.'

'So you're not visiting just to delight in my scintillating personality then?' Hamish sounded a little disappointed.

'That too,' Ally confirmed, laughing. 'If it's OK with you, I'll be up there in about twenty minutes.'

Twenty minutes later, she found Mrs Fraser polishing up the wrought-iron furniture on the huge oak door. 'The earl said to go straight in,' she said. 'Through the hall, second door on the left.'

Ally thanked her and made her way through the enormous hall, which, today, thanks to beams of sunlight, looked marginally less gloomy than before. She knocked on the second door on the left.

Hamish was seated at his desk in a sea of paperwork and fiddling with a computer.

'These things are invaluable when they do what you want,' he said, sounding exasperated, 'but a bloody pain in the arse when they don't. Excuse my language, Alison! Shall we have some tea?'

'No thank you; I've just had some,' she replied, knowing that Mrs Fraser would not be well pleased at abandoning her polishing to produce tea. 'This really is a flying visit. I want to dig back through the earls of Locharran, if that's OK with you?'

'There seems to be records only of their births and deaths,' Hamish said, 'so I hope you're not bothered about who they married?'

'Births and deaths will be fine,' Ally said, watching him turn the pages of yet another enormous tome. 'I'm interested in Robert Sinclair, fifth Earl of Locharran, and, in particular, when he died.'

Hamish frowned. 'That'd be about the middle of the nineteenth century then?'

'Try 1851 onwards,' Ally suggested, hoping against hope that there would be some useful information.

After some page-turning and sharp intakes of breath, Hamish finally stopped. 'Here we are,' he said, sliding the book across to where Ally was standing.

What was recorded was the death of that same Robert Sinclair, fifth earl of Locharran, on 13 September 1851, due to a riding accident, and which would have been less than two months after his marriage to Jessie.

'Would you mind if I photographed that?' she asked, getting out her phone.

'Not at all,' Hamish replied. 'I do remember now my grand-father talking about the tragedy. He was such a young man, in his prime, when he died. Terrible thing; fell off his horse jumping a fence. His brother succeeded him, of course.'

'Very sad,' Ally agreed, taking a couple of photographs. 'And it's very kind of you to let me see this. Thank you so much.'

'Here we are,' said Hamish, pointing further down the page. 'He was succeeded by the sixth Earl of Locharran, Malcolm Sinclair. His brother.'

Ally photographed the entry. 'Thank you.'

'You're very welcome, my dear. Is this something to do with Carrington's stupid claim?'

'Well, it could be. I promise to let you know.'

'Stuff and nonsense!' said the earl. 'Sure you won't stay for some tea?'

'No, thank you. I must be on my way.'

'You off to see the vet, eh?'

'Bye, Hamish,' Ally said, replacing her phone in her pocket.

'So we still don't know whatever happened to Jessie after that?' Ross asked a while later as Ally showed him the photographs she'd taken. 'I mean, she was the Countess of Locharran surely, however briefly?'

'And now we know who succeeded him,' Ally said. 'Hamish confirmed that it was the brother, Malcolm Sinclair.'

'So, what on earth happened to poor Jessie when her

husband died after only two months?' Ross asked, looking bewildered.

'My guess would be that she was bundled off to America,' Ally replied.

'Who do you think would do that?'

'My money would be on the sixth Earl of Locharran, Malcolm Sinclair. I doubt she went voluntarily,' Ally said, 'and, if it became obvious that she was pregnant, they would have paid her a great deal of money to get her out of the way. And I doubt a simple girl like Jessie would have known that her child, if it was a boy, would be the heir.'

'So, Wilbur Carrington *was right*,' Ross said. 'That, presumably, was the proof he was looking for?'

'And ended up with a knife in his back, before he could lord it over everyone.'

Ross sighed. 'Which points to poor old Hamish Sinclair, I suppose. Or the brother! What did you say his name was?'

'Tyler. Tyler Carrington.'

'Meaning that this Tyler guy could now be the legal heir!'

'Oh my God!' Ally stopped in her tracks. 'But he's so adamant that he doesn't want to know about the earldom! That he's nothing like his brother!'

'And you believe him?'

'I honestly don't know any more,' Ally replied, 'but he can't have killed his brother because he was in America. What the hell do we do now?'

'I'll tell you what we do; we take this information to Rigby straight away,' Ross said very firmly. 'It's important for many reasons, not least because you could be living under the same roof as a killer, Ally. I know you believe he was in America, but what if he wasn't? Or what if he paid someone to commit the crime? That could explain why Ian Grant was killed. I think you're going to give this Tyler some story about needing his bedroom and getting him moved down to the Craigmonie or somewhere.'

'Let's see what Rigby says first,' Ally said. 'That's if he's *there*, because he might have gone back to Inverness. Not that he was in the slightest bit interested in the documents in the folder I gave him.' She was experiencing a mixture of emotions: fear, because Tyler could well be a killer; sorrow, because the other likely suspect could be the earl, and she'd become fond of him; and a nice, warm glow because this very nice, attractive man actually cared that she might have a killer underneath her roof.

'Let's go see Rigby right now,' Ross said. 'We'll demand to see him because we have some vital information. If necessary, I'll take you to Inverness.'

'Thanks so much, Ross.' She paused. 'I bet you're beginning to wish you'd never set eyes on me and not become involved in this unholy mess!'

He placed his hand underneath her elbow as he steered her across to the temporary police station. 'I've no regrets whatsoever,' he said, 'and I'm intrigued by this case.'

PC Chisholm, he of the prominent Adam's apple, was on duty at the entrance and looked up enquiringly as they came in.

'We have some important information for Detective Inspector Rigby,' Ross said. 'Is he here?'

Chisholm shook his head. 'He's in Locharran, but he's out at the moment. He should be back soon.'

'Can you hurry him up, please?'

The policeman looked at them both doubtfully. Then, seeing their faces, he picked up the phone. 'Two people with important information for you, sir.' He listened for a moment. 'The vet, sir – Mr Patterson, senior, and Mrs McKinley from the malthouse.' He listened again. 'Yes, sir.' Then, turning to

Ally and Ross, he said, 'Take a seat. He'll be back in about five minutes.' He looked at Flora. 'That's a nice wee dog. I hope she's house-trained?'

Ally was thankful, and not a little relieved, that Flora had peed profusely on the lawn as they left the malthouse. 'She'll be fine,' Ally said.

They sat down on the two uncomfortable grey plastic chairs which had been placed underneath the large noticeboard, meaning that no one sitting there could read any of the 'important' messages on it, and exchanged glances.

'Well, at least you won't have to drive to Inverness,' Ally said, feeling a little guilty but relieved.

'You know I would have done it gladly,' Ross said with a smile.

'Well, well, well,' said Rigby as he led them into his office. 'And to what do I owe this honour?'

His sarcasm was not lost on Ross. 'You owe this honour to the fact that we've been doing some detective work for you, Inspector.'

Rigby plonked himself down behind his desk with a sigh, indicating that they should sit themselves on another two of the grey plastic chairs opposite. Ally reckoned they must have got them as a job lot.

'Fire away,' he said.

'You weren't very interested in the contents of the folder I gave you,' Ally said. 'You didn't think it important that, back in 1851, a Jessie McPhee married someone called Robert, with the initial S at the beginning of his surname.'

Rigby looked from one to the other. 'That could have been anyone.'

'Well, it wasn't *anyone*,' Ally continued. 'It was the then Earl of Locharran, Robert Sinclair.'

Rigby's eyebrows shot up. 'You've proof of this?'

'Yes,' Ross said. 'We've checked the records for Murchan Church, going back to the 1800s, which is where Mrs McKinley here finally found evidence of McPhees, and we duly contacted the minister.'

'Who just happened to still have the old records,' Ally added, 'which included the entry of marriage of one Jessie McPhee and one Robert Sinclair, Earl of Locharran. And guess who else had been asking to see those records?'

Rigby shook his head.

'None other than our late friend, Wilbur Carrington.'

'OK,' said Rigby, 'so this Jessie McPhee married the earl. What about it?'

'The earl died in an accident a couple of months later,' Ross said, 'and his younger brother inherited the earldom.'

Rigby frowned. 'So?'

'There is no further mention of Jessie,' Ally said. 'She seems to have vanished into thin air.'

'She probably moved away somewhere,' Rigby said.

'Except we know she moved to the States,' Ally added. 'And if you'd taken notice of what was in that green folder, you'd have come to the same conclusion.'

Rigby had started to scribble some notes on a piece of paper. 'Why would she go to America?'

'We don't know for sure,' Ross said, 'but it seems very likely she was pregnant and was probably paid off by the new earl.'

'Don't forget that she was a housemaid,' Ally said, 'and was used to doing what she was told.'

Rigby scribbled some more, then scratched his head. 'There's a lot of guesswork going on here,' he remarked after a moment.

'Supposing Jessie was pregnant?' Ally said. 'That would explain a lot, although she might not even have been aware of it herself when her husband died.'

'You're saying that Wilbur Carrington was carrying all this paperwork around with him because he believed that he was a genuine descendant?'

'That all depends on the date Jessie's baby was born and whether it was a boy. And Wilbur would have known that. He'd probably got further proof from records in the States,' Ally said. 'Which means his brother, Tyler Carrington, is now the rightful earl.'

Rigby stopped scribbling. 'But he's insistent that it doesn't interest him. Are you suggesting that he came over here to kill his own brother, to inherit an earldom that he didn't want?'

'An earldom he *says* he doesn't want,' said Ross.

Rigby surveyed them both with a glimmer of a smile. 'But Tyler Carrington was in the States when his brother was murdered,' he said triumphantly. 'We've checked that very thoroughly. He was actually at a conference in New York at the time he got the news. This has been verified. He got the British Airways evening flight to Glasgow, and his name is on the passenger list. He then flew from Glasgow up to Inverness to identify his brother's body and to hire a car. Tyler Carrington is not his brother's killer.'

Ally glanced at Ross. 'But what if he *paid* someone to kill his brother?'

'Like who?' Rigby asked, frowning.

At the same time, Ross and Ally said, 'Ian Grant.'

TWENTY-SEVEN

'Well, so much for that theory,' Ally said despondently as they made their way back up to the malthouse a little while later. 'That probably leaves Hamish as the most likely suspect now.'

Rigby had smiled when he'd informed them that Ian Grant had been at a wedding in Fort William on the night of Wilbur Carrington's murder. 'He stayed there overnight and that has been verified, I'm afraid. Sorry to burst your sleuthing bubble, Mrs McKinley!'

'Looks more and more like it,' Ross said sadly, 'but I hope not. Hamish has always been one for the ladies, but he's quite a gentle person really.'

'I know. And I hope not too. At least I don't need to worry about Tyler piercing me with a skean dhu in the middle of the night!'

'Maybe not,' Ross said, 'but I'd keep your bedroom door locked anyway.'

Ally patted him on the arm. 'I always do. Thank you so much for accompanying me today, Ross. I wouldn't have got anywhere if I'd been on my own. Let me get you a drink.'

'I'd love one, but unfortunately I'm on duty shortly for four hours, but I'll have one tomorrow afternoon, if you're available? And I'd also like to see more of what you've done with this old place,' Ross added, waving a hand in the direction of the malthouse.

'I'll look forward to it,' Ally said.

After he'd gone, Ally felt restless. She took the picture down from the wall, turned it over and removed Tyler from eleven o'clock. He certainly couldn't have been in two places at once. Flora was still looking energetic, so this, Ally decided, might be a good time to wander down to The Bistro and give Linda the news of her new friendship. She sincerely hoped that Linda wouldn't think that she was gloating, because she wasn't, but she badly needed to tell someone.

'I just thought I'd pop in to tell you that—' Ally began, ten minutes later.

'That you've snatched the lovely Ross Patterson from under our very noses!' Linda interrupted with a grin. 'I've just been to the shop, and the news is all round the village: *Mrs McKinley and Ross Patterson have been walking around together, hand in hand!*'

'Oh my God!' Ally exclaimed. 'We only went to see the minister, and we were not – *not* – hand in hand!'

'Queenie is convinced that you went to see Donald Scott about getting married!'

Ally rolled her eyes. 'That is utterly ridiculous! We were trying to trace some old church records which might, or might not, prove that Wilbur Carrington was the rightful heir.'

'I believe you!'

Linda handed her a mug of coffee and produced some chocolate cake. 'So, tell me, *have* you?'

'Have I what?'

'You *know*! Have you been to bed with him?'

Ally laughed. 'For heaven's sake, Linda! I've only known him for a few days.'

Linda snorted. 'But you'll be seeing him again?'

'Well, yes, but—'

'But you will. End up in bed with him! Lucky old you!'

'Do you know what? I honestly haven't had time to even think about that, what with hunting round old churchyards, trying to get some sense out of the minister and telling Rigby today what we found out.'

'Ah, but there's always tomorrow! And I'd avoid the shop for a couple of days if I were you! Wait until they find someone else to gossip about. At least it's given them some relief from the murder of poor old Ian Grant.'

When Ally got back to the malthouse, an exhausted Flora flopped straight into her basket and fell fast asleep, while an equally exhausted Ally poured herself a large glass of white wine and wandered out to the garden seat, beneath the rowan tree, on the west side of the house. It was early evening, it was pleasantly warm and she needed time to gather her thoughts together. She'd only taken one sip when a female voice called out, 'Coo-ee.'

'Oh, hello, Mamie,' she said, resigned to the peace being shattered.

'I'm not disturbing you, am I?' Mamie was attired in a pink-and-white-striped blouse and bright-pink pedal pushers.

Ally sighed. 'Not at all,' she said brightly.

'Oh good, so you don't mind if I join you?' Without further ado, Mamie lowered herself into the old rusty and wobbly garden chair, which creaked threateningly.

'Have you had a nice day?' Ally asked politely.

'Oh yes, I have. I've been walking across the moors, and the weather has been just lovely. I think I might have been bitten, though.' Mamie scratched her foot.

'You must watch out for midges,' Ally told her. 'They come out when it's warm, and they can eat you alive. You'll need some insect repellent.'

Mamie ignored this and cleared her throat. 'I hear that Callum whatever-he's-called, from the Craigmonie Hotel, has been *released*! I cannot *believe* it!'

'They can't keep anyone in custody indefinitely if they don't have proof,' Ally reminded her.

'But,' said Mamie, shaking her head, 'I understand that his DNA was found on Wilbur's body.'

'Because,' said Ally, 'there was a bit of a fracas at the Craigmonie the night of the murder because Wilbur had had a few too many, he'd upset several of the locals and he then refused to leave. I think Callum had to manhandle him to get him out.'

'Nonsense!' exclaimed Mamie. 'My Wilbur would *never* have behaved like that!'

'Perhaps,' Ally said gently, 'there was a side to him that you didn't know?'

'I wouldn't have *entertained* the idea of marrying a violent man, Ally! You have to believe me when I say that Wilbur was a decent, God-fearing person!'

'Perhaps you never saw him lose his temper?' Not for the first time Ally wondered how much Mamie really knew about this fiancé of hers when she lived on the other side of the continent. 'And you must realise that a lot of people witnessed the scene, Mamie.'

'Well, they'd probably all stick together anyway,' Mamie retorted dismissively. 'Ah, here's Tyler!'

Tyler was crossing the lawn towards them, carrying a large carrier bag which was clinking merrily, probably full of bottles.

'Is this a private conversation, or can anyone join in?' he asked jovially. He looked around as he sat on the one remaining garden chair, which creaked under his weight. 'This is a great view, isn't it? I can see the mountains from here, and there sure are some great rock faces up there that I'd love to climb.'

'That sounds rather dangerous on your own, surely?' Ally said.

'Not if you know what you're doing,' Tyler replied. 'I've scaled rock surfaces all over the place, and I reckon I could tackle these without too much trouble.'

Ally sighed. She'd have to offer them a drink now.

But Tyler appeared to have been reading her mind because he said, 'I've just bought some wine straight from the chiller down in the shop, so if you could find a couple of glasses, Ally...?'

As she made her way back into the house, Ally wondered how much she should ask – or tell – Tyler. Did he also have proof of Jessie McPhee being an ancestor? Jessie *Sinclair* more correctly! And, even more incredibly, could Tyler now actually be the *real earl*? She found a couple of wine glasses, came back outside, and handed one each to Mamie and Tyler.

As Tyler unscrewed the bottle of Sauvignon Blanc and filled Mamie's glass, Mamie asked, 'Tyler, did *you* know that Wilbur sometimes drank too much and could become a little' – she hesitated, searching for the word – 'belligerent?' She gulped some wine.

'Yup!' replied Tyler. 'He liked his drink, and he didn't like it if someone upset him.' He stared unblinkingly at Mamie. 'I guess there was a side to him you knew nothing about!'

'Anyway,' said Ally, desperate to defuse the situation yet again, 'I've discovered that a certain Jessie McPhee probably married the Earl of Locharran way back in 1851, and he died not long after, which is why Jessie ended up in the States.'

'That's right!' exclaimed Tyler, downing a large gulp of wine. 'She was our great-great-grandmama!' He smiled. 'Have I missed out a "great" or added too many? But you *know* what I mean!'

Ally tried not to appear astounded, which she was. 'And you *knew* that?' she asked.

'Of course I knew that! Wilbur was obsessed by it and never stopped talking about it!' Tyler lifted his eyes to heaven. 'Mind you, I think he might have wanted to get that confirmed, find more proof.'

'And it seems he found it?' Ally said.

'Then I guess he was the rightful Earl of Locharran for a couple of days!' Tyler said cheerfully. 'And thank God I was at that Leisure and Sport Conference in New York when he was killed, otherwise I guess I'd be the chief suspect.'

'But, Tyler, this means that you yourself might now be the rightful Earl of Locharran,' Ally said, exchanging glances with Mamie, whose mouth was hanging open.

There was silence for a moment before Mamie, somewhat recovered, said, 'So who then would have killed Wilbur, and why?'

'Well then, it's gotta be the earl,' Tyler said, 'because he sure as hell had a motive.'

'Oh, it *can't* be!' Mamie wailed. 'He's *such* a gentleman! He'd never do anything like that!'

Tyler shrugged. 'Well, it has to be someone round here, and it sure as hell ain't me!'

Ally wondered if she should mention the entry of marriage, which she'd photographed on her phone, and then decided not to. 'Maybe,' she said, 'you should go and talk to the earl again, Tyler?'

Tyler shrugged. 'I've told you, and everyone else in this damned village, that I'm not in the slightest bit interested in being an earl, or a lord, or a duke, or the bloody king! I just want my brother's body released so that I can fly home and arrange for a burial. Is that too much to ask?'

'And you know what?' said Mamie, wiping her eyes. 'I'd kinda like to go back with you, Tyler, *and* my Wilbur, when all this is over.' Her eyes had filled with tears again as she looked back at Ally. 'I often wonder when this is gonna be over, Ally.'

Ally sighed. 'I often wonder too.'

'But I've almost completed my jigsaw,' Mamie said triumphantly. 'Just a few pieces missing.'

There were indeed, Ally thought as she carried the glasses indoors, just a few pieces missing, and not only in Mamie's puzzle.

Ross arrived the following afternoon as arranged, with a bag of tulip bulbs. 'I've been thinning these out,' he said, 'and I thought you might like some. I wasn't sure what exactly was in your garden up here.'

'Thanks so much,' Ally said. 'There's not a great deal in the garden because, obviously, it wasn't anyone's home before now. I've had it tidied up, but it's somewhat lacking in spring flowers.' *And summer flowers too*, she thought. 'Would you like to see round before I make the coffee?'

Ross said that he would and, with Flora at their heels, Ally led the way into the utility room and her little office, before leading him up the old staircase at the back of the building. 'This section had to be kept separate,' she explained, 'because the wall between here and the west side of the malthouse is at least four feet thick. It was certainly built to last.' She opened the first door at the top of the stairs. 'This one's mine,' she said, glad that she'd had a good tidy-up, knowing that she'd be showing him around.

'I'm really glad you're up a different staircase from your guests,' Ross said, looking into the room briefly. 'Lovely sunny room,' he added.

'And this one,' said Ally, opening another door, 'is for

friends and family, if they ever decide to visit me. Though I don't think they're currently over-impressed with the crime rate round here! And this is the bathroom which both bedrooms share.' She opened the third door, and Ross glanced in briefly. 'Now, follow me!'

Ross followed her down the old staircase, through the kitchen and into the hall, where she showed him the dining room and sitting room. 'These rooms are primarily for guests,' Ally told him, 'or for formal entertaining, although I don't expect to be doing a lot of that.' She opened a further door. 'And this is going to be my own little snug. It's got a log burner, a comfy couch and the TV, and this is where I'll be on cold winter evenings.'

He was looking around with interest. 'You've made a great job of all this! When I think of what a draughty old barn-like place this used to be!'

Ally smiled, pleased at his approval. 'Now, let me show you the guest bedrooms,' she said, leading the way up the smart wooden stairs, Flora scurrying behind them and sliding on the polished steps.

'This,' said Ally, opening the first door, 'is Room One, where Wilbur Carrington stayed, and which I had to keep locked up for days.'

'And this,' said Ross, heading towards the window, 'is the famous desk?'

Ally nodded, opened it up and showed him how to access the secret drawer which, obligingly, slid out.

'Wow!' Ross said. 'This is real mystery stuff! I really thought secret drawers only existed in Agatha Christie films and the like.'

'Oh, they do indeed exist,' Ally confirmed, closing the drawer and pulling Flora out from the far corner of the room, where she was about to overturn the wastepaper basket.

'Now we come to Room Two,' she said, locking Room 1

behind her, 'and this is Mamie's room – that's the fiancée.' She led the way into the bedroom and opened the door to the en-suite bathroom. Conscious of a howling sound, she said, 'What on earth's wrong with Flora?' She turned round to see the puppy sitting down outside Room 2, emitting a loud wailing sound. 'Maybe she's not keen on looking at Mamie's under-wear!' Mamie had festooned three pairs of lacy pink knickers across the towel rail in the bathroom.

Ross looked thoughtful. 'Which is the room where Willie drank himself to death?' he asked.

'Well, this one, I suppose,' Ally replied, 'or the bathroom, to be more exact.'

'There's your answer then.' Ross was laughing. 'The dog *knows!*'

'Oh, come *on!*' said Ally. 'She'll come in in a minute.' She called Flora and, looking out of the door, saw that the puppy had retreated further along the landing and refused to move.

'I told you so,' said Ross, highly amused. 'Animals can always sense something spooky, and it would appear that Willie is still very much in residence!'

Ally was finding this very hard to swallow. 'You don't really believe all that old rubbish, do you?'

Ross shrugged. 'Who knows? Well, the dog certainly does...'

'She's probably just tired,' Ally said, approaching Room 3. 'Now, this is Tyler's – the brother's – room.' She looked down, amazed to find Flora had rejoined them and was happily exploring the room. Could Ross possibly be right about Room 2? She'd need to have a further word with Morag to see if she'd experienced anything weird in there when she'd been cleaning the bathroom.

Back in the kitchen, Ally busied herself making coffee, while Ross threw a ball around the floor for Flora.

'I like your still life,' he remarked, indicating the picture on the wall.

'Yes, I do too. It belonged to my grandmother,' Ally said, hoping that there weren't any Post-it notes showing round the edges.

'It adds a touch of the Mediterranean,' Ross said. 'Talking of which, would you like to go out for an Italian meal next week sometime? Nothing fancy, just down at Concetti's? They do great pasta dishes as well as fish and chips, you know.'

'That would be great,' Ally replied, 'but only if you let me pay my way. We had that wonderful meal at Seascape the other day, which must have cost you a fortune, and I'm *not* having you paying out again!'

'Why ever not?' he asked. 'Are you one of these independent, feminist-type women?'

'I suppose I must be,' Ally admitted. 'Furthermore, I *am* earning money, so I'd like to pay please.'

'We'll talk about that next week,' he said with a wink.

TWENTY-EIGHT

Ally couldn't avoid it any longer; she had to visit the village shop. She needed some milk and she'd almost run out of dishwasher tablets, but it was anyone's guess how Queenie was likely to react in view of the current gossip.

Her first thought had been to drive to Fort William or Inverness and do a big shop, but she really didn't need that much. *And why*, she asked herself, *would I drive miles just to avoid a gossipy old woman?*

Leaving Flora in Morag's care, Ally meandered down to Locharran Post Office and Stores, taking a deep breath before she ventured inside. She was able to pick up the dishwasher tablets from the display near the doorway before making her way to the counter to ask for the milk. For reasons best known to Queenie and Bessie, the fridge containing milk and dairy products had been positioned on their side of the counter, and so milk always had to be requested.

Queenie was, as always, stretched across the counter, keeping an eye on a toddler who, while his mother was looking at biscuits, was busy helping himself to packets of Smarties from the opposite display.

'Watch that child of yours!' bellowed Queenie, scowling.

The woman turned round and scowled back. 'I was going to pay for them, so what are you on about?'

'Oh no you *weren't!*' Queenie yelled back.

'Oh yes I was!' snapped the woman.

The child began to wail when his mother grabbed the Smarties from his little hands and shoved them back in the display. 'We'll get our shopping somewhere else, Aidan, won't we?'

Aidan continued to howl loudly as his mother marched him out through the door, slamming it behind her.

Ally hoped the woman had a car because there was nowhere else for miles around where Aidan was likely to get his Smarties.

'Tourists!' Queenie retorted with great contempt, completely ignoring Ally who was still waiting at the counter.

While this little fracas was taking place, Bessie had emerged from the storeroom. She was wearing a shabby purple sweater with her usual droopy grey skirt. Ally reckoned that the woman was probably around her own age and, if introduced to some make-up and decent clothes, might actually look reasonably attractive.

Ally had never seen Bessie smile before, but she was smiling now, displaying a gap where one of her front teeth had been removed. 'What can I get for you, Mrs McKinley?'

Ally couldn't believe what she was seeing or hearing. She'd hardly ever heard Bessie speak before either. 'Oh, just a couple of pints of milk, please, Bessie.'

Bessie trotted across to the fridge. 'Nice day,' she remarked.

Both Ally and Queenie were now looking at her in astonishment.

'Yes, it is, Bessie,' Ally agreed, casting a sidelong glance at Queenie.

'What's got into *you?*' Queenie asked her sister crossly.

'Nothing,' Bessie replied, placing the milk on the counter. 'I'm just happy for Mrs McKinley.'

'For *me*?' Ally looked from one to the other in amazement. 'Why?'

'Yes,' said Bessie blithely, 'because I think that Mr Patterson needs a nice lady friend after all the tragedy in his life.'

Ally was struck dumb.

Queenie rounded angrily on her sister. 'What are you talking about?'

'Well,' said Bessie, 'you said you weren't going to talk to Mrs McKinley again because she was man-mad, and that would have been very rude.'

For once, even Queenie was speechless.

'But I think it's nice,' Bessie continued, 'and it's not her fault if the men are flockin' round her!'

'But they *aren't*!' Ally spluttered. She turned to Queenie. 'We had this conversation last time I came in here, Queenie, and nothing has changed in the meantime. I've become friendly with Mr Patterson purely because he's been treating my puppy.' She turned back to Bessie. 'I'm glad you think it's nice, Bessie, because he's a charming man.'

Bessie beamed. 'Queenie and me have always rather fancied him, haven't we, Queenie? And if we can't have him, then I'm pleased he's found somebody nice.'

Queenie had come alive. 'For God's sake, woman! Of course *I* don't fancy him! You speak for yourself, Bessie!' She was breathing heavily. 'I don't know how you can talk such nonsense, particularly at a time when we're all mourning for poor Ian. You should be *ashamed* of yourself!' Not once did Queenie meet Ally's eye.

Bessie had finally come out of her shell and, as she hitched up her droopy skirt, she took Ally's money and smiled.

'Thank you, Bessie,' Ally said. 'It was very sweet of you to say that. You must come up to the malthouse sometime for a cup of tea.'

Queenie's jaw dropped.

'That would be a real treat,' said Bessie.

Ally couldn't help herself from smiling as she walked back up to the malthouse.

The moment Ally stepped into the kitchen she knew something was wrong. Morag was standing in front of the table, coat on, eyes narrowed, face grim.

'Are you all right, Morag?' Ally asked anxiously, looking around and relieved to see Flora fast asleep in her basket.

'No, I am *not* all right!' Morag snapped.

As she spoke, Ally noticed the empty space on the wall and the upside-down picture on the table, Post-it notes fluttering in the breeze from the half-open window.

'Morag, I can—'

'I dinna want to hear it!' Morag interrupted loudly. 'Just as well I decided to give the kitchen a clean this mornin' and noticed the bloody great cobweb on that picture!'

'But—'

'But nothin'!' Morag shouted. 'I can see what ye're trying to do – make Murdo and me look like killers!'

Ally resisted the temptation to say, 'But you were only at four o'clock!' Instead she said, 'I only listed the people I thought could be affected if Carrington's theory was true.'

Morag inhaled deeply. 'Meaning that ye think we were capable of killing him? And poor Ian too? And Mrs Fraser! And Mrs Jamieson! And *Queenie*! Are ye out of yer mind?'

Ally sighed as she took off her jacket and placed it on the back of a chair. Why the hell had she not noticed that damned cobweb and removed it herself? 'You've got it all wrong, Morag!'

'No, I bloody well haven't! I've never been so insulted in my whole life. Ye come up here from Edinburgh thinking yerself so high and mighty that ye can judge us all! I will not be workin' here again – ever!' With that, she picked up her shopping bag and made her way towards the back door.

Ally moved quickly, barring her way. 'Please don't go. As you can see, I've listed some very unlikely people – my friend Linda for one. Do you honestly think that I'd suspect any of you as killers? Of course not!'

Morag pushed past her. 'Then ye shouldn't have stuck our names on there! Ye should be concentrating on the most likely suspect, and that's the earl! But, of course, the rest of us haven't been winin' and dinin' you, or giving ye dogs, have we?' She turned round. 'Find yerself another cleaner!' She then marched furiously out of the back door, slamming it with as much force as she could muster, leaving Ally standing, stunned.

After a moment, she took a deep breath and sat down at the kitchen table, surveying her suspect clock. It took a further couple of minutes for it to dawn on her that Morag, and Murdo, were now very likely to spread this news all around the village. Soon no one would be speaking to her. What had she *done*?

Ally's happy mood was replaced with black despair. As she no longer had a cleaner, she knew she should check to see how far Morag had got to before she discovered the Post-it notes. Leaving them still on display, she ventured slowly upstairs to check the bedrooms and discovered, with great relief, that they'd both been done. As she descended again, Ally discovered that the dining room hadn't, and the floor was covered with crumbs, as usual, from Mamie's consumption of croissants at breakfast. Ally put four or five of these out each day, originally assuming that Tyler would eat two, and Mamie would eat two. In the event, Tyler rarely ate one, leaving Mamie to demolish the lot.

As she cleared up and vacuumed, Ally could only hope that

Morag would calm down, see sense and, hopefully, come back tomorrow.

When she'd finished, she made herself a sandwich and a cup of tea – after she'd replaced the picture on the wall. Then a sudden thought occurred to her. The earl had a cousin, didn't he, who was the heir to the estate? Could the cousin have got wind of Wilbur Carrington's plans and nipped them, *and* Wilbur, in the bud? She needed to talk to the earl but, if she phoned, it would very likely be Mrs Fraser who'd answer the phone and would doubtless be listening into the conversation as well. She didn't know if Hamish had a mobile but, if he did, she must note the number. Now her only hope was to take Flora for a walk across the moor and hope, like that first time, she might bump into him. It was worth a try.

The weather had improved greatly and it had conveniently rained each night, leaving the days sunny and breezy with scudding clouds. Still, you could never really depend on the weather in this neck of the woods, and so Ally donned her waterproof hooded jacket and set off with an excited Flora. She went in the direction of the castle, climbing up through the heather for about half a mile, before she sat down for a brief rest in the shepherd's hut, as she had before. However, there was no sign of either the earl or his dogs on this occasion, and Ally was about to turn back when she spotted Angus Morrison in the distance and made her way towards him.

Angus was surrounded by dogs, and so Ally lifted Flora up and held her tightly, unsure if she was permitted to mix with them.

'Aye,' said Angus by way of a greeting, squinting against the sun as she drew near.

'Oh, hello, Angus,' Ally said. 'I was hoping to run into the earl because there was something I wanted to ask him.'

Angus sniffed, then wiped his nose with the back of his hand. He pointed up towards the castle. 'He's at the stables with his new mare.'

'Thank you.' Ally continued climbing up to where she thought the stables might be. For once her sense of direction led her straight to where Hamish was placing a saddle on a beautiful grey horse.

'Hello, Alison, and what brings you here?' he asked with a grin. 'Have you changed your mind and want to make mad, passionate love to me?'

Ally laughed. 'No, Hamish, I have not.'

He bent down and stroked Flora. 'How are you coping with this one?'

'She's absolutely fine, thanks. And thank you again for such a wonderful gift.'

'I hear you have a new man in your life now? Am I no match for the vet?'

'We're just friends, thanks to Flora here.' Ally couldn't believe that the news had actually penetrated the castle walls too. 'But what I wanted to talk to you about was this cousin of yours – the one who might be your heir.'

The earl regarded her quizzically. 'What about him?'

'I just wondered if he might have wanted to protect the earldom, for his own benefit,' Ally said as tactfully as she could.

'Are you asking me if I think he could be a killer?' Hamish asked, feeding a carrot to the horse.

Ally gritted her teeth. 'The thought just crossed my mind.'

'Unlikely, although I suppose he could have dashed up from London to do the killings and then dashed back again. I suspect, though, that his red Ferrari might have been noticed somewhere along the way, don't you think?'

'Perhaps he used a different car? Or flew?' Ally asked, beginning to feel a little foolish.

'I doubt it, but I'll check. I must admit he'd be quite fit to do the deed, but I don't think somehow that he did.'

'I don't like the idea of you being the prime suspect,' Ally said truthfully.

Hamish smiled. 'That's very sweet of you, Alison. Actually, Rigby hasn't been interrogating me for a couple of days so perhaps they *have* found another prime suspect. No harm in hoping, I suppose. Maybe it's time *we* had another outing, you and I? You need to give the vet some competition, you know!'

'We'll talk about that another time!' Ally replied, laughing, as she turned to walk back. She was increasingly sure that Hamish had nothing to do with Wilbur's murder, but in spite of his comments, she still felt there was a strong possibility that the cousin could be involved.

TWENTY-NINE

The following morning Ally dispensed breakfasts single-handedly, hoping that both of her guests would be going out so that she could get on with cleaning their rooms. Already she was sorely missing Morag, who kept the kitchen tidy, kept the coffee going, stacking the dishwasher and cleaning the bedrooms, including changing any bedding and loading the washing machine.

As she left the dining room, Mamie said, 'By the way, I heard some funny sounds from my bathroom again during the night. I think I might have mentioned that before, and you really need to get the pipes checked. It's quite a weird sound.'

'I will, I will,' Ally said, gritting her teeth.

She set about dusting the sitting room while she waited for Tyler and Mamie to vacate their rooms, noting that Mamie had almost finished her jigsaw puzzle. A couple of pieces were missing, as she'd said, presumably lost.

It was eleven o'clock before she could start cleaning. Ally hadn't realised quite how untidy Mamie was, with make-up smeared over the dressing table, cast-off clothes strewn across the bedroom floor, damp towels on the bathroom floor, and two pairs of lacy pink knickers hanging from the towel rail. Ally sighed and tackled the jobs, with no sound nor sign of Wailing Willie. Ally decided she would get the plumbing checked although she didn't honestly think there was much wrong with it.

Tyler's room was tidy by comparison. It was a bed-changing day, and Ally removed the duvet and pillow covers before pulling off the fitted undersheet. And that was when something caught her eye. Wedged between the mattress and the wooden footboard there were in fact two items: one was a mobile phone, and the other was a pair of lacy pink panties which, it had to be said, seemed unlikely to belong to Tyler.

Ally stood riveted to the spot for a moment, staring in complete bewilderment at the pink knickers, which were an exact match for the two pairs in Mamie's bathroom. But why were they in Tyler's room and stuffed down at the bottom of the bed?

There was only one answer, and that was that Tyler and Mamie were sleeping together! Perhaps at some point Mamie must have decided that, as Wilbur was no longer on the scene, she'd settle for Tyler instead. But that didn't make a great deal of sense because she seemed to be genuinely grieving for Wilbur and, anyway, she and Tyler did not appear to be hitting it off. Or was that some sort of pretence? But why would they do that?

The phone had to be Tyler's because she'd seen Mamie using hers and it was – surprise! – pink. But what was his phone doing wedged at the foot of the mattress alongside Mamie's pink panties? Something very strange was going on here. Then the house phone rang, and Ally, feeling dazed, walked carefully down the stairs to answer it.

It was Tyler. 'Sorry to bother you, Ally, but I think I may have left my phone somewhere in the room. So if you or Morag come across it in the course of the day, could you just leave it on my dressing table, please?'

Turning the phone over in her hand, Ally said, 'I'll look out for it, Tyler.' She thought for a moment. 'So, where are you ringing me from?'

'I'm out on the moors. Luckily I met a hillwalker who's very kindly allowed me to borrow his phone. Anyhow it's gotta be in the bedroom somewhere.'

After he rang off, Ally went back upstairs and stared at the phone and the knickers. What was going on? If only she could get into his phone, she might be able to find out a thing or two. Ally thought for a moment. There was always the chance that he might have used his birth date, as so many people did, but she needed to find out what that was. It would be in his passport, of course, if she could find it. It was unlikely he'd carry it round with him while he climbed rocks or whatever, so it must be in this room somewhere.

Very carefully Ally began to check the drawers in the chest, looking beneath neatly folded socks, underwear, T-shirts and sweaters. There was no passport there. Then Ally moved across to the dressing table where the two top drawers yielded mainly toiletry items and belts. When she pulled out the larger drawer underneath, she found a conglomeration of books, papers and a passport!

With shaking fingers Ally opened it to see a younger Tyler staring back at her. He'd been born on 20 October 1963. Could he possibly have used that? She picked up the phone again with shaking hands and attempted to steady them sufficiently to be able to tap in 102063. Not for one moment had Ally expected any kind of success, and so she could scarcely believe that it did work – here she was with Tyler's phone *open* in her hands!

Ally placed the passport carefully back in the drawer, then sat down on the chair by the window, just in case she might see Tyler return at any moment. Having reassured herself that she was completely alone, Ally clicked on the email inbox. Much to her relief, all of the emails had already been opened, and so there was no harm in her opening some of them up. As she scrolled down the list of incoming emails, the one that kept reappearing was from a certain Milton & Ferber, Real Estate. She clicked on the most recent.

Hi Tyler, it began. *Thank you for the copy of Wilbur's death certificate. The really great news is that we now have everything we need to be able to proceed with the documentation of your ownership of the earldom of Locharran, the many thousands of acres that go with it and the houses thereon.* There followed a paragraph of legal jargon, and it ended up with: *Looking forward to joining you for some hunting, fishing and shooting! Thanks so much for the invitation!*

Ally couldn't believe what she had just read. How could this be possible? Was Tyler about to oust poor Hamish and claim these thousands of acres as his own? Not as a theme park but as some Highland sporting escape for, presumably, the British gentry and rich Americans? But what about Wilbur? Who then had killed Wilbur? It had been proved conclusively that Tyler had been in the States when Wilbur was murdered, so it couldn't have been him.

To reassure herself, Ally opened up some of the previous emails from Milton & Farber, all of which confirmed one way or another that they had been preparing this documentation while awaiting a certified copy of Wilbur's death certificate. Astounded, Ally placed the phone on the dressing table, as Tyler had asked.

Nothing made sense. Ally tried to think straight so she could decide what to do next.

Should she phone Rigby? Yes, of course she should!

Ally, still shaky from her discovery, carried Tyler's phone downstairs. She would read out these emails to Rigby, if necessary, and he'd definitely want to see them. Hopefully Tyler wouldn't come back early and go looking for his phone.

With trembling fingers, she clicked Rigby's number, which, as she expected, was answered by the constable. 'I'm afraid he's tied up at the moment.'

'This is really urgent!' Ally shouted. 'Please, I need to talk to him *now*!'

'I'll get him to call you—'

'No, *now*!' Ally interrupted. 'I have vital information about the Carrington case!'

She heard him sigh and mutter into another phone, during which time Ally tried to calm herself down so that she'd sound coherent when Rigby came on the phone.

'Mrs McKinley?'

'Oh, thank goodness!' Ally sighed with relief. 'I've just been servicing Tyler Carrington's bedroom and, in the bed, found not only his mobile but a pair of Mamie Van Nuyen's panties!'

There was a moment's silence before Rigby spoke. '*This* is the urgent case-solving information that I've just interrupted my meeting for?'

'No, no, there's much more! But if she's been sleeping with him, doesn't that mean that they're in this together?'

She heard Rigby sighing.

'What it means, Mrs McKinley, is that she's determined to be the Countess of Locharran and, if she can't have one brother, she'll settle for the other.'

'But I find that hard to believe because she was so upset about Wilbur's death and—'

'Remind me where's she from?' Rigby interrupted.

'Somewhere in California.'

He sniffed derisively. 'Was there anything else?'

'Yes, as a matter of fact there is. I managed to get into Tyler's phone.'

'How on earth did you manage that?'

'Guesswork. I thought he might have used his birthdate as a password, and so I found his passport and decided to try. And hey presto!'

'Tell me more.'

She could tell he was interested now. 'I found several emails from his lawyers, all confirming that he was now the rightful earl. Apparently, they'd been waiting for Wilbur's death certificate.'

'Where's that phone now?'

'On the kitchen table. Here.'

'Get that into a safe place right now! That's the final piece of evidence we need. *Right now*, Mrs McKinley, please!'

'OK, hold on.' Ally took the phone into her little office and locked it in her personal papers drawer.

'Have you done that?'

'Yes, I have.'

'OK, I can tell you this now. We had reason to suspect him anyway because underneath the Land Rover we found a hair. One hair, which was a close match for Wilbur Carrington's DNA.'

'But Wilbur Carrington's dead!' Ally exclaimed.

'He is... but it could belong to his brother.'

'So, you think Tyler cut the brakes?'

'A distinct possibility, particularly in view of what you've just told me.'

Ally could scarcely believe what she was hearing. 'But why would he want to kill poor Ian Grant?'

'Because, presumably, Grant must have known or discovered something relevant. He was about to tell me something just before he was killed.'

'But this doesn't make sense,' Ally said, 'because you told us Tyler was in the States when his brother was killed.' She was feeling increasingly frustrated; why had Rigby not given her suggestion about a hit-man more weight before now?

'He could have an accomplice, as you suggested before. Now, I'm coming right over for that phone. The man is dangerous and, if he comes back in the meantime, keep everything as normal as possible. He must not suspect that we're on to him.'

As Rigby was speaking, Ally thought she heard a slight sound and turned quickly towards the kitchen door, which she'd left ajar in her hurry to make the phone call.

And there, framed in the doorway and with a menacing smile on his face, stood Tyler Carrington.

THIRTY

'That sounded like an interesting conversation, Ally.' Tyler leaned against the door frame nonchalantly, his expression anything but nonchalant.

'H-how long have you been standing there?' Ally stammered, placing her phone on the table without disconnecting it. She prayed that Rigby was still on the line and could hear everything.

'Long enough.' He advanced towards her slowly, still smiling. 'I guess you were talking to the policeman?'

Ally stepped backward, terrified. She heard the front door open and, behind Tyler, she could see Mamie walking slowly across the hallway. 'Tyler?' she called.

'Keep out of this, honey,' he said, staring fixedly at Ally.

Ally took a deep breath. 'Detective Inspector Rigby is on his way here right now.' She saw him hesitate for a moment.

'Come on, baby,' Mamie cajoled from behind him. 'Please don't harm Ally. She's been real good to us...'

As she spoke, he turned and walked past her towards the front door. 'We gotta stick to our plan now, Mamie; the cops will be here any minute.' And with that, he opened the door and disappeared through it.

There was a shocked silence. Ally looked across at Mamie, seeing the angst written all over her face.

'I've gotta go after him!' she said.

'But, Mamie...' Ally began.

'No, I *must* go!' Mamie screamed.

'Mamie, *stop!*' Ally grabbed her elbow. 'Let him go!' She looked out of the front door. 'He's not taken his car so he won't go far.'

Mamie shook her head furiously. 'No, he'll climb.'

'Climb? Why would he do that? Anyway, he hasn't taken his gear either!'

Mamie grabbed his climbing gear from the hook. 'I gotta get this to him!'

'How on earth are you going to do that, Mamie?'

At that moment, they heard the sound of sirens, and the police car drew up.

Ally rushed out of the front door.

'Where's Carrington?' Rigby asked, leaping out.

'I don't know,' Ally said. 'He dashed out a few minutes ago.'

'Sir!' yelled the young constable with him. 'I think I see him. There's somebody running across the moor towards the crags!'

'I'll take the car,' Rigby shouted back, 'and try to cut him off. You follow him on foot.'

'Leave him alone!' Mamie yelled. 'You ain't gonna catch him! He's too good for you – you'll never get him!'

'We'll see about that,' Rigby said, getting back into his car. He set off, at speed, on the coast road which edged on to the moors.

Mamie had started to run out towards her car. 'I gotta get to him!' she said again.

Ally raced after her and managed to wrench the car keys from her hand. 'Give it a minute,' Ally said, pulling her back towards the door. 'Wait for a few minutes, *please*, until you calm down.' She took Mamie firmly by the arm and shepherded her into the kitchen. 'I don't pretend to know what's going on, but you need to calm down. Let me make you some tea – or would you prefer something stronger?'

Mamie shook her head violently. 'No, no, you don't understand, Ally! I gotta meet him!'

'Where?'

'*Where?* Why should I tell *you* when all you'll do is tell that stupid policeman?'

'Mamie, the policeman is hot on Tyler's heels and will possibly have caught up with him by now.'

Mamie was pulling back towards the door. 'I've gotta get outta here! Tyler will be halfway up that rock face by now...'

It was obvious to Ally now that Tyler had involved Mamie in this somehow. She knew she was taking a risk, but she couldn't let Mamie get away.

'No, Mamie, I can't let you go on your own in this state!'

'Well, I'm *going*.' Mamie said, grabbing back the keys, 'and more fool you if you wanna come along.' And with that she headed towards her car, Ally racing after her.

As she leaped into the passenger seat of Mamie's little car, Ally knew that she was very unwise to accompany her but felt she had no choice. Mamie, with tears streaming down her face, switched on the ignition, then put her foot down hard on the accelerator.

'Whoa, Mamie, take it easy!'

Mamie did not appear to hear her and took off up the steep mountain road, through Glen Locharran, at high speed. Ally swallowed. This road passed the top of some high crags before heading down and out towards the coast.

'Where are we going?' she asked after a moment.

'I'm going to pick up Tyler,' Mamie said, wiping her eyes on her sleeve. 'I know exactly where he's climbing.'

A couple of minutes later, she pulled in abruptly to the right, parked and was out of the door with Tyler's climbing gear in her arms, heading towards what was plainly the top of a rock face.

Ally looked around briefly at the miles of mountain road stretching into the distance, without anywhere or anyone in sight, and then followed Mamie, who was running across through the heather and the bracken to the crag top, calling out, 'Tyler! Tyler!' What was this crazy woman going to do now?

Reaching the top of a sheer rocky crag face, Mamie stopped, looking down over the edge. 'Come on, baby,' she yelled. 'I'm *here*, waiting!'

Ally approached cautiously. She didn't like heights and was terrified to get as close to the edge as Mamie was. 'Mamie, stand back, for God's sake!'

Instead of standing back, Mamie was now on her hands and knees, then flattening herself so that she was hanging over the edge with only the lower part of her body on solid ground. 'Tyler, you're nearly there! I'm *here*! Take my hand!' She was waving her hands in the air.

Ally, trying to overcome her vertigo, made herself walk to the edge. Tyler was a good three-quarters of the way up, even without his climbing gear, desperately seeking a foothold and grunting loudly. Below him, staring up, was Rigby, accompanied by two uniformed policemen. Rigby had a loud hailer. 'Come down, Tyler Carrington! For your own safety! *You can't get away!*'

But Tyler was paying no heed, finally finding a foothold and hoisting himself up with only a few feet left to climb.

'Take my *hand*!' Mamie was shouting, reaching out with her arms to try to help him up, but he was ignoring her.

'You're too near the edge, Mamie!' Ally shouted, but Mamie seemed not to hear.

Then, with a crashing sound, the turf and rocks beneath

Mamie's weight began to break loose, showering stones down into the abyss. Ally stepped back and grabbed Mamie's legs, pulling her roughly away from the edge.

'No, no, *no!*' Mamie was shouting hysterically. 'He's nearly got to the top...'

Ally, brave because she was beyond being terrified, made herself look over again.

Tyler Carrington was being bombarded by the falling rocks. He lost his grip and, with a scream Ally would remember to the end of her days, crashed down the rock face, falling onto a huge outcrop directly below as she and Mamie watched.

For a moment there was total silence. Ally was almost certain that Tyler was dead. No one could survive that fall, and onto a *rock*, surely. Still, she watched as Rigby felt for a pulse and heard him say, 'Well, that's *that.*' He looked as shocked as she felt. The two constables were studying Tyler's spreadeagled body and shaking their heads.

Mamie, in the meantime, was now hysterical, still lying on the ground, pounding what remained of the fragile earth beneath her. 'I *gotta* go to him, Ally,' she screamed. 'He's going to be so badly injured and he'll *need* me!'

'Mamie,' Ally began gently, 'I don't think—'

'You don't think *what?*' Mamie asked, getting to her feet, her eyes ablaze.

Ally took a deep breath. 'I don't think he survived the fall, Mamie. Let's go back down and find out for sure. I'll drive if you like?'

'No, no, *I'll* drive!' Mamie was now racing back towards her car, tears streaming down her face, Ally at her heels.

As Ally got into the passenger seat, she realised that she should have insisted on driving, because Mamie was now hysterical, pounding at the steering wheel, shouting, 'Tyler, Tyler!'

But before Ally could say anything, Mamie had started up the car and was reversing back onto the still deserted road.

After a moment, Mamie spoke. 'We were going to be *married*!' Her voice broke, and she gave some great, shuddering sobs.

This was all so incredible that Ally forgot her terror for a moment. 'You and... Tyler? So you were never with Wilbur?'

'Of course not!' Mamie looked outraged at this idea. 'He was such an idiot, always going on about his stupid plans for his theme park. He had to be removed, or he might have become the earl. *Tyler* was the earl! And *I* was about to become the Countess of Locharran!'

At this moment, Ally realised with horror that they were not going the way they came; instead, Mamie had turned towards the coast and had her foot down hard on the pedal. 'Where are we going?' Ally asked tremulously as the car gathered speed. Her mouth was so dry that her lips were sticking to her teeth.

Mamie did not reply. She increased the speed, and Ally began to fear for her life. This whole scenario was so incredible that she decided to ask the question that had been in her mind ever since she'd found the panties in Tyler's bed. 'So was it *you* who killed Wilbur?'

She was desperate to know but at the same time wondered if she was going to be alive long enough to tell anyone the way Mamie was driving.

Mamie gave a hysterical cackle. 'Well, of course I did! I would have done it outside the hotel that night, but I couldn't keep up with him and had to follow him all the way to your malthouse.'

Ally felt her throat constrict, all hope of escape now gone. The car was racing round the bends at breakneck speed, too fast to consider opening the door and jumping.

'And you know what?' Mamie continued triumphantly. 'No

one would ever have known if it wasn't for that goddamn chauffeur! He saw me the day I killed Wilbur, and then recognised me later when I got back. Tyler had to get rid of him before he could open his big mouth.'

As they skidded round another bend, Ally wondered when mild-mannered, sweet little jigsaw-loving Mamie had morphed into this cold, ruthless killer. There was a heart-stopping moment when she realised for sure that Mamie had nothing to lose now, but she, Ally, did. She wasn't going to come out of this alive unless she thought of something – and fast.

Her heart pounding, Ally saw, in the wing mirror, that there was a police car some distance behind. Mamie did not appear to have noticed it and had pressed the accelerator down to the floor, the car now roaring along at ninety miles an hour and beginning to protest.

'For God's sake, Mamie!' Ally screamed frantically. 'You'll kill us both!'

'Ever seen the movie *Thelma and Louise?*' Mamie now seemed frighteningly calm.

Ally had seen the movie, where the two women, at the end, headed over a cliff towards certain suicide. The car was now revving and making a rasping noise, weaving from side to side on the narrow road, a steep embankment on the right and a sheer drop on the left. Her heart racing in fear, and with trembling fingers, Ally hauled herself across Mamie, as far as her seat belt would allow, grabbed the steering wheel and then wrenched it sharply to the right.

All she remembered afterwards was the horrific crashing sound into the steep bank.

THIRTY-ONE

'Your mother's going to be OK,' the nurse said reassuringly to Jamie McKinley, who'd flown up from Edinburgh to Inverness as soon as he'd heard the news and was then accompanied by Rigby to Raigmore Hospital. 'She's got some cracked ribs, a broken arm and a lot of bruising.'

'Oh my God,' said Jamie.

'It could've been worse,' the nurse said cheerfully. 'It'll all mend!'

Ally, propped up in bed, with her arm in plaster, was feeling drowsy from the painkillers.

'God, Mum, you gave us such a scare! I've got hold of Carol and the gang, who're sailing around the Greek islands somewhere, and told her that there's no need to come back and that her crazy mother is doing well. But she said they'd be home by the weekend. Simon still has a week's leave, and she's coming up to see you on her own.'

'Good,' Ally said, 'no point in buggering up their holiday. Is Rigby still around?'

Rigby, apparently, was standing outside the door, awaiting permission to enter.

'Do you want to see him? Are you sure you're strong enough?' Jamie asked.

'Yes, I do.' Ally waved her good arm towards the door. 'Let him come in.'

The door opened to admit Rigby holding, of all things, a gigantic display of the most beautiful flowers Ally had ever seen.

'They're from everyone in Locharran,' he said, looking embarrassed as he deposited the floral display on the floor. 'It's too big to go on any of the surfaces,' he added, looking around.

'It's *beautiful*,' Ally said. 'Thank you so much for delivering it. But, tell me, what about my wee dog?'

'Your wee dog's fine,' Rigby replied. 'Morag McConnachie came up to the malthouse shortly after you left, and she's taken Flora home with her.'

'*Morag?*'

'Yes.' Rigby shrugged. 'She said something about wanting to come back. I didn't even know she'd left.'

Ally sighed with relief. 'What about Tyler?'

Rigby shook his head. 'God only knows why he thought he could scale that sheer face. I suppose he might just have lived if he hadn't hit that big rock.'

'He did kill Ian, you know, and—'

'Tell me in a minute,' Rigby put in. 'Believe it or not, he'd almost got to the top. He was some climber.' Ally could hear what sounded like admiration in his voice.

'And?'

Rigby cleared his throat. 'I'd sent another police car along the road where, if he'd survived, he was likely to emerge, and that was when they saw Van Nuyen's car careering along at over ninety miles an hour.'

Ally digested this news for a moment before asking, 'And what about Mamie?' She was feeling increasingly terrified that she might have been responsible for Mamie's death by her own action. In spite of everything, she'd become very fond of her.

'Mamie's still here in the land of the living,' Rigby replied, 'but she's got both arms and legs broken, and she's going to be here in hospital for a long time before she goes to jail.'

'I think that's enough for Mum at the moment,' Jamie interrupted. 'When she's fit enough, I'm going to take her back to Edinburgh with me to recuperate.'

Ally turned her head to look at her son. 'No, Jamie, I'll be going back to Locharran, but that's a very kind thought.' She turned back to Rigby as she sipped some water. 'Let me tell you what happened after you left the malthouse.' Ally gave him an account of her horrifying ordeal.

'*Thelma and Louise!*' spluttered Jamie when she was finished. 'She really *was* out to kill you!'

'No, she was out to kill herself, but she'd have taken me with her,' Ally said sadly, turning to Rigby again. 'I still don't understand how she could have killed Wilbur and then disappeared off the scene until she arrived at the malthouse days later?'

'We've checked her out,' Rigby said. 'Apparently she flew in from Los Angeles two days before killing Wilbur, having bought a skean dhu in a souvenir shop, would you believe. After she'd done the deed, she flew all the way back home.'

'What on earth for?' Jamie asked.

'So she could fly back again a few days later,' Rigby said triumphantly, 'having supposedly just been told of her fiancé's death.' He sniffed. 'But he wasn't her fiancé and never had been. She was engaged to Tyler Carrington *not* Wilbur Carrington. When we checked her out earlier, which we did, we only came up with her arrival from California on the *second* occasion.' He shook his head, a little embarrassed. 'We didn't think to go back to look for any earlier flights.'

'All those flights must have cost her a fortune,' Jamie remarked.

'She was probably convinced it would be worth it,' his mother reminded him, 'because she reckoned she was going to be the Countess of Locharran, with a castle and thousands of acres. I wonder if Tyler really loved her, or was he just using her?'

'I don't suppose we'll ever know,' Rigby said, 'but when we checked her background, Mamie Van Nuyen turns out to be an unsuccessful Hollywood actress.'

Ally sighed. 'So, presumably there will now be no further claims to the earldom?'

'We've checked. There were only the two brothers, both now deceased. They did have a legitimate claim, but now it's reverted back to Hamish Sinclair, who is extremely relieved, although he had a few bad moments when he found out that he could have been out of a job! So, business as usual!'

'I wonder whatever happened to poor Jessie McPhee?' Ally asked with a sigh.

'Well, we've unearthed a few details,' Rigby said. 'Yes, she was banished to Boston and sailed from Glasgow in December 1851, when she was five months pregnant. Her son was born the following May, the birth was registered and the father's name simply listed as Robert Sinclair. It appears Jessie married again, to an Edward Barker, but then we lost trace of her until her death was recorded in 1864.' He cleared his throat again. 'I suppose I should have studied that file you gave me more closely, but it didn't seem terribly relevant at the time.'

Ally nodded but said nothing.

'Anyway,' Jamie said, 'I still think you should come back with me, Mum.'

Ally patted her son's hand. 'Thanks, but I want to go home to Locharran. I'll manage with Morag's help, and I want to be with my puppy and my ghost!' She suddenly remembered how Mamie had heard wailing the night before the next day's drama. So Willie *was* still around!

'You're going to be getting another visitor,' Rigby added with a smile. 'There's a certain vet who's been in touch asking if he can come to see you, and if you'd like him to come to take you home to Locharran when you're discharged.'

Ally felt herself blushing – how ridiculous was that? She hadn't blushed in years!

'So you're definitely going back to Locharran?' Jamie said, grinning. 'Even after everything that's happened? And who is this vet?'

'Oh, just a friend,' Ally replied casually. 'You should get a dog again, Jamie. You meet some lovely people!'

The little procession made its way along the hospital corridor. Katy, who'd been Ally's favourite nurse, led the way, weighed down with Rigby's enormous flower arrangement. Behind, Ally walked slowly, her ribs hurting with the exertion, leaning on Ross's arm. She bade farewell to the little group of nurses who'd come to see her off, and now she was going home; home to Locharran!

Then she stopped short in the corridor, noticing that Constable Chisholm was now standing outside one of the doors.

'I need to have a word with him,' Ally said firmly.

'I'm not sure that's wise,' Ross said.

'Probably not,' Ally said, 'but I want to do it anyway.'

'But—' began the nurse, staring in disbelief as Ally approached the policeman.

'Are you guarding Mamie Van Nuyen now?' Ally asked him.

'I'm not allowed to let anyone in there except staff,' he said a little hesitantly.

'I think I might be an exception,' Ally replied calmly. She pointed at her arm in plaster. 'I'm not about to do any damage!'

'I guess you're armless,' he said, sniggering at his own wit.

'But why would you want to see someone who nearly killed you?'

Ally didn't reply to his question. 'You can come in with me if you must.'

He shook his head and opened the door.

The little room was dimly lit because the blind had been partly lowered, but Ally could make out Mamie's outline, in a pink nightie and with plaster casts on both arms. As she drew nearer, she could see that Mamie appeared to be asleep, and she saw the cuts on Mamie's face, one of which had been stitched and narrowly missed her eye.

'Oh, Mamie,' Ally said quietly.

Mamie opened her eyes. 'Oh God, it's *you!*' and she closed them hastily again.

'I think I've come out of this better than you have,' Ally said with a hint of a smile.

Mamie gave a deep sigh but kept her eyes shut. 'I should have died,' she muttered, 'and you should not have been in the car at all. I would have killed us both. I'm really sorry, Ally.'

Ally wasn't sure if she was sorry because she *hadn't* killed them both, or sorry because Ally had been in the car. It was difficult to know what to say because she could hardly offer platitudes such as 'You'll soon be up and about again!' when the woman was almost certainly destined to spend the rest of her life in jail. Instead, she asked, 'Are you in a lot of pain?'

'Doesn't matter – nothing matters now that Tyler's dead,' she said as tears rolled down her cheeks.

Ally pulled a tissue out of the box on the bedside table and gently patted Mamie's face dry. 'I'm sorry, too, Mamie; I really am.' Ally knew that Mamie had done what she'd done for Tyler because women will sometimes do anything for the men they love. Had he really loved Mamie, or had he just used her? Poor Mamie.

Blinking back her own tears, Ally headed towards the door,

which was ajar. The policeman had plainly been listening in. He didn't speak but closed the door firmly behind her.

Ross, now alone and holding the flowers, put his free arm around her. 'Come,' he said. 'Let's get you home.'

'Oh yes please,' said Ally, already dreaming of her malt-house, her new friends, the moors, and the castle and the slightly batty village. Home.

•

A LETTER FROM DEE

Dear Reader,

Thank you for reading this book and I hope you enjoyed meeting Ally McKinley. It's set in the part of Scotland where I myself come from, and I hope I've been able to describe adequately the beauty of the area. Ally's likely to pop up again soon, so if you wish to keep up with her, or any of my other books, you can sign up on the following link:

www.bookouture.com/dee-macdonald

Your email address will never be shared, and you can unsubscribe at any time.

If you liked this book, I'd appreciate it if you could write a review because I like to know what my readers think, and your feedback is invaluable.

You can get in touch via Facebook and Twitter (now X).

Thank you,

Dee

facebook.com/AuthorDeeMacDonald
x.com/DMacDonaldAuth

ACKNOWLEDGEMENTS

A huge thanks to my brilliant editors at Bookouture, Lizzie Brien and Natasha Harding, for their help, encouragement and enthusiasm – not to mention their endless patience!

Thank you to the wonderful team who publish and promote my books, including Ruth Tross, Alba Proko, Melissa Tran, Peta Nightingale, Mandy Kullar, Stephanie Straub, Occy Carr, Kim Nash, Noelle Holten, Jane Eastgate, Laura Kincaid and Lisa Brewster.

And my sincere apologies to anyone I've accidentally omitted.

Thanks to Amanda Preston – my lovely agent at LBA. She, too, is so supportive and constructive when it comes to reading through my manuscripts.

Every writer should have a 'writing buddy' too, someone to cast an eagle eye over one's work and who isn't afraid to say what's lacking in plot, planning and grammar! Mine is called Rosemary Brown, and I am greatly indebted to her.

Not least, thanks to my husband, Stan, who gives me peace to write and provides liquid refreshment, and to my son, Dan, and family who sort out my technical problems.

Finally, thanks to you, dear reader, for buying my books!

PUBLISHING TEAM

Turning a manuscript into a book requires the efforts of many people. The publishing team at Bookouture would like to acknowledge everyone who contributed to this publication.

Audio
Alba Proko
Melissa Tran
Sinead O'Connor

Commercial
Lauren Morrissette
Hannah Richmond
Imogen Allport

Cover design
The Brewster Project

Data and analysis
Mark Alder
Mohamed Bussuri

Editorial
Lizzie Brien

Made in the USA
Las Vegas, NV
29 August 2024

94574248R00143